Praise for Pa~~~~
NASCAR Library Collection titles

TOTAL CONTROL

"This new installment in Britton's NASCAR series is the best yet. The story is heartachingly real but also wonderfully hopeful. It's an incredible read."
—*Romantic Times BOOKreviews*

"Fans of the world of NASCAR will love this action-packed ride that will take your emotions around the track at 200 mph. Ms. Britton has written characters that are realistic and will touch your heart on many levels."
—Wendy Keel, *The Romance Readers Connection*

TO THE LIMIT

"A fun lighthearted NASCAR romance."
—Harriet Klausner, *The Best Reviews*

"An edge of the chair, heart racing, can't put down read."
—Wendy Keel, *The Romance Readers Connection*

ON THE EDGE

"Britton writes the kind of book that romance fans will read and reread on gloomy days."
—*Publishers Weekly*

IN THE GROOVE

"*In the Groove* is a fun, light-hearted love story with racing as the backdrop and a feel-good ending."
—*Racing Milestones*

PAMELA BRITTON

titles in the NASCAR Library Collection

"Miracle Season"—a novella in *A NASCAR Holiday 2*
Total Control
To the Limit
On the Edge
In the Groove

And also by Pamela Britton

The Cowgirl's CEO
Cowboy Vet
Cowboy M.D.
Cowboy Trouble
Dangerous Curves
Scandal
Tempted
Seduced
Cowboy Lessons
Enchanted by Your Kisses
My Fallen Angel

PAMELA BRITTON

On the **move**

H

HQN™

ISBN-13: 978-0-373-77222-3
ISBN-10:   0-373-77222-X

ON THE MOVE

This one's for my BFFs. Melissa, whose love and laughter always brightens my day. Lisa, whose kindness and compassion soothes my soul. Kori, whose blunt honesty makes me see the light. Kelli, who always listens. Piney, who's never out of coffee and always has a warm shoulder to cry upon. And Michael, who is, well…the best friend of all. You guys are the foundation that supports me through the good times to the bad. I would not be the person I am today without you. I love you.

On the move

PROLOGUE

Open Season
By Rick Stevenson, Sports Editor

YEARS AGO, it used to be that drivers swapped rides late in the season. In one fell swoop—and over the course of a couple months—you knew who was taking over what rides and for how long.

No so anymore.

Nowadays, drivers start talking contract negotiations before the season's barely begun, never mind when race season's drawing to a close. You could know in March that so-and-so won't be renewing his contract in December, and then spend the rest of the year speculating where that driver will go. About the only driver whose fate I knew at the end of *last* season was Brandon Burke's.

Brandon Burke.

Now, there's someone I wish I didn't know. Let's recap his stellar career:

Wrecked the leader of the Indy 500.

On the last lap.

When Mr. Burke was twenty laps down.

Has broken the cameras of numerous photographers. Rumor has it Indy 500 photographers took to carrying pepper spray. Rumor also has it that he punched out his father not long ago, and that the brawl had a lot to do with Brandon being booted out of the IRL.

One thing's for sure, KEM Motorsports bringing Brandon Burke to NASCAR was about the silliest thing I saw done this past season. And I don't know about you, but I suspect the silliness isn't over.

Preseason

"Some drivers thrive on winning races. Others love to cause trouble. It's the latter that gives racing a bad name. Brandon Burke is one of those drivers."

—Finish Line magazine

CHAPTER ONE

THERE WERE, in Vicky's opinion, three types of men: Those that made you go, "Eww." As in, *yuck, I wouldn't touch that with a ten-foot pole and a pair of rubber gloves.* Those that made you think, "Hmm." As in, *if I was tired, tipsy and just a little bit desperate, I might take him home.* And those that made you exclaim, softly, of course, "Oh, my."

Brandon Burke was a solid *"Oh, my."*

She'd known that. Of course she'd known that. The thing was, it didn't make it any easier to approach him. So she hung back, peering around the edge of one of the many buildings located at the South Carolina racetrack, every once in a while walking forward only to stop suddenly and turn back, the large bag she'd slung over one shoulder hitting her in the spine.

Back to hiding.

You're being ridiculous. He's just a man.

It was a busy day at the drag race motorsports complex. People heavily laden with salty-scented sunblock rushed past her, spectators, track officials and crewmen alike. The sweet smell of hot dogs and hamburgers hung in the air, as if everyone were at an outdoor barbecue rather than a drag strip. On the asphalt behind her, cars took off at regular intervals, their engines so loud, Vicky resisted the urge to cover her ears.

Come on, Vicky. Sooner or later you've got to do it.

She took another peek.

And her whole body just sort of went *oomph*.

Brandon leaned against the side of a big rig that hauled his drag bike from track to track, looking very…very…

She thought for a moment.

Gladiator-ish, if there *was* such a word. He was watching a mechanic work on his bike. Yellow Do Not Cross This Line tape kept fans at bay. Above him someone had pulled a white awning out from the side of the rig. It cast a translucent glow over his darkly tanned skin—as if he stood beneath a photographer's umbrella—and turned his black leather gear a shade of gray. She didn't know how he could stand to wear those leathers on a hot, sunny day like today, but she had to admit, he looked, um, *hot* in them.

She wiped a trickle of sweat off her *own* forehead. *Go on,* she silently urged, watching as he leaned forward and said something. But Vicky had never been aggressive where men were concerned. Out on the track, the deafening roar of a race car in the middle of a qualifying run filled the air yet again, but she could still hear the two of them laugh over the sound.

Do it.

Now!

She readjusted the straps of her indigo bag, and headed for him.

He became more beautiful with each step. Race-car drivers were not, as a rule, pretty…at least not in her experience. But this guy was gorgeous in the same way as a Calvin Klein model. Razor-stubble chin. Blond sideburns in front of his ears. Michelangelo's lips. Botticelli's wide-armed physique, and the swept-back, shoulder-length blond hair of Perseus. She'd minored in Art…a degree that wasn't useful in her current job, but terrific for spur-of-the-moment metaphors.

She paused outside the tape, clenched her

hands, then sternly told herself to stop being ridiculous. She'd graduated at the top of her class. With honors.

"Hi, Brandon," she said.

Dizzyingly blue eyes—the same color as oceans south of the equator—gave her a puzzled stare.

"I'm Vicky," she said, ducking beneath the yellow tape. "Vicky VanCleef."

Brandon glanced at his mechanic, gave him a don't-worry-I'll-handle-this look, albeit one tinged with amusement, and pushed away from the side of the semi.

"Can I help you?" he asked, those eyes of his sweeping her up and down.

Not much to see, I'm afraid. "You don't recognize the name, do you?"

"No," he said, his drawl more pronounced when it was oozing male sensuality. "Should I?" he asked suggestively.

Whoo-wee, the man should come with a Warning: Smile May Cause Electric Shock. She felt that sexy grin all the way down to her toenails. And it figured he didn't recognize her. She'd only worked for SSI, Sports Services Inc., for a couple of months.

"We've actually talked on the phone a few times," she said. "I work for SSI."

"SSI?" he asked, as if he didn't recognize *that* name, either. But of course he did. They might be new to representing him, but they weren't *that* new.

"SSI," she repeated, shifting the bag to the other shoulder so she could lift the wide flap and pull out a business card. "Sports Services, Inc. I'm Scott Preston's assistant."

He glanced at the card, recognition dawning. Again, the eyes scanned her, and for the first time Vicky found herself wishing for a six-foot-one frame, voluptuous cleavage and sexy, pouty lips. Alas, she was five foot four, average looking, and with hair as light brown and wispy straight as an Afghan hound's.

"What are you doing here?" he asked.

All amusement had fled. There was no longer any hint of a smile. No word of greeting. Just the steely-eyed glare of a man who wasn't happy to see her. Well, she'd expected that. After all, he'd been ducking her calls for days.

"Actually, Mr. Knight requested that I come. Well, Mr. Knight wanted my boss, *Scott,* to come. But he's too busy. One of his star football players broke his leg. Terrible thing. End of his career.

Scott went down to, um—" tell the player SSI was through with him, too. But she couldn't tell Brandon that. He might suddenly comprehend what a complete and utter jerk of an agent Scott was, and so she said, "Console him."

"What does Mr. Knight want with me?" he asked, one of his dark brown eyebrows lifting. He crossed his arms in front of him, something that made his shoulders appear twice as wide.

He knew. He *had* to know. Mr. Knight owned the car Brandon drove and he'd have to be stupid not to know what his team owner wanted, but if he wanted to play dumb… "Well, *he* thought, and Scott thought so, too, that maybe you'd forgotten that you're not supposed to race any type of vehicle other than stock cars." She put on her best we-all-make-mistakes smile. "It's in your contract," she added, patting her square bag where a copy of said contract rested. "Although it appears as if you didn't see that particular clause."

He smirked, and it was one of those not-quite-a-grin looks that wasn't really an attempt at a smile. She *hated* when people did that.

Another drop of sweat trickled down her back. "Ahem. So," she said, resisting the urge to wipe her hands on the front of her pants, and having to raise her voice to be heard above the sudden roar of yet another engine. "I know this is kind of bad timing, but I'm afraid you can't race today. Not if you don't want to violate your contract with Mr. Knight."

"Tell Mr. Knight to go blow."

"Excuse me?"

He'd started to unzip his leather race gear. Vicky felt her mouth go dry. The black material slid off his shoulders, exposing a white cotton tank beneath. Arms so sculpted they belonged on the cover of a fitness magazine flexed as he shrugged out of the material.

"Mr. Burke," she quickly added when it became clear that he wasn't undressing because he'd taken her warning to heart—*or* to make her mind go blank. Which it did. Momentarily. "I understand your reluctance to pack up and leave, but *obviously* I can't tell Mr. Knight to, um, *go blow.* We only just signed with him, so I don't think it'd be wise to go against his wishes."

All Brandon did was shrug before he turned away. She watched him cross to an orange-and-white cooler where he pulled out some sort of purple-colored drink. When he turned back, he almost seemed surprised to see her still standing there.

"I'm not giving up my drag bike," he said after cracking the lid. "I told Scott that same thing. He said we'd work it out."

And why wasn't Vicky surprised?

"If we can't," Brandon said, "then I'm not interested in driving for Mr. Knight."

What!

Her mouth hung open for a moment. He made it seem as if they could just rip up the thirty-page contract in her bag. "You can't just arbitrarily decide not to work for KEM."

"I can do whatever I want," Brandon said, walking away.

"Mr. Burke, please," she said, trying not to panic as she moved to catch up to him. "This is obviously some kind of misunderstanding, and until we have it all sorted out, I think we should at least talk it over with Mr. Knight."

He turned back to her, tipped the minijug back, then proceeded to down half the bottle in a few loud gulps. Vicky watched his Adam's apple bob with every swallow. He had a muscular neck, thick cords running up the side of it; she wondered what they'd feel like beneath her fingers....

Vicky!

He uncoupled the bottle from his lips with a

suctioned pop, released the breath he'd been holding and looked over at her once again. "Out of the question. Don't have time to talk to anyone right now."

"You mean, you're going to race anyway?"

"Yup."

She forgot how good-looking he was at that moment. Forgot that just a second ago she'd been fantasizing about swiping the sideburns that hugged the shell of his ear. Forgot everything in the wake of the realization that Brandon Burke was an ass.

"And I'm here to tell you that you can't," she said, trying hard to keep the conversation professional.

What a jerk.

What did you expect, Vicky? He has Scott as an agent. Like attracts like. And Scott is the king of jerks.

"Actually," he said, taking a step toward her. "I doubt you're in a position to tell me anything."

His ploy almost succeeded—the one he'd no doubt used to keep women in line. He tried to discombobulate her with his good looks. Five minutes ago it would have worked. Five minutes ago she might have completely forgotten what she wanted to say in the wake of his tangy, masculine scent, one she caught a whiff of as he tipped away from her.

But that was before he questioned her authority.

She reached inside her briefcase once more. Inside were glasses which were—for the most part—for show, but for some reason always seemed to give her self-confidence.

She slipped them on.

Next she pulled out the copy of his contract. She tipped her head down so she peered over the top of the glasses. "According to paragraph twenty-five, article B, if you do not listen to me, you will…" She flipped through pages, found the aforementioned paragraph and read, "Invalidate your contract with KEM, otherwise known as Knight Enterprises Motorsports, should you race, ride or otherwise endorse any vehicle other than ones owned by KEM. Such acts will be deemed in direct violation of Driver's contract." She looked back up at him and said, "Said driver being *you*."

Good, Vicky. That's the spirit. Keep him on his toes. Put your degree in law to use. Nothing like a bit of legalese to put a man in his place.

"Oh, yeah?" Brandon asked, somehow scooting even closer to her. "And what will Article B do to stop me?" His leather race gear creaked as he leaned toward her.

"It will," she paused and swallowed. "I mean, *we* will do whatever we deem necessary to get you to stop," she said, holding his gaze with an effort that damn near exhausted her.

"Really?" he asked softly, drawing out the syllables. "Then I guess you're going to have to do your worst, Miss VanCleef, because I am very definitely racing this bike."

He turned away.

Vicky felt like a balloon suddenly cut from its tether. "Hey," she called.

He ignored her.

Damn it. Now what did she do? Should she follow him inside the truck/big rig/car transport… thing?

Brandon slipped between two glass doors. He closed them with a bang.

"Excuse me," a voice said.

Vicky jumped.

Brandon's mechanic gave her a look. Vicky realized she stood in front of his toolbox, one he evidently needed to get into.

"Sorry," she muttered, stepping away.

Okay. So, obviously reasoning with Brandon Burke was not an option. That meant she'd have to resort to Plan B.

If only she had a Plan B.

The mechanic opened a long, narrow drawer, rooted around, then slammed the thing closed with a grunt of disgust. He brushed by her without a second glance, leaving her and the bike all alone as he followed in Brandon's wake.

And an idea began to germinate.

It wasn't a particularly *good* plan. In fact, it was very definitely one of those desperate-times-call-for-desperate-measures ideas that she'd likely regret the next morning.

But Vicky didn't care.

She'd spent months trying to get hired by SSI, and while it wasn't her first choice of agencies to work for, it would do. For now. A foot in the door, she'd called it. Sooner or later she'd go to work for a *real* agency, one with agents who had ethics and clients she didn't want to kill.

Brandon Burke would *not* stand in her way.

Oh, no. He would learn that she wasn't the type of woman to bow down to any man, even if he was spine-tinglingly handsome.

CHAPTER TWO

BRANDON WATCHED Vicky VanCleef walk away, although why the hell she'd patted his bike, he had no idea. He shook his head, turning away.

There was more to *that* woman than met the eye. Well, good for her.

"What was that all about?" Jon, his mechanic, asked, pausing in the middle of the aisle that ran up the length of the hauler. He stopped before a cabinet full of drawers, opened one up and began to fish through it.

"Nothing," Brandon said, shaking his head.

"Didn't sound like nothing." Jon might be six foot one, big, burly and covered with tattoos, but he wasn't dumb. "You bucking the system again?"

"What of it?" Brandon asked, turning his attention to a race card someone had left on the counter. It was a picture of him standing next to his bike. A Hog on steroids, that's what he called his bike with its two-hundred-horsepower engine, fat tires and spiderlike wheelie bars jutting out from behind. The thing topped out at over one hundred and eighty miles per hour, and the feel of it between his legs gave him a rush unlike any other. Okay, maybe there was one other thing that was better.

"Look," Jon said, whatever he was looking for apparently forgotten, "I know you're used to doing as you please. But after everything that's been going on, are you sure thumbing your nose at your new boss is wise?"

Obviously, Jon was worried about his next paycheck. Brandon didn't blame him. If Brandon didn't start making some serious money, then his hobby racing bikes would disappear like tire smoke at a starting line.

"Don't worry about it, Jon. I've got it handled."

Jon flicked his chin up. "Yeah, sounded like it."

But Brandon just shrugged. What could he do? He needed to race. He needed to win the damn purse money, but nobody knew how perilous his financial situation had become. And nobody *would* know. Sure, if he raced, his new boss—Mathew Knight—might get torqued, but he'd get over it. Owners always did.

He glanced out the sliding doors, but he couldn't see Vicky *or* his bike from where he stood.

Gone. Good.

He turned back to his lead mechanic, not because he wanted to talk to him, but because he'd spotted some race fans who looked as if they wanted his autograph. They hung out near the back of his hauler, autograph books plainly in sight, one of them raising a hand to his eyes and leaning forward as if trying to peer through the tinted glass. He wasn't in the mood to sign anything, although he supposed he should be grateful for the few fans he had left.

Stop it, Brandon. Your career hasn't sunk that far yet.

Yeah, the latest headlines had made him look bad. But it'd all blown over. And now he'd found a new job—driving stock cars in the NASCAR Sprint Cup Series—and so his name would soon be front-page news again. Money would start rolling in. Things would get back to normal.

He hoped.

"Troy Goodman told me he thought he saw your dad floating around here earlier," Jon said.

Brandon felt his spine snap erect. "When?"

"About an hour ago."

He forced his vertebrae to relax. "So? He knows better than to come around here."

Jon gave him a look. Not surprising. The feud with his father was well-known. Dear old dad had a mouth about as big as his gut. He also had a habit of showing up at the worst possible moment. That's all Brandon needed right now—someone else chiming in about how he shouldn't do this or shouldn't do that.

Damn it.

"You want me to start with the 05-sized jets," Jon asked in a very obvious attempt to change the subject.

"Use the 05s. Or maybe the 06s," Brandon said, turning away and leaving the hauler. He needed some fresh air.

"Mr. Burke, can I have your autograph?" one of the waiting fans immediately asked.

"Sure," Brandon said, forcing a smile. He couldn't afford to alienate what few fans he had left.

"Thanks," the guy said. A good-looking woman with blond hair and a lanky frame sidled up to have her book signed next. Brandon felt his mood improve.

"You want to take a picture with me and my

bike?" Brandon asked, pointing over his shoulder to where his bike waited.

"Sure," she said.

"What bike?" the guy, maybe her boyfriend, asked.

"You have a camera?" Brandon asked, ignoring him.

"Yeah," the blonde said excitedly. "In my purse."

"What bike?" the guy commented again.

"The one over there," Brandon said impatiently. No wonder blondie here was making eyes at him. Obviously her boyfriend was a few cans short of a six-pack.

Brandon glanced toward his bike.

It was gone.

"ARE YOU SURE it'll fit in there?"

Vicky eyed the bathroom in question before turning to one of the crew members who'd helped her get the bike to its current location outside a stucco building where the public restrooms were located.

"Trust me, honey," one of the four men said. He was a tall, lanky guy with a shock of red hair and freckles all over his face. "It'll fit. You just need to make sure no one's inside."

But Vicky *still* wasn't certain this was a good

idea. When she'd spied Brandon's bike sitting on its rollerized jack stand, unattended, she'd reacted without thought. Only as she'd pushed the thing away had she begun to realize she'd bitten off more than she could chew.

Thank god someone had offered to help. Actually, several someones. Crew members in short-sleeved, dark blue tops with the name of one of the armed services emblazoned across the front had come to her rescue. At first she'd thought they were really from the armed services, but the many multicolored sponsorship patches on their shoulders and shirtsleeves had dispelled that notion. They'd asked what she was doing and Vicky had said without thinking, "Pulling a prank." They'd bought it, especially after she'd shown them her business card and explained that she worked for Brandon's agent.

"Let me go see if anyone's inside," she said reluctantly. She glanced back in the direction they'd come, but there was no sign of an irate Brandon bearing down on them. Not that she had a clear view. They'd traversed the length of the garage, numerous car trailers, pedestrians and outbuildings blocking Brandon's rig from her line of sight. But it wouldn't be hard for him to follow.

All he'd have to do was ask which direction a girl and a drag bike had gone.

Maybe you should bring the bike back.

And maybe I shouldn't, a little voice answered. The man deserved to be thwarted, she thought, pushing on the heavy door that led into the restroom.

"Hello?" she called out, her voice echoing off the concrete interior. "Anybody here?"

A toilet flushed. A woman wearing a white T-shirt and enough makeup to spackle a Roman colosseum emerged from a stall. "You looking for someone, honey?" she asked, her big hair and equally large breasts causing Vicky to step back.

"Um, no. I was just checking to see if the bathroom was empty."

The woman nodded, but not before giving her a puzzled stare. Vicky just stood there, half hoping someone else would come in so she could go back outside and tell the guys this wasn't going to work.

You're going to get canned, she thought to herself.

But if she couldn't get Brandon to pull out of the race, she was done for anyway. Her boss, Scott, was just enough of a tyrant to fire her on the spot. She'd heard the horror stories. She had almost quit at least a dozen times in the past couple of months because of Scott's pushy, abrasive and jerklike behavior. She had a law degree, for goodness' sake. Worst case she could find a job in a law firm someplace.

But that was just it.

She didn't want to work in a boring law firm. She wanted to do something fun and exciting. Working for a sports agency had seemed so different, so cool. When Scott had offered her a job it'd seemed like a dream come true.

The bathroom door closed. Vicky reluctantly headed back outside.

"Look, maybe we should—"

"All clear?" one of the guys asked. The name Rick was emblazoned across his chest.

"Yeah, but I'm thinking maybe this wasn't such a good—"

"Come on, guys," Rick said, encouraging the others to push. "This is gonna be a riot. Brandon's gonna flip."

"He deserves to flip," she thought she heard someone mutter.

One of the other guys held open the door. To Vicky's surprise and, yes, dismay, the bike glided right through.

"There," a guy named Art said, his smile from ear to ear. "Easy peasy."

"Ah, yeah," Vicky said, by now having *serious* second thoughts. "Easy peasy," she echoed.

"I think maybe you should put an Out of Order sign on the door," Rick said.

"Yeah, good idea," Art said.

"And maybe move that garbage can so it blocks the door," someone named Tony said.

"Perfect," Rick said.

"Wow," Art said, glancing around. "Women's restrooms look really different than ours."

Rick slapped Art in the head. "You're such an *idiot*. Go make us an Out of Order sign."

"No, really," Vicky said, sweat beginning to bead on her brow. "I can do that." And maybe push the bike back outside when they were gone. Had anyone noticed it'd disappeared? Maybe she could put it back before that happened.

"That's okay," Art said, already on his way out. "I've got it."

He returned a few minutes later with the sign and a lock, too. The guys chuckled as they wrapped a chain around the door and then secured the padlock in place. Vicky had a mental image of a hole being dug, one that continued to get deeper and deeper, her body pushed into it by a man who looked suspiciously like Brandon.

"I wish we didn't have to go qualify," Art said, handing her the key to the padlock. "I'd love to see the look on Brandon's face when he finds out his bike is missing."

"You have to tell us what he does," Tony said.

"Sure. Um. You've got it," Vicky said.

Now, please, leave.

Because once they did that, she'd be able to unlock the door, pull the bike out and push it back to its original spot, hopefully without Brandon being the wiser.

"Crap, crap, crap," she muttered, watching as her coconspirators walked away, Rick slapping Art's arm again.

You dug the grave, Vicky. Time to lie in it.

Still, she turned back to the door, wondering if she should maybe go find Brandon, confess all, then slink back to New York with her tail tucked between her legs.

"What the *hell* have you done?"

Okay. So maybe a confession was out.

"Where's my bike?" Brandon all but snarled.

"What bike?" she asked, hoping to brazen it out.

He closed the distance between them. Vicky

gulped. His irises changed color when he was angry. She knew this because she had a close-up view of the spectacularly blue orbs, only now those irises were tinged with green.

"You, Vicky VanCleef, are in deep, deep trouble," he said softly. "You better come clean before I have you arrested."

She really *was* in deep trouble, and not because of what she'd done. Oh, no, she was in trouble because even as Brandon stood there, smoke just about steaming out of his ears, even as horrified as *she* was by what *she'd* done, Vicky wondered what it'd be like to kiss a man like him. Someone with such oozing, potent male sexuality that she was certain locking lips with him would be an experience a girl would never forget.

"Arrest me, please," she muttered. "I think I need to be locked away."

CHAPTER THREE

BRANDON STARED down at her, wondering if he'd misheard her. "Did you just say you *wanted* to be arrested?"

"No, I—" She glanced toward the bathroom door as if she hoped to make an escape. Fortunately for him, the facility was out of order. "I said you *can't* have me arrested."

"Oh, yeah?" he asked, taking a step toward her. "Watch me."

He turned away, fully intent on finding a security guard.

"No, wait, don't," she said, her hand resting on his arm.

"Look, Brandon. I know you're furious, and I don't blame you," she added quickly when he was about to tell her just exactly how furious he was. He could feel his cheek twitch, something that usually only happened when he was around his father.

"Let's not be too hasty," she said. "Right now the last thing you need is more bad publicity."

"Excuse me," he said, crossing his arms. It'd grown quiet. Well, as quiet as a racetrack ever got. Spectators still strolled by, a few of them gave them curious looks, but out on the drag strip the steady roar of engines was gone.

Drag-bike qualifying would start soon.

"What if I…ah… What if the person who arrests me goes to the press with this story?"

"Are you kidding? *You're* the only one who's going to get bad press, because as soon as this meet is over, I'm calling your boss."

"That's not a good idea," she said quickly.

"Where's my bike?"

"If you call my boss, you'll have to explain that you want your bike back so you can race it. Scott knows that's in violation of your contract. He'll read you the riot act. You don't want that. Trust me. I'm an official riot-act recipient."

"He wouldn't dare thwart me," he said, leaning down and going nose to nose with her. There were freckles on that nose, he noticed. Lots and lots of them. How could such hell on heels have *freckles?*

"B-but he would. That's why he sent me down here. To, ah, thwart you."

"The bike, please," he said, trying hard not to lose control of his quickly rising temper. Bad things occurred when that happened.

Such as fistfights with his dad. Or his car owner. Or his teammates.

Little cute babies. That's what his anger management counselor had told him to think of whenever he felt his temper slipping out of control. The thing was, he hated kids.

"I can't let you have your bike," she said quickly, as if she had to get the words out fast in order to ensure they were said. Her cheeks reddened. He saw her blink a few times, but she held his gaze.

"Where is it?" he said again. Damn it. He didn't have time for this.

"I can't let you have it."

"Why not?"

"Because if I tell you where it is," she said, "you'll race it. And I can't let you do that. You'd be in direct violation of your contract."

"I violate contracts all the time."

"Well, not this time. If you do, SSI will have no choice but to fire you as a client."

"Excuse me?"

"SSI will not tolerate your flagrant disregard

of the contract you signed with KEM. If you won't listen to us, we'll have to, um... We'll have to let you go."

"Really?" he asked, crossing his arms.

"Yes, really," she said, although she appeared to doubt that was true. Suddenly the fight seemed to drain out of her. She ran her hands through her wispy brown hair, then looked around for a moment. When she met his gaze again, there was a new look in her eyes, one that almost seemed full of concern. "Mr. Burke, can we talk candidly?"

"I thought we already were," he replied equally softly.

"Yes, I suppose we are," she said. "Look, I've read your file, and I have to be honest, I don't think it's in your best interest to do something that would cause SSI to terminate your contract."

"And why's that?" he asked.

"Are you kidding?" she said, eyes wide. "Do you really have to ask after all the trouble you've been in in recent months? Walking out on that open-wheel guy, Bob Manly—the man that owned the Indy 500 car you used to race. Aren't you still in legal trouble with him? Then there's the bad press. You didn't exactly make a good impression at your first NASCAR Sprint Cup

Series race last year, did you? You're not king of
the racing hill anymore and so I'm thinking you'll
have a heck of time finding another agent. I mean,
the racing industry will only give you so many
chances, right? Surely your time is drawing to an
end."

"You think so?"

"I do," she said with a firm nod.

"Shows you how little you know about the
racing industry. I can find a new agent like
that," he said, snapping his fingers. "And a new
ride, too."

"Oh, really?" she said. "Because I have to
wonder, where are all those offers now? Your file
isn't exactly brimming with prime opportunities.
We had to practically beg Outlaw Bail Bonds to
sponsor you, and in the end they only agreed because your bad-boy reputation fits their corporate
image perfectly. Trust me when I say our phone
wasn't exactly ringing off the hook when Scott
was trying to find you a car to drive."

"Things will turn around," Brandon said, holding on to his patience by the thinnest of threads.

"Oh, yeah? How? You may not be driving a
race car for the next several months. Did you skip
over the clause in your contract that says if you

breach your agreement with KEM, then you can't go drive elsewhere?"

"Where's my bike?" he asked again, his cheek beginning to twitch.

"Let's say you do happen to find another job. What will you do when KEM files a lawsuit against you? Because you know they will. Can you afford to fend off another legal dispute?"

"You don't know anything about racing," he said. "And I'm tired of standing here. Either tell me where my bike is, or I call your boss."

"All right, fine," she said. "You're right. I don't know a whole lot about racing, but I do know the law. You'll be in deep trouble if you ignore KEM Motorsports' dictums. But here," she said, tossing him something. It was a key. "I'm tired of dealing with men who think they rule the world. Go ahead. Take your bike. Have fun riding it. It'll be the last time you drive something fast for a while."

She turned away.

"Wait," he yelled. "Where is it?"

"In the bathroom," she called.

The bathroom? He eyed the Out of Order sign, then the lock on the door. What the—

Why that clever little…

His gaze shifted back to her. Did she have a

law degree? he wondered, unlocking the door. His hands shook. He clenched them, glancing back at her. He'd have to admit, she looked like an attorney in her tailored pants and no-nonsense blouse.

When he pushed against the bathroom door, he stopped.

Have fun…it'll be the last time you drive something fast for a while.

Yeah, right. KEM would look the other way when he raced his bike. Team owners always did.

Can you afford *another legal dispute?*

So what if he couldn't. He'd be making money hand over fist soon enough.

Not if you're not driving for KEM, he thought.

"Son of a—"

He pushed on the door with more force than necessary. The wood connected with the wall with a loud boom. He'd be speaking with her boss, just as soon as he finished racing today, because if there was one thing he knew for certain, it was that Vicky VanCleef had crossed a line.

She'd be the one getting fired.

CHAPTER FOUR

SHE WAS GOING to get fired.

Vicky knew this the way she knew blondes got all the guys and brunettes all the leftovers.

She told herself not to think about it as she rode the subway into work the Monday after Brandon's race, her oversize purse slung over one shoulder. The train from Brooklyn was, as usual, packed with wall-to-wall people.

After she got off the train, she walked to the offices of SSI which were located on Manhattan's east side. The building where she worked loomed over her as she darted out of the way of a taxicab.

Maybe I should have stayed at home.

Scott didn't need to see her to fire her, right? She could have stayed in bed, read a book, eaten a box of chocolates.

Go on, Vicky. No sense in delaying the inevitable.

She reluctantly entered the building and took

the elevator to the twelfth floor. The double doors that led to the office's hallowed halls displayed the company's logo, the SSI letters jutting out like the *S* on a Superman T-shirt. She'd been impressed when she'd first spotted the massive front desk with its half-round front and marble top three months ago when she'd started the job. Behind a harried-looking receptionist was a wall with a door to the left of it. Behind the glass, executive assistants, office clerks and junior agents moved between shoulder-high cubicle walls. Senior agents sat in offices that were set around the perimeter wall, the glass fronts allowing the assistants to see their bosses, and sunlight to filter in from outside. Vicky headed to the far right corner and her own cubicle just outside of Scott's spacious office.

Scott, her erstwhile boss, was busy tossing a basketball into a miniature hoop attached to a bookshelf across from his desk. He'd removed his silk jacket; Vicky could see it hanging off the back of his chair. His lips moved nonstop, the headset on his head glowing red, which told Vicky he was on the phone.

There was a yellow Post-it note on her desk. *See me.*

She sank into her office chair.

Damn.

Her eyes skated around the beige-colored cubicle. Her gaze focused on the picture of her parents she'd pinned to the fabric-covered walls. She stared at the stern countenance of her mom and dad. Mom, with her stunning good looks, her collagen-enhanced lips trying to smile. Dad, with his perfectly coiffed gray head held high and solemn expression. The photo had been taken at a posh Manhattan restaurant, right after she'd told her mom and dad that she didn't want to join VanCleef & VanCleef. She wanted to do something fun with her degree. Something different.

They hadn't approved.

Her thoughts were interrupted by her phone beeping. Scott's gravelly voice all but roared over the intercom. "Vicky, front and center."

Two weeks ago Vicky would have complied tacitly. Today she snapped, "Aye aye, Captain," without missing a beat. Maybe dealing with Brandon had taught her to be more aggressive. Or maybe, like any condemned prisoner, she recognized she had nothing to lose by talking back.

She slid her purse off her shoulder, straightened her suit, slipped off the tennis shoes she wore while commuting and slid on the heels she wore around the office.

"You wanted to see me?" she asked, entering Scott's office.

"Sit down," Scott said, his bright blue gaze eyeing her up and down, manicured hands drumming on his dark oak desk. He always scoped her out. At first Vicky had thought he was coming on to her, but she'd quickly learned he was merely giving her the once-over. Scott put great stock in appearances. When she'd come to work one day in casual pants and a cotton shirt, his ocular scan had been followed by a lip-curling grimace of distaste. She'd taken the hint.

"Brandon called me this weekend," he said without preamble.

"Oh, yeah?" Vicky asked, her ribs vibrating beneath the assault of her heart.

Scott nodded, then leaned back in his chair. The thing creaked in protest. Vicky had a mental image of it tipping over backward, Scott's loafers thrust skyward as he tumbled over into the credenza behind him.

"Good work."

Huh?

Scott smiled now, his arms lifting as he hooked his hands behind his neck. "Hiding his bike. Genius. I laughed my ass off."

Vicky blinked, thinking for an instant that she couldn't have heard him correctly.

"Brandon gave me an earful," he continued, the smile turning into a smirk. "The jerk wanted me to fire you."

"But you're not?" she asked in a weak voice.

"Hell, no," he said, leaning forward so suddenly the wheels of his chair slapped the plastic carpet protector. "You got him to change his mind about racing."

"I did?"

Scott didn't say anything for a moment. "You mean, you didn't know?"

She shook her head. "After throwing the key to the lock at him, I pretty much walked away."

"You *locked* the bathroom *door?*" Scott asked, chuckling.

She nodded again. Vicky was still reeling with the realization that she'd somehow managed to get through to Brandon.

"No wonder he was so pissed off." Scott picked up a pen off his desk, signing his name with a flourish at the bottom of a sheet of paper.

"Here," he said, sliding the page across his desk. "Take this to accounting."

"What is it?" she asked.

"It's a cash advance approval form. You're going to need some money and a company credit card."

"Uh, why?"

"For managing Brandon," he said. That was the thing about Scott. He always assumed she could read his mind. It drove her nuts.

"And how, exactly, will I be managing Brandon?"

He glanced up at her, giving her a look that made her feel stupid. That was the other thing about Scott. He couldn't be bothered to explain things.

"You're going down to North Carolina," he said, each word pronounced succinctly, as if Vicky were hard of hearing. "And keeping an eye on him."

"North Carolina?"

He shook his head, looked toward the heavens as if seeking help from above. Vicky felt sorry for his girlfriend—the one whose picture sat on the credenza behind him. The woman must be a saint to put up with Scott.

"You'll be staying in North Carolina for the

next few weeks. You've gotten a promotion, Vicky. You're a junior agent, and your first client, your *only* client, is Brandon Burke."

CHAPTER FIVE

"WHERE THE HELL IS HE?"

Brandon glanced at his watch, then around at the lobby of the posh luxury hotel. He'd been ordered to pick up his agent at 7:30 a.m.—sharp—only to get here and discover the man was a no-show, damn it.

"I should have told him to find his own way to the damn meeting," he muttered.

And he would have, too, except something about Scott's tone warned Brandon that his chauffeur services weren't so much a request as they were a command performance. At least the digs were nice, Brandon thought, doing a slow sweep of the hotel lobby. He stood in an atrium, one that rose up at least twenty stories high. Fancy, wrought iron railings rimmed the interior. Each room had its own balcony, one that overlooked the center of the hotel. A waterfall tinkled in the distance. Plush trees and carefully placed potted palms shielded guests from other visitors' views. It felt and smelled like a rain forest, the air thick with moisture and the scent of fresh earth.

"There you are."

Maybe all that carbon monoxide had affected his brain because that sure sounded like...

"You ready? Let's go. We're late. Took me forever to get to the lobby."

Brandon's brain refused to reconcile what his eyes observed. Standing before him, looking as calm and cool as the lawyer Scott professed her to be, was Vicky VanCleef in a dark blue skirt suit, hair smoothly slicked back.

"What are *you* doing here?" Brandon asked.

"Surprise," she said, the brown briefcase that she held brushing her knee-length skirt. "Scott sent me to handle this meeting."

"Excuse me?"

She wore thick-rimmed glasses today, the kind that were supposed to make her look stylish and elegant. All they succeeded in doing was to make her look more like a bookworm.

"I'm supposed to accompany you to your meeting with Mr. Knight," she responded.

"But...I thought Scott said he was firing you."

She scooted closer to him. Hell, she even leaned in and peered up. "'Fraid not, Brandon," she said, a smile spreading across her face, one that wasn't the least bit amused. "Not for your lack of trying, however."

Actually, he hadn't mentioned firing her to Scott at all. It was his agent who'd suggested the idea after Brandon had called to complain about the bike-stealing debacle. Once Brandon had calmed down he'd realized Vicky might have a point, and in the end he'd decided not to race. He was still pissed that she'd dared to touch his bike, but he'd changed his mind about getting her canned.

"So you *haven't* been fired?"

"Nope," she said quickly. "In fact, I got a promotion."

Why did he have a feeling he wasn't going to like what was coming next?

"I'm your new agent. Well," she quickly amended, "I'm technically a junior agent. Scott was so impressed with the way I handled you in South Carolina that he thought I should do it from here on out—you know, manage you as if you were my client."

"No way."

"Yes, Brandon." She looked so damned smug

about it, Brandon felt his cheek begin to twitch. What was it about her that always managed to do that to him?

"Scott's my agent," he snapped. "I signed with *him*. You can't be my agent."

"Oh, he's still representing you. But after what happened in South Carolina he thinks you need a little extra—" she pursed her lips, tipped her head side to side "—push to behave, and so I'm it."

Brandon reached for his cell phone.

"Don't bother. He'll just ignore you."

"Then I'll leave a message."

"He'll ignore those, too."

"You're not my agent."

"Junior agent."

"Whatever."

"And I'm afraid you have no choice. It's in your contract with SSI. Paragraph 22, section A. Agent can, if Agent so desires, appoint a Junior Agent to handle Client if the Agent deems it necessary." She lifted a brow. "Or did you not read that, either?"

"I read it. Of course I read it. I read every page of my contract." In a way. He'd just fallen asleep after the first page. "But just because I read it doesn't mean I have to agree to it."

She released a laugh that was damn near a snort. "Yes, Brandon, it does. You *signed* that contract, thereby agreeing to every word. But if you don't like it, fire Scott."

That robbed him of speech for a moment. "Excuse me?"

"Look," she said, "I don't want to work with *you* any more than you want to work with *me*. If you fire Scott, then you'd be doing me a favor. We wouldn't have to work together and I wouldn't be at fault so I could keep my job."

She didn't want to work with him?

"Then what was all that crap about never finding another agent?" Brandon asked.

"I lied," she said. "In my briefcase I have a list of agencies who might be willing to work with you. I'll give it to you if you want."

"You're a piece of work," he said.

"I'm just trying to make it easy on us both."

"No," he said. "I'm not firing Scott. You're stuck with me."

"Are you sure?"

"Positive," he said, although damned if he knew why.

"Fine. Let's go."

He didn't follow.

"Or not," she said. "I can do this alone. I have a feeling whatever Mr. Knight has to say won't be pleasant. But don't worry, I can take it on the chin for you. That's my job."

"You're not seriously going without me."

"Yes, Brandon, I am."

AND SHE DID. Vicky hailed a cab, gave the cabby KEM's address, and headed off to Knight Enterprises without breaking a sweat.

Well, all right. Maybe her hands shook. And maybe her heart beat as fast as a hyperactive poodle's. And maybe she had to resist the urge to close her eyes and groan.

Had she really told Brandon to fire Scott?

She had. But to be honest, she was tired of it all. Scott was such a tyrant. And Brandon appeared to be no better. And now she was forced to do Scott's dirty work. Rumor had it Mr. Knight had asked his lawyers to join him at this meeting with Brandon, probably because they, too, could see the handwriting on the wall. Brandon needed to be brought under control, and with Vicky's boss being as slimy as he was, she wouldn't doubt that Scott had known about the meeting before giving her Brandon as a client. More than likely Scott hadn't wanted to deal with the matter and so he'd sent her in to take the rap.

"You trying to get a job with Knight Enterprises?" the cabdriver asked.

"Actually, no," she said, glancing out at the landscape.

"You a reporter or something?"

Who was this guy? The FBI? "Actually, no," she said, hoping that he'd get the message that she didn't want to talk. She should probably take another look at Brandon's contract with KEM. She'd pretty much memorized its various clauses on the way down to Charlotte, but it never hurt to take a second look.

"Not much of a KEM fan, myself," the cabdriver said. George was his name, at least according to the Operator's Permit that hung on the dashboard.

The snaps of Vicky's brand-new briefcase flicked open too fast and caught her thumb. She gasped in pain, instantly sucking it into her mouth.

Ow, ow, ow.

"I think Todd Peters is a jerk," George continued. "And that new guy they hired, Brandon Burke, he's even worse."

"I know," Vicky murmured. Boy, did she ever

know. She pulled out a legal-sized document, one that was at least twenty pages long.

"Don't know what Mr. Knight was thinking hiring that jerk. I heard he mouthed off to some of the drivers last season."

"Yeah?" she said, her eyes skimming the first page. Terms, indemnity and termination. Those were the clauses on the first page.

"Yeah," the man said. "Apparently he called—"

Vicky's seat belt slammed into her shoulder.

"What the hell?" her driver yelled, braking as if a herd of elephants blocked him. "What does that jerk think he's doing?"

Vicky looked up, just in time to see a foreign-looking car swerve in front of the cab to the shoulder of the road. The cabdriver did the same out of self-defense. Both vehicles ended up sliding onto the gravel easement.

"Was he trying to avoid hitting something?" Vicky asked, turning to peer behind them.

"No—"

Vicky heard the man gasp.

"I don't believe it," George said.

"I know," Vicky said, facing forward again. "The way people drive always amazes me, too. But this is nothing. You should see New York."

George didn't reply. Vicky wondered if he was having heart problems or something— shock could do that to a person. She glanced out the front window, and the reason for George's speechlessness became immediately apparent.

Brandon Burke walked toward the cab.

"Oh, crap," she muttered. "What the heck does *he* want?"

"You know him?" George asked.

"Unfortunately, yes," she said, watching as Brandon crossed to her side of the car.

He opened the door. "I need to talk to you," Brandon said.

"So you *ran* my *cab* off the side of the road?"

"I wanted to talk to you right away."

"And you couldn't call my cell phone?"

"I don't have it."

Oh. That's right.

"You could have waited until we arrived at KEM."

His shoulders slumped. It was strange, because Vicky could see the fight just drain right out of him.

"I'm sorry." He said the words quickly. It was as if he had to get them out fast before he lost the ability to say them. "I should have just waited until we arrived at KEM. I'll just meet you there…"

He turned away and Vicky found herself calling, "No wait," before she could think better of it. He looked so much like a remorseful schoolboy that she couldn't resist asking, "What did you want to talk to me about?"

He didn't answer right away. She waited. Out on the road a car whizzed by. She watched as the wind from its passing caused a lock of his hair to fall over one eye. He flicked it away impatiently.

"I'm sorry," he said. "I have this horrible temper. I need to learn to control it better. It's not your fault Scott switched things up. I shouldn't have snapped like that."

Vicky glanced at the cabdriver. The guy's eyes were glued to his rearview mirror, as if he were watching daytime TV.

"Hang on," she said, slipping out of the car. They'd stopped near a wooded area, Vicky's heels sinking into gravel and the wet earth as she moved a safe distance away from the side of the road. Brandon followed. When she turned back to him, she crossed her arms in front of her.

"I think you're right," she said. "I think we got off on the wrong foot."

"We did," he said with a nod. "I'm not the easiest person to work with. I know that. It's just that Scott switching things up without even calling me really made me mad. I'm sorry I took it out on you."

Vicky released a breath that was pure relief. "Well, if it's any consolation, Scott's pretty good at stepping on toes."

"I can see that."

She looked away. To be honest, she had to shift her gaze to somewhere else because Brandon with kindness in his eyes was a Brandon that made her legs turn into spaghetti noodles. "Apology accepted."

His gaze settled on the cab. "You sure you don't want to ride with me to KEM?" he asked. "No sense in wasting a cab fare."

She didn't want to ride with him. That meant sharing a car. Being close to him. Having a *conversation* with him.

"That's okay," she said quickly.

"You sure?" he asked. "Seems kind of silly to take two cars when mine's right there."

She glanced at his car. It was bright red, low-slung and it looked more as if it belonged on the Autobahn than city streets. White racing stripes intersected its middle—like a giant, white equal sign. Probably an expensive import of some sort.

She jerked upright.

"Hey," she said. "You're not supposed to be driving foreign cars."

"Relax," he said. "It's a GT made by my sponsored manufacturer. I'm legal."

"Oh," she said, and for some reason, she had a hard time meeting his gaze.

"Come on," he said. "I'll give you a ride."

"No, no. That's okay."

"I insist," he said, his big hand cupping her back.

Vicky just about jerked away. She looked up at him in shock, but only for a moment because she couldn't look him in the eye...again.

Curse it all, she thought, she couldn't *possibly* find him attractive still? No *way*.

But she did.

It didn't matter that five minutes ago she'd been muttering expletives that included his name. It didn't matter that he'd tried to get her fired. A rush of purely irrational and completely unexpected lust caused her body to tingle in places it had *no* business tingling, heat that radiated out from the very spot where his palm rested against the small of her back.

Which just went to show how completely illogical the human brain could be where sexual attraction was concerned.

"Come on," he said. "We'll go tell the cab-driver his services aren't needed anymore."

She didn't want to tell the cabdriver anything. She wanted to get in the yellow car and take off. The sooner the better.

But she knew if she kept on protesting, it would seem odd. Just as she knew there was a part of her—a tiny part—that wanted to be alone with Brandon. Even if it was for the fifteen-minute drive to KEM's headquarters.

"We won't be needing your services anymore," Brandon said to the driver, taking his hand away from the small of Vicky's back so he could reach for his wallet. "Here, let me get you some money."

"Actually, that's really not necessary, Mr. Burke," the cabbie said. "Really. We've only gone a few miles."

"Yeah, but you would have gone a whole lot farther if I haven't stopped you. Here," he repeated, handing George a twenty-dollar bill. "I insist."

"Thanks, Mr. Burke."

Brandon had just found himself a new fan, Vicky thought, using her briefcase as a shield in front of her. The cabdriver even went so far as to call out, "Good luck at the race this weekend."

Unbelievable.

He placed his hand in the small of her back again. Vicky just about closed her eyes.

You have the hots for him.

"Come on," he said, and when Vicky looked up at his smiling face, Vicky knew it was true. She very *definitely* had the hots for him. "You're going to love my car."

He opened the passenger-side door, the smell of new car filling the air, and then he touched her again, helping her into the car with a guiding hand.

Oh, lord.

She noticed then that he had creases that branched out from the edges of his eyes. And that he had rock-star hair—the strands swept back from his head and left long and curly around the nape of his neck. And that he had a way of looking at her that made her feel exposed and vulnerable.

And that, miraculously, she'd started to like him.

CHAPTER SIX

"Stupid idiot," Brandon thought he heard her mutter.

He slid into the leather driver's seat and glanced over at Vicky one last time.

She had the hots for him.

Oh, yeah. She wanted him. No mistaking the blush that spread around the collar of her I-want-to-be-taken-seriously suit.

Well, well, well.

He started his car, five hundred horsepower roaring to life with a near feral growl. When he found his gaze resting on Vicky yet again—despite warning himself not to turn and stare—she was gazing out the window, hands in her laps, her fingers contracting over and over again.

"Hey, listen," he said, placing a hand on her thigh.

She flinched like a dog whose nose had just been smacked.

"Don't," she said.

"Sorry," he said, biting back a smile. "It's a habit of mine, touching women when I talk."

"And I'm a person who enjoys personal space." She made a box out of her hands. "My space," she said. She motioned outside the box. "Your space. No touchy-touchy."

He almost laughed because he knew that despite what she said, she wanted him.

"Let's go," she said impatiently.

He started the car and punched the gas pedal.

"Hey," she yelled, thrust back in her seat by the force of his acceleration.

He set his smile free.

Nothing like horsepower to put him in a good mood. That was one of the perks of his job. Not only did he get his choice of cars—as long as they were made by his race car's manufacturer—but he got to drive them for free, compliments of one of the local dealerships.

"Sorry," he said. "I have a tendency to do that."

"Go figure," he heard her mutter.

It was one of those early spring days where the sky was as blue as pool water. Warm, too. It made him want to roll the windows down and turn up the radio.

He took his foot off the accelerator. A glance at his passenger revealed she'd gone deathly white. "You okay?" he asked.

"No," she squeaked. "I'm not."

"Too fast?"

"What do you have under the hood? A space shuttle engine?"

"No," he said with a shake of his head. "It's a supercharged, 5.4 liter V-8."

"Whatever that is," she replied.

Brandon wondered why he felt the need to play with her a bit. Maybe because he wanted to get back some of his own control. He still couldn't believe she'd asked him to fire Scott just because she didn't want to work with him.

"It means it's got a very," he said, leaning toward her, his eyes darting between her and the road, "*very* big engine."

The look she gave him could have melted the interior dashboard and *that* was made of carbon fiber.

"Like me," he added, just in case she'd missed his point. He rested his palm on her thigh again.

She picked up his hand as if it was roadkill.

"Box," she said, making a square out of her hands yet again. "Remember?"

He'd expected her to blush. Maybe even wilt into the seat. She did neither. That surprised him. He had considerable experience with the opposite sex, and he'd recognized the look of sheepish dismay he'd seen earlier. It'd been followed by a curse and a blush, a sure sign he'd gotten her hot and bothered.

"Look," she said, reaching for the briefcase she'd set at her feet. "Since you seem so bored right now, perhaps we should go over your contract again."

Bored? Did she think he was flirting with her to pass the time?

Well, wasn't he doing exactly that?

Yeah, he admitted. She was an uptight, undersexed woman—exactly the type he liked to avoid. Unfortunately, it seemed as if they'd be stuck together for a while.

But maybe that wouldn't be such a bad thing?

"Sure," he said. "Go ahead and refresh my memory."

She pulled out a legal document that made Brandon's stomach turn just looking at it. Words. He hated words.

"Okay, so," she said, settling the document on her lap. "I don't think we need to go over the first paragraph. It just spells out the names of those people who have a fiduciary interest in the contract. The next paragraph is the Indemnity paragraph. It just states that you agree not to sue KEM Enterprises or its employees if something they do results in legal action…."

Brandon nodded, though to be honest, he was listening with half an ear. What if she asked him to read something? What then?

Relax, Brandon. You're driving. She's not going to ask you to do that.

"Are you listening?" Vicky asked.

The words intruded upon his deliberations.

"I'm listening," he said, pressing down the accelerator so he could merge onto Interstate 77.

"Then what did I just say?" she asked.

Brandon glanced over at her. She was leaning against her seat, her eyes narrowed as though she was about to order him to the corner of the room.

And it hit him then what he could do to keep her a little more malleable.

Seduce Vicky.

Okay, so maybe not seduce her. Just flirt with her

a bit to distract her. Sure, it wasn't exactly ethical. But the truth of the matter was, he was desperate.

But something told him it'd take a lot of work to get Vicky alone.

Ah, but wouldn't it be fun to try? His eyes caught on the legs that peeked out from beneath her business suit. They looked surprisingly tanned and toned.

Yup. Maybe not a bad idea at all.

"Brandon?" she said, looking at him over the top of her glasses.

It was that look more than anything that sealed the deal. He had a feeling seducing Vicky would be a challenge—and he loved to be challenged.

"Oh, I was listening," he said, reaching out and touching her again. "Your voice can really turn a guy on."

Vicky didn't react. Not at all. Wait, she blinked at him. He knew this because her glasses magnified her eyes and he could see the way they stared at him intently, her own gaze darting between his two irises as if debating which one to jab a finger into.

And then, to his shock, she left his hand on her thigh. "Let's just go back to the point where you

tuned out, okay? Or did you want to try and seduce me right now, in which case I'll just put this
contract away so I'll be unencumbered while I
laugh my head off."

Seduce her? How did she know?

"What makes you think I'm trying to seduce
you?" he asked, pulling his hand away and
clenching the steering wheel. His fingers felt
weird, probably because her leg had been surprisingly warm.

She tipped her head down and stared at him
over the rim of her glasses. "Your voice can really
turn a guy on." She mimicked his masculine
voice. "Pish," she hissed. "I've heard better."

"Better what?"

"Your whole flirt-with-the-plain-Jane-lawyer-
to-get-out-of-work thing. I'm not buying it."

"You think I'm flirting with you to avoid dis-
cussing my contract?"

"What else could it be?" she said.

"Maybe I'm genuinely attracted to you."

"Yeah, right." She looked away, shaking her
head.

"Maybe I am."

"Years of being the class president—*not* the
prom queen—has illustrated the fallacy of *those*

words." She smiled, and it appeared as if she *really* didn't care.

"I'm smart, not pretty. And that's okay," she said quickly. "I *like* being smart. From what I've observed, being gorgeous is vastly overrated. It takes twice as long to be taken seriously. Most women hate you on sight. You have to wear make-up wherever you go because, God forbid, you should ever look less than perfect. Obviously, I don't have that problem. I don't care about make-up. I'm smart, and that's more important than looks because looks fade. So if you don't mind, let's stop the kidding around. I'd like to finish going over your contract with you since you seem to have forgotten the bulk of it."

He stared at her in shock for a full five seconds, all the while peeking glances at the road in front of him. When he finally pulled his gaze away, it was just in time to spot the road he needed. "Hang on," he said, jerking the wheel right.

"Jeesh," he heard her mutter as she clutched the armrest.

"You know," he said, shifting gears and ignoring her complaints. "I've often heard smart women are hot in bed."

"That's exactly my point," she immediately

countered. "You've *heard*. Ergo, you have yet to experience it yourself. You have no firsthand experience and thus lack the skill set which would enable you to make a fair assessment of the situation."

Skill set?

He almost burst out laughing. And if they hadn't been in such a hurry, he'd have pulled over right then. Maybe used his "skill set" for both their pleasure.

Later.

Much later. If there was one thing Brandon was good at, then it was learning new things. That was the reason why he'd switched from IRL to the NASCAR Sprint Cup Series, and why he'd continue to drive for whoever wanted to put him behind a wheel. He'd never met anyone like Vicky before, although at this point he wasn't sure if that was a good thing or a bad thing. She made him want to laugh, and it'd been a long time since a woman had done that to him.

"Now," she said. "Are you ready to stop playing around and get to work?"

Oh, he'd get to playing around again. With her.

"Shoot," he said, because there was something else Brandon was good at—being patient. He would kiss her, if only to prove to her that he was right. Beneath the business suit was a ferocious kitten, one who would *enjoy* his touch.

He would make sure of it.

THE MEETING WASN'T quite what Vicky expected. There were no KEM attorneys present, and Mathew Knight showed a remarkable amount of restraint as he read Brandon the riot act.

"I thought I made myself clear," Mr. Knight said. He didn't wear a suit, something that surprised Vicky since she'd have thought the owner of Fly For Less Airlines would dress in Armani. But no. He wore a red shirt with the Fly For Less logo on it and dark brown slacks. "I don't want you strapping into anything other than a stock car."

Vicky's gaze moved to Brandon and she was tempted to kick him under the table just so he'd look at her and she could give him an "I told you so" glare.

But all he did was lean back in his chair and cross his arms, like a petulant boy who'd just been told to stop shooting spitballs.

"I don't think I can stress this enough, Miss VanCleef," Mr. Knight said, his eyes shifting to hers and glinting like cold emerald chips. "If your client doesn't begin to toe the line, he's out. We were very careful to include several clauses in his contract that will give us full recourse should he cross the line. KEM is not afraid to take legal action."

No doubt. In her professional opinion, Brandon's contract was ironclad. If Brandon continued to ignore KEM's dictums, not only would he forfeit the right to race someone else's stock car, but KEM would demand reimbursement for the anticipated revenue he'd earn them over the remaining years of his contract—an estimated five million dollars.

Vicky glanced at Brandon, trying to gauge if any of this was sinking in. Judging by the look on his face, it wasn't. His eyes showed about as much emotion as a piece of wood.

She turned back to Mr. Knight, trying to appear poised and confident when what she felt was way, way out of her league.

"I appreciate your candor," she said, proud that her voice sounded steady. "And I realize that you're being very gracious in giving Brandon a chance to prove himself. Trust me, SSI wants Brandon to succeed as much as you do."

"Undoubtedly," Mr. Knight said, glancing at

Brandon as if he expected the driver to finally say something. "But with Daytona only a week away, we need Brandon on his best behavior."

"I'm not racing this weekend," he said.

"Excuse me?" Mr. Knight asked, cocking a black brow.

"If you won't let me race my drag bike, I'm not going to race your stock car."

"You can't do that," Vicky and Mathew Knight both said at the same time.

"Brandon, we talked about this on the way over," Vicky added. "You're bound by the terms of your contract for the next two years. Remember the Breach of Contract clause I read to you. If *you* don't drive, *we* get in trouble."

He knew that. Of course he knew that. He was just being difficult. The question was, why? she wondered.

"No team owner I've driven for in the past has enforced that clause," he said, leaning forward in a sudden rush, his muscular arms flexing as he rested them on the glass-covered table.

"I'm not most owners," Mr. Knight said. "And if you climb on that bike, you'll be hearing from my lawyers."

Right then a beep sounded. They heard a disconnected voice on the intercom say, "Mr. Knight, your fiancée's on line two."

"Okay, thanks," Mr. Knight said. "Excuse me a moment."

He got up, but he didn't leave the room. Vicky quickly grabbed a piece of paper, slid it across the table's smooth surface to Brandon, and wrote: *What are you doing?*

Brandon glanced at the paper, his eyes growing—if possible—even more emotionless just before he shook his head.

Are you trying to blow this? she wrote next, tapping the paper with her pen to get his attention when it became obvious he wouldn't look in her direction. Once again, all he did was shake his head.

Fine, she wrote next. *Be a jerk. But tell me you're bluffing about not racing this next weekend.*

Nothing. Nada. Not even a shake of his head. By then it was too late. Mr. Knight rejoined them. "Sorry," he said. "Where were we?"

"I'm not racing," Brandon said again.

Vicky just about clutched her hair and screamed.

"That's right," Mr. Knight said with a narrowing of his eyes. "And I was about to tell you that I'll do whatever it takes to keep you *off* said bike."

Vicky didn't doubt Mr. Knight's word for a

moment. Mathew Knight wasn't one of the richest men in the world for nothing. Fly For Less, the airline he'd built from the ground up, was one of the highest grossing carriers in the industry. That kind of success didn't come from letting people walk all over you. During a time when other airlines had closed their doors, Fly For Less had continued to grow, offering deeper and deeper discounts and yet somehow managing to increase their profits. If Mr. Knight wanted to play hardball, he had the money and resources to do exactly that.

"Brandon," Vicky said. "Maybe we should talk outside for a second." She gave Mr. Knight an "I'll handle this" look.

"We've done enough talking," Brandon said.

"Outside," Vicky repeated, more sternly. She even placed a hand on his shoulder, leaned in and said, "Now," in a voice that had always worked on children whenever she'd used it.

Brandon looked as though he might refuse. She tightened her grip. He slowly stood, although not before giving his team owner a look, one that clearly said this wasn't over until it was over.

"Why are you being such an ass?" Vicky asked

the moment they were out of earshot. "I don't know why you feel the need to bait Mr. Knight, but you really should stop."

"He's trying to control me."

Vicky glanced back toward the glass doors of the conference room. Undoubtedly, Mr. Knight could hear them. She led Brandon farther down the hall. "He's not trying to control you," she said as they entered the main lobby, a massive space that featured glass walls to their left and right. There was a showroom to her right and to her left a store that appeared to sell team merchandise judging by the racks of T-shirts and jerseys. "It's just business to him."

The receptionist chirped a happy, "Have a nice day," as they walked by her desk.

"We'll be right back," Vicky mumbled, heading for the tinted doors directly ahead of them. She needed to walk, the faster the better. If she didn't burn off some of this energy, she'd end up stuffing Brandon's mouth with his own contract.

"Where are we going?" Brandon asked.

"To talk outside," she said, pushing open the front door and entering a courtyard sandwiched in between the U-shaped building.

"What makes you think I'll listen to you any

more than I did Mr. Knight in there," Brandon said, motioning over his shoulder.

"You'll listen to me because, despite all evidence to the contrary, you're a very smart boy." She stopped beneath the shade of one of the trees that lined either side of the sidewalk. Grass stretched out beyond, ending at the base of the glass-covered building.

"Boy?"

"Man. Whatever. I don't know what happened to you the moment you walked into the conference room, but I don't like it. You've gone right back to being a jerk again. The attitude stops. Right here. Right now. If it doesn't, that's it. SSI and you are through."

"I thought that's what you wanted? For me to get fired. Or for me to fire SSI."

He *would* bring that up, she thought, squinting against a spot of sunlight that poked through the leaves. The fact of the matter was, she'd just been bluffing. Or had she been? Damn. She didn't know what she'd been doing, she just knew that in the meeting with Brandon and Mathew Knight she'd felt a sudden urge to make things right—despite the way he'd been joking around with her earlier.

She *liked* representing Brandon. Maybe it was

the feeling that for once in her life, *she* was in control. Well, sort of. Maybe it was sitting across from a man like Mathew Knight—someone who inspired her with his success. She wanted to help make careers. And, yes, damn it, she wanted to *be* close to the glamour and glitz of professional athletes. She wanted to be somebody, someone other than the daughter of the übersuccessful and ultrawealthy VanCleef family. Maybe, ultimately, that was it—she wanted her own identity, and if this was as close as she got to "being somebody," then so be it.

It was time to start acting like an agent.

"Look, Brandon," she said, spying their reflection in the glass across the grassy yard. The man looked handsome even from a distance. "We don't have much time. Mr. Knight isn't the type who likes to wait. Therefore it's imperative you heed my words. Don't cross the boss. Go back inside, smile at the man, and tell him you've seen the light. I know you can do it. You did it with me earlier. Somewhere inside you is a reasonable human being. I'd like that same man I saw earlier to make an appearance in the conference room now."

He looked ready to argue again, but just as it had out by the side of the road, the fight seemed to drain out of him. "Do you really think he'll come after me if I race?"

"I do," she said with an emphatic nod.

"All right, fine," he said. "But I want something in return."

"What's that?" she asked warily.

He gave her a smile, one laced with wicked charm. "You," he pronounced happily.

CHAPTER SEVEN

BRANDON HAD NEVER SEEN a woman blush like Vicky...and he loved it.

"What?" she asked, her eyes wide behind her glasses.

"You," he said again, trying hard to keep from smiling. She looked like a cat whose tail had been stepped on.

"You're out of your mind," she said.

"Come on, Vicky," he said softly, lifting a hand to her face and touching her cheek. She had really soft skin. "How much is it worth for me to behave?"

"You're insane," she said, stepping back so fast she almost fell off the edge of the sidewalk. "You can joke around all you want, but in about thirty seconds, Mr. Knight is going to walk out of that conference room—if he hasn't already— and something tells me that if that happens, then you can expect a summons from his attorneys shortly thereafter."

"I'm not kidding," Brandon said, although he really was, but he was also curious about what she'd say next.

"Of course you are. That's what you do." She rolled her eyes. "You say whatever outrageous thing that comes to mind. It doesn't matter if you actually believe it or not, just as long as you shock the people you're talking to. I've watched your media clips, the ones you sent Scott when you asked him to rep you. If an interview isn't going your way, or if a reporter has pissed you off, then you always say something outrageous. It catches them off guard, maybe stirs the media pot. I was shocked at how many times something you've said made front-page news. I almost think that's why you do it. One way to get your sponsors some attention."

How the hell did she know that?

"You did that the first time you drove for KEM, too. You went into the driver's meeting and insulted everyone in the room. That stirred up a hornet's nest. I couldn't believe the number of bloggers who posted something about it. Your friends in the media were pretty vocal about it, too."

"Yeah, so?"

"But it's not just a way of getting attention. It's a defense mechanism, too. Whenever you don't like what someone's done to you, or said to you, you lash out." Suddenly her face softened. She even slid off her black frames, her green eyes an incredible shade when they weren't shielded by glass. "You're going to ruin your career."

"You think so?"

She nodded again. "Look, Brandon. Back at the office I saw something you should know about. A legal brief, one written by SSI's attorneys. Apparently Scott asked them to look into the possibility of filing a civil suit against you should you breach your contract with KEM."

"What?" he asked, shock making him forget for a moment that she really did look adorable.

"It's actually a clever idea," she said. "Leave it to my boss to think it through. The legal department thought it a good idea, too. They told him that based on the contract you signed with SSI, specifically the indemnity clause you agreed to, they felt it *might* be possible to bring suit against you for the unearned money you would have brought SSI if you hadn't breached the contract. Granted, SSI would have to file a lawsuit and then actually *win* the case, but if they were successful, you'd end up owing our firm a potential million dollars or so, and you'd probably set a precedence for other athletes who blow it and indirectly screw their agents. I'm surprised it hasn't happened before."

"You're kidding," he asked again, feeling sweat trickle down the back of his neck, and not because it was warm outside.

"Unfortunately, I'm not. Anyone can file a civil suit, I just don't think a sports agent has ever sued a client before. It's unheard of, but not impossible."

"Why that no good, money-hungry, piece of—"

"Wait, Brandon," she said, clutching his hand. "Don't let it get that far. Listen to what I'm saying. Toe the line. You won't regret it if you do."

She held his gaze with an intensity that made it impossible to look way. Beneath the shade of the tree they stood underneath she looked worried. And concerned. She still held his hand, too, her fingers clutching his own now. Hell, it almost appeared as if she actually cared.

Yeah. She cares…she wants the money you'll earn her if she keeps you in line—just like her boss.

"Why do you work for such a putz?" he asked.

She leaned away, dropped her hand and he was sorry for that, he admitted. He liked her touch.

"Because it's my job," she said, her left hand fidgeting with the glasses she held. "Working for Scott pays the rent. I'll find another job with a different sports agency once I gain more experience." She frowned. "I probably shouldn't be admitting that to you, either."

But he was glad she did. Not many people were that honest with him. In fact, he could hardly think of a single person.

Sad, Burke. Really sad.

"All right," he said, turning away.

"Wait," she said, rushing to get in step with him, heels clattering on the concrete. "Are you saying you'll behave?"

He stopped, looking down at her. She hadn't replaced her glasses and out from beneath the shade of the oak tree, he noticed that her eyes were a true green—not muddied by brown or blue—but an intensely flawless emerald color that was striking.

"Oh, I'll behave," he found himself saying. "Some of the time."

"What do you mean?"

"You'll see," he said, his mood suddenly improving. "You'll see."

YOU'LL SEE.

The words worried Vicky.

But contrary to her fears that his "some of the time" meant he'd hassle Mr. Knight when they got back inside, Brandon managed to do a credible job of apologizing. Still, her shoulders were as taut as a stretched rubber band up until the moment Mr. Knight turned the meeting over to Brandon's new public-relations manager, Flora Parsons. The gray-haired woman's addition to their meeting had been a surprise. Vicky reasoned out later that Mr. Knight had refrained from introducing the elderly Ms. Parsons until he'd been certain Brandon could be brought to heel.

"It'll be Ms. Parsons's duty to assist you at the racetrack," Mr. Knight said. "She'll be your liaison with members of the press." He glanced at Brandon, narrowed his eyes and said, "You know the drill."

Brandon apparently did because he nodded. But Vicky had to wonder, were all PR reps this old? Flora Parsons had to be pushing seventy. She reminded Vicky of the woman who used to run her high-school library. Maybe it was the bagel-shaped bun on the back of her head. Or the pinched mouth. Or maybe it was the frumpy ruffled shirt peeking out from beneath a somewhat older brown suit. Or maybe, Vicky suddenly realized, it was the don't-mess-with-me eyes. The look had been trained on Brandon from the moment the two met.

"Nice to meet you," Brandon said, reaching across the table and shaking her hand.

That's the ticket, Brandon, Vicky thought, nodding her approval.

"I suppose we'll see if it'll be a pleasure to work with *you,*" Ms. Parsons volleyed back and Vicky was tempted to let the woman borrow her glasses. That frown she gave Brandon would have been much more effective had she been peering over a pair of spectacles.

"Well, I suppose so," Brandon echoed. He gave the woman a smile that Vicky felt certain was meant to charm the lady, but it didn't.

This, Vicky decided, might turn out to be interesting.

"I've never had a PR rep that looked…" It was obvious Brandon searched for words that would flatter the woman. Equally obvious was that he couldn't seem to locate any. Vicky almost laughed.

"Old," Mrs. Parsons finished with a tight smile.

"I was going to say *seasoned,*" Brandon said with another grin.

"Mrs. Parsons has been with Knight Enterprises for nearly thirty years," Mr. Knight said. "She's been head of publicity for years. You should consider yourself fortunate that she agreed to take you on as a…" Now it was Mr. Knight's turn to search for words. "Special project. You couldn't ask for a better media liaison."

"I see," Brandon said.

Two seconds later, the meeting drew to a close. Brandon was given his schedule for the next week and Vicky noticed he was due to race that weekend which meant she'd be attending her first NASCAR event.

"I expect to see you at the track on Friday," Mr. Knight said, looking no less stern than he had at the beginning of the meeting.

"Aye, aye, Captain," Brandon said, giving his boss a mock salute that caused Mr. Knight and Ms. Parsons's eyes to narrow.

"Come on," Vicky said, grabbing Brandon's arm before he could say another word. "Thank you, Mr. Knight, Ms. Parsons, for your time." She marched her client out of the room like a mother with an unruly child.

"Well," Brandon said after they'd left the room. "That went well, don't you think?"

"Um, yeah," Vicky muttered, letting go of his arm. "After you settled down." He had really warm skin. It made her fingers tingle.

"Can you believe the uptight biddy they hired as my PR rep?" he said with a glance back at the conference room.

"Something tells me that 'uptight biddy' will be good for you."

"Yeah, but she sure doesn't look like any PR rep I've ever seen before." He shivered theatrically.

Yeah, well, here was further proof that Mr. Knight was a smart man. She wondered if Brandon had a reputation for trying to seduce the women he worked with. That would explain his "sexy voice" remark to her earlier and his "I want you" comment. Obviously, it was impossible for the man to look at a woman—any woman—and not think of sex. Ergo: Ms. Parsons.

"Look, Brandon," she said. "I'd really like to go over some things before the race this weekend. And we should probably finish reviewing your entire contract, since it appears as if you didn't read it. Also, I'd like to go over how you want our relationship to work."

They'd crossed the courtyard and reached Brandon's fancy car, the red paint nearly blinding her it was so bright outside. "I'll be moving down here temporarily," she added. "And so I'd like to know what you expect of me. In turn, I'd like to give you a list of what I expect of *you*."

"I told you what I expect of you," he said, his car chirping as he pressed the unlock button.

"And what was that?"

"Sex."

"Very funny," she said. It was really strange because for a second or two she'd actually felt a little bit hurt that he was back to teasing her again.

"I'm not trying to be funny. I'm serious."

"And that's first on my list of things *I* expect from *you*. I'm not going to tolerate being the butt of your jokes anymore, so stop playing with me."

He crossed around the front of his car. "Honey," he drawled, "when I'm playing with you, you'll know it."

How did he do it? How did he make her cheeks erupt like barbecue briquettes? She might vow to stop lusting after him, but lord help her, it was damn hard when she came face-to-face with his potent male charms.

"Quit," she said, turning back to his car. Brandon was the last person she should allow under her skin. He was the type of man who'd take what he wanted and then leave. And she'd had enough of that in her life already, thank you very much. "I'd like to get back to the hotel, if you don't mind. I have a couple of apartments I'm supposed to look at this afternoon."

"Vicky," he said, somehow inserting himself between her and the vehicle. "Look at me."

She told herself not to. She really did. Nothing good could come from looking up at him. Already her cheeks were radiating like the roof of the car. Only that heat had started to spread to other areas, too. It was a crying shame—not to mention vastly unfair—that she was so attracted to the man.

"Honestly, Vicky," he said softly. "You're selling yourself short every time you think I'm not interested in you."

Her gaze shot to his. When their eyes met, Vicky felt as if she'd jumped off a horse at full gallop.

"Besides," he murmured, his hand reaching up to stroke her cheek. "You don't need to find an apartment."

"No?" she asked, heart pounding. "Why not?"

"Because," he said with a smile that should grace the cover of a magazine, "you're moving in with me."

CHAPTER EIGHT

"MOVING IN WITH YOU?" she cried.

He was joking, she realized. Of course he was pulling her leg because right after he said the words he stepped back from her and opened the door.

"In you go," he said with his perky charm.

She didn't want to "go" anywhere. She wanted to go back inside KEM, maybe find herself an air-conditioning duct, one she could stand in front of to cool her face.

Man, she wished he'd quit messing with her. "Thanks," she said, mouth dry.

When he opened his own door and slid inside, she expected him to continue the conversation, but instead he said, "Hey, you mind if we run an errand on our way back to town?"

Mind? Of course she minded. All she wanted to do was get away from him fast. To forget about how nice it'd been to have his palm cup her face.

"No," she choked out. "Of course not."

"Great," he said, leaning toward her and resting a palm on her thigh.

She flicked it off.

"Oops, sorry," he said. "There I go invading your box again, huh?"

She could tell that he wasn't sorry at all. She looked out the window, struggled with a way to bring up the subject of her supposed "moving in" with him, but in the end she chickened out. Besides, he'd obviously been pulling her leg. He was inhaling something other than exhaust if he thought they'd ever live together.

"I'm *not* moving in with you."

He flashed her a grin that echoed the twinkle in his eyes. "I know," he said. "I was just pulling your leg. Although I *do* have nanny quarters."

"Oh," she said, feeling like a fool for buying into his joke.

She should have known it was all a jest. "Where are we going, by the way?" she forced herself to say.

They'd pulled out of the parking lot, tall trees blocking the sun. Vicky pretended an interest in their surroundings, but in fact, it was all she could do not to scoot to the farthest edge of her seat.

"I want to go look at some homes."

"To build?" she immediately asked.

"Something like that," he murmured.

She didn't like the idea of going sightseeing with him *at all*. What if he pulled off the road? Tried to kiss her? Maybe attempted to prove to her that he really did want her?

You've been inhaling more than exhaust fumes, too, a little voice said. Relax, Vicky. It's not as if he's going to force himself on you.

She knew that. She just didn't like the thought of being alone with him any longer than necessary.

"Um, what kind of house are you going to build?" she asked, more to distract herself than anything else.

"You'll see," he said noncommittally.

And that was it. That was the extent of their conversation. He never touched her again. Never said another word, and Vicky found herself feeling—all right, she could admit it—disappointed. She liked him flirting with her.

And you, Vicky, have lost your mind.

They arrived at their destination less than fifteen minutes later, although it was not where Vicky expected. She'd assumed they'd drive though North Carolina's countryside, perhaps pull over and study some of the area's more palatial mansions. Instead, they had driven into Cousin Larry's Modular Home Sales and Repair.

"You want a *mobile home?*" she asked in shock, staring out the front windshield at row after row of manufactured buildings.

"Actually," he said, pulling into a parking lot that bordered the busy road they'd just pulled off of, "I do."

When he slipped out, Vicky wondered if she should just stay in the car. That's what she wanted to do. But Brandon came around and opened her door for her, so Vicky was left with no choice but to slip into humid, North Carolina air.

"This won't take long," he said, having to raise his voice over the sound of the cars that zoomed along the busy road.

"Brandon," someone boomed. Vicky turned and immediately realized this must be the "Cousin Larry" mentioned on the sign. "Glad you could make it," he said, clapping Brandon on the back as if they were old friends.

"Me, too," Brandon said. "Larry, this is my agent, Vicky VanCleef."

"An agent, huh?" Larry said, his blue eyes

sweeping her up and down. "I didn't know agents could be so pretty."

"So what have you got for me?" Brandon said.

"Well," Larry said. "I think we have several designs that would suit your needs. Down at the end there's a few three-bedroom models that would work well. You could put bunk beds in each room and sleep six at a time. Or double up and sleep twelve. That's the siding I was talking about," Larry said, pointing toward a log-cabinlike home that loomed three feet off the ground. "Really looks like wood, doesn't it?"

"It does," Brandon agreed.

"Slap that puppy down on some of your acreage and it'll look just like the label of a syrup bottle. Go on," he said. "Look around. They're all open. A few of them even have furniture. Let me knows which models you like and I'll work up a price."

"Okay, thanks," Brandon said. "I will."

"You really want a modular home?" Vicky said the moment they were out of earshot.

"What if I do?" Brandon asked, amusement clearly tingeing his voice.

"Nothing. I mean, there's not a thing wrong with modular homes, but I would have thought someone with money would want to—you know—build something custom."

"Mr. Burke," Larry called. "I almost forgot. I'll give you however many homes you need at just above cost if you make sure Cousin Larry's is mentioned in all your print advertisements and whatnot."

As many homes as he needed? What was Brandon building? A compound? Vicky wondered.

"That's great, Larry. I'm sure we can work with that."

"And I just wanted to say that I think it's a real great idea. Children today, they need all the help they can get. A boys' ranch is just what this area needs."

"Well, thanks, Larry. I think so, too."

Vicky stared up at Brandon in shock. He glanced down at her. "Come on," he said. "Let's go check these things out."

He didn't give her time to respond, and in all honesty, Vicky didn't know what to say, anyway. She was left standing there, staring after him, her mind reeling in surprise.

Brandon Burke wasn't such a tough guy after all. In fact, she admitted with a growing sense of dismay, he might just have a heart.

SHE LOOKED SHELL-SHOCKED, Brandon thought, trying hard not to laugh. "You coming?" he asked from the porch of the first home. He'd turned around only to realize she hadn't followed.

"Um, yeah," she said with a little shake of her head.

"These are nice, aren't they?" he asked, holding open the front door.

He saw her brows lift when she caught a glimpse of the inside. This was one of the furnished ones and so it had a couch in the family room off to their right. To the left were the bedrooms, and straight ahead was the kitchen, tall windows allowing light to spill into the interior.

"I always thought they'd look, you know, cheap," he said. "But this is great. The boys will love them."

She didn't say anything. When he glanced back at her, he noticed she hadn't moved away from the door. "What's the matter?" he asked.

"Why didn't you tell me what you wanted to do?"

He shrugged. "Why would I? It's my own little pet project. SSI has nothing to do with it."

She peered up at him, and Brandon thought to himself, yet again, that she really was pretty in a no-

nonsense way. He liked that she didn't wear a lot of makeup. He felt intrigued by the suit she wore— or more specifically—what might be underneath. And when he'd touched her earlier, he'd recognized something else, too. They had chemistry.

Man, did they ever have chemistry.

She was shaking her head.

"What? Do you think it's a dumb idea?"

"No," she said, meeting his gaze at last. "I think it's a great idea."

He felt his shoulders relax. "You do?"

She nodded. "I just have to wonder, you know, why?"

"Why what?"

"Why a boys' ranch?"

He shrugged. "It's just something I've always wanted to do."

"Yes, but *why?*"

Leave it to Vicky to ask such a question. He hadn't known her all that long, but he could already tell she was like a dog with a bone when it came to getting to the bottom of a matter. "Maybe because I know what it's like to grow up lonely."

"Do you?"

"Of course. Traveling like my family did. Racing every weekend. I didn't have time for friends.

When I did get a weekend off, I was an outcast. I was that kid that didn't go to school. Didn't get to take a girl to prom. Didn't do anything but race."

"Yes, but what does that have to do with wanting to open up a boys' ranch?"

"I just told you," he said. "I want a place where lonely kids, like I was, can gather and meet other kids like themselves."

"Was your father hard on you, Brandon?"

"Okay, that's enough," he said, turning away. "Let's check the place out. I bet there's a bed in that room down there."

She didn't follow and when he stopped at the end of the hallway, she still stood in the family room, a sad expression on her face.

"Come on," he urged.

He saw her pull in a deep breath, saw her throw her shoulders back. She must have realized she'd trod too closely to a subject he didn't want to discuss because she didn't push him further and for that he was grateful. The last thing he wanted to discuss—ever—was his father.

"Wow, look at the size of that bed," he said after peeking into a room. "Bet we could have some fun on that." He flung himself onto the mattress in question, bouncing up and down on it for good measure.

She must have changed her mind about pushing him because he heard her say, "I know about the fistfight you got into with him."

"Seriously, Vicky. Enough. The subject of my father is off-limits."

"Why? Because he was hard on you?"

"Enough," he said again, shooting off the bed. He couldn't take the compassion in her eyes. And the sorrow and the pity. His childhood wasn't that bad. He'd learned to race cars. That was all that was important.

"Let's go," he said.

She grabbed his hand as he passed by. "I'm sorry," she said.

"Vicky," he said, biting back an oath of impatience.

"You can talk to me about it if you want."

He tried to think of what to say, but in the end he did the unthinkable.

He kissed her.

He didn't know why, except he suspected he did it so he could shut her up. What he didn't expect was the jolt that nearly knocked him to his knees.

"Brandon," she cried.

The chemistry he'd noticed earlier kicked in, and before he knew it, a simple kiss had turned into something far more. His hands dropped to her shoulders, pulling her even closer, trying to pull her up against him so she could press that sweet little body of hers against his...

"Brandon," she gasped.

"Wow," he said softly, and then, "Wow," again. She tasted like caramel mocha—sweet.

Suddenly she said, "Let me go."

He did exactly that. They stood there, light streaming in from a window over the bed, Vicky panting and Brandon thinking yet again, *Wow*.

"I'm calling Scott."

"Why?"

"This isn't going to fly."

"What isn't?"

"Our working together. Not now. Not after—"

"Our kiss?"

She nodded, and she was already reaching for her cell phone. Her hands shook.

"Vicky," he said softly. "Don't call your boss."

"I have to," she mumbled, pressing some numbers.

He took her phone away.

"Hey," she cried.

"I'm sorry," he said.

"You should be."

"You're not going to quit," he said.

"You *kissed* me."

"I promise not to do it again."

Something sparked in her eyes. Something that'd looked an awful lot like...

Disappointment?

"I can't be your agent," she said again.

"Vicky," he said softly, studying her closely. Had she *liked* his kiss? "I know you're upset, and I don't blame you. But don't quit."

He couldn't let her do that, he suddenly realized. He *needed* her. He *liked* her. Vicky had compassion—something that was rare in his life. Not only that—she had ethics and that was something he also needed in his life, although it was a little late to be recognizing that now.

"Look, I'll make you a deal," he said. "We'll try this out for a week. If we don't mesh, I'll call your boss. I'll tell him you're doing a great job, but that I like being represented by men. That sounds plausible, and that way you won't look as if you're walking out on me, something I'll bet your boss won't like."

She peered up at him. Brandon tried not to

look at her lips. Her totally natural, beautifully shaped lips. Damn, he wanted to kiss her again. It shocked him just how much.

"I'm sorry, Brandon," she said softly. "But when I get back to the hotel, I'm going to call Scott and resign."

CHAPTER NINE

BRANDON DIDN'T SAY A WORD the whole way back
to the hotel and that was all right with Vicky because, truthfully, there was nothing left to say.

She *had* to quit.

"Vicky," he began as she exited the car.

"Bye, Brandon," she said, practically bolting
for the hotel. But as she let herself back into her
hotel room, her stomach turned at the thought of
calling Scott. Quitting meant going back to New
York as a failure. It meant finding a new job.
Maybe moving back in with her parents.

Staying meant dealing with Brandon. After
that kiss, she knew that wouldn't be wise. She
was starting to like him, and not in a purely professional way, either. That just wouldn't do. Bad
enough that she had a horrible track record with
men. She'd been dumped so many times she'd

lost count. Throw in the fact that she was Brandon's agent and they were doomed.

She picked up the phone.

It rang in her hand. She dropped it. "Son of a—"

The phone rang again. Reluctantly, she checked the display.

It was her mother.

Vicky almost ignored it, but she knew if she did, her mom would only call back again. And again. And again.

With a sigh of resignation, she pressed the accept call button.

"Are you ready to come home yet?" her mother asked.

"Mo-om," Vicky moaned. "I just got here."

The sniff of disdain was barely audible, but Vicky heard it. "I know. But I should have thought a few hours would have been sufficient time to convince you to leave."

As a matter of fact, a few hours *had been* enough—but she couldn't tell her mom that. Theirs was a…difficult relationship, complicated by the fact that Elaina VanCleef wasn't really her mom. Oh, Elaina had raised her, but Vicky's real mom had died when Vicky was only two. Her dad had remarried with surprising haste. Such haste, in fact, that Vicky had always wondered if there hadn't been a little hanky-panky going on between her father and Elaina when her mother had been alive.

"I know it's not New York," Vicky said. "But it's actually really pretty here. I'll be doing a lot of traveling to Charlotte in the future."

If she could find another job with a sports agency.

"Honey, I know you've momentarily convinced yourself that you want to be an agent, but do you really have to *move* there? The Met's benefit is next week. There's a big gala at the zoo. Fashion Week is just around the corner. I know you won't want to miss that, right?"

Actually, she did. That was the difference between her and Elaina. Elaina loved clothes. Vicky barely tolerated shopping. Elaina enjoyed weekly manicures. Vicky bit her nails. Elaina entertained. Vicky hid in her room. It'd been a source of stress between the two of them for years.

"Mom, I hate to disappoint you, but I'm really committed to my new job."

"Yes, but you can do that job from New York, right?"

"I have to go where I'm needed."

"*I* need you, pumpkin."

That was so typical of her mom. When all else failed, try guilt. But Vicky knew better than to fall for it. Her mom didn't really need her. She never had. Even though Vicky knew she loved her, and Vicky loved Elaina, there was still a part of her—a tiny part of her—that wondered if it was all an act. Her mom and dad had never had any more kids. Vicky had overheard Elaina explain once that she didn't want the hassle of another child. That had stung. Even though Elaina had always treated Vicky like her own, there was still a sort of…distance between the two of them.

"Mom, I know you miss me, but I'll be back home for a visit soon." Probably sooner rather than later.

Another long pause, and then a sigh followed by, "Fine. Just remember, if it doesn't work out, there's always the firm."

"I know, Mom. Thanks."

Another sigh. "Call me when you've found a place to live."

You can move in with me.

Vicky winced at the memory of Brandon's words. "I will."

The phone snapped closed with more force

than Vicky intended. Why had she answered it? She should have known her mom would only muddy the waters of her mind.

Call Scott now, she told herself.

Instead Vicky just sat down on the end of the bed. She knew Scott wouldn't lose any sleep if she quit. And if she told him she didn't want to work with Brandon anymore, which was another option, she had a feeling he'd tell her that SSI didn't want to work with her, either.

"Crap," she muttered to herself.

But working with Brandon…

What if he kissed her again? What then?

Let him.

After all, she'd resisted him once. She could do so again. It wasn't as if he was serious. He was just playing some stupid game, although why he'd decided to play it with *her,* she had no idea.

The phone rang again. She checked the display. It was Scott. She pressed the no button when the display asked her if she wanted to take the call. But two seconds later, the walkie-talkie feature kicked in with a *chirp.*

"Vickyyyyy," drawled a seriously irritated voice over the microphone system that allowed her to hear her boss speak. "Oh, Viiiick-yyyy."

Drat it all. She'd forgotten about Direct Connect.

"Look," she heard him say. "Brandon told me what happened and I have a feeling that's why you're not answering my calls."

Brandon had told Scott about kissing her?

"You don't have to be afraid to tell me you need to go home. I might be your boss, but I'm not completely inhumane. I mean," he said, "I can't imagine what your mom must be going through."

Wait. What the hell was he talking about?

"I'm sure you'll want to be there when the doctors give your mom the prognosis. Any idea if she's ever going to walk again?"

Reluctantly, she pressed the connect button. "Hey, Scott," she said with false brightness.

"Vicky. There you are. Great. How's your mom?"

"Um, she's doing just fine, Scott," wondering what the heck Brandon had told him.

"Look, I'm not a *complete* jerk. I can't believe you were afraid to call me and ask for time off. Look, I'll have one of the administrative assistants arrange a flight back home. Take a couple weeks. When your mom's stable, you can come back to work. Of course, it'll have to be unpaid leave. Human Resources says you haven't accrued any time off. But I'm sure you'll cope. All that matters is your mom."

And at last Vicky understood what Brandon had done—given her a way out.

"Scott, really, I don't think it's necessary that I leave."

Vicky couldn't believe she said the words.

"Vicky, honey, you sure?"

"I'm sure," she said. "I'll stick around. Wait it out. My, um, dad said he'd call if there was any change."

"Wow, Vicky, way to be a team player," Scott said. "I'm impressed."

"Um, thanks," Vicky said.

What was she doing? She ought to get out while the going was good because there was no denying the truth. She wasn't really mad at Brandon for kissing her, or worried that he'd do it again. He was just that kind of guy—the kind of man—that liked women. What had her worried was that there was a chance that she wouldn't have the willpower to stop him if he kissed her again.

"That's just great, Vic," Scott said. "Frankly, I was a little worried if you took a week off, we might have to let you go, but you just reassured me that I made the right choice when I hired you. How are you and Brandon getting along, by the way?"

"Great," she muttered. "He invited me to move in with him."

"He did? That's great!"

Vicky blanched. "Scott, it was a joke."

"But it's a great idea. Last time I was down there, he offered to let me use his nanny quarters. I didn't end up staying there, but why shouldn't you? After all, if you moved in, you'd be able to keep an even closer eye on our boy."

"Scott, no, I really don't think that'd be wise."

"Oh, but I think so."

"I need my privacy. And, frankly, I doubt Brandon would go along."

"He'll go along."

"No, Scott. It's a bad idea."

"It's a *great* idea. Remember, Vic…personal attention. That's how we're going to make him a star. Go out and take a look, at least. Couldn't hurt."

"But, Scott—"

"Got to go. I'll check in with you tomorrow." She heard one last chirp, and then her boss was gone.

"Bye," Vicky mumbled, clutching her head. Why the heck had she mentioned moving in with Brandon?

NANNY QUARTERS, Brandon thought. The idea was insane. Just what the heck had Vicky been thinking when she told Scott about his offer to let her move in? He'd been kidding. And why hadn't she taken the "out" he'd given her earlier? She could have kept her job and saved face all in one shot. He hadn't wanted her to quit because he'd been stupid enough to kiss her.

"Damn," he muttered, the word echoing off the stucco ceiling in his tiny kitchen.

Now Scott wanted Vicky to look at his nanny quarters? Was the man serious?

"Damn," he said again.

Obviously Scott had been serious. If Brandon wasn't mistaken, that was Vicky coming down his driveway. He moved closer to the window.

Sure enough, that was her. Already.

"Damn," he muttered again. Now what?

He watched as she got out of the car and looked around. He knew what she would see—and it wasn't much. No palatial estate. No landscaped lawn. No sparkling lake in the background like most of the other drivers on the circuit. His home was a tiny, run-down farmhouse nestled atop a small hill near the outskirts of Statesville.

Nothing but a couple dozen acres and a big red barn behind the two-bedroom house.

He ran a hand through his hair, then turned away from the window. A few moments later, she knocked on the front door. He stood there for a moment contemplating what to do. He'd never felt so out of sorts. After his dad had made a wreck of his finances, he'd been careful to keep his secret destitution exactly that—a secret. And he'd succeeded, too. No one bothered him way out here, mostly because no one cared about Brandon Burke, ex-Indy driver.

She knocked again.

"Hang on," he said, reminding himself he had nothing to worry about. If she made a comment about the way he lived, he'd tell her it was just temporary.

"Where's the nanny quarters?" she asked the moment the door opened.

"Yeah, about the nanny quarters. Bad idea."

Her hair was loose today, no bun. She wore jeans, too.

Vicky VanCleef looked *good* in jeans.

"I couldn't agree more, but Scott says I should go look at them, so let me go look."

"Why'd you tell Scott you didn't want any time off?"

She looked momentarily pained, but she hid her expression quickly. "Because I'm a big girl," she said. "And no man's going to chase me away from a job I worked hard to obtain."

Good for you, he almost said. "Well, if it's any consolation, I'm glad you didn't resign."

She looked even more pained. "It's not. Now, if you could just point the way…?"

"No need," he said. "Just tell Scott you took a peek and the nanny quarters don't suit. Frankly, it's a dumb idea and I resent the fact that Scott thinks I need a live-in babysitter."

"I couldn't agree more, about the dumb idea, but if there's one thing I know about Scott, he'll ask me a million questions about your place in order to convince himself I really did as he asked."

"I'll just describe them to you. He'll never know."

"Just let me go take a peek, that way I can look him in the eyes. Are the quarters above the barn? Is that where they are?" She turned away and headed in the barn's direction.

Brandon rushed after her. "Look, Vicky. I'll

call Scott. Tell him how much I resent the hell out of him sending you here."

"Fine, you do that." She stopped suddenly, Brandon nearly crashing into her. "Is that where you want to put the boys' ranch?" she asked, pointing to a low-slung valley out behind his barn. A long time ago the fencing that delineated the property line had been painted white, now it was a sort of muddy gray.

"Yeah," he said. "Not too far away from the main barn. Out in that meadow there between the trees."

"That'll be nice."

"Yeah," he said, scrubbing a hand through his hair. "It will."

"I really respect how humbly you live."

Oh, man…he wished she'd quit looking at him like that with compassion. He was starting to think she might actually like him and that troubled him greatly because the truth was, he'd begun to like her, too.

"Yeah, well, it's just temporary," he said. "One day I'll remodel the house."

"Yeah, but I bet you won't tear it down."

"No," he said with a shake of his head. "I'm just going to add a second story, maybe some dormers. Turn it into more of a contemporary ranch house."

"That would look nice," she said with a smile.

She headed toward the barn again. "By the way, you can try and call Scott. But you know how it is, once he gets an idea, he's like a dog with a bone...and he thinks the idea of me living with you is absolutely brilliant, even though we both know there's not a chance in hell it'll ever happen. But go ahead...call." From her back pocket, she produced a phone which she flipped open.

"No, that's okay," he said, because he suddenly realized that she was headed for his barn.

His barn.

"Here," she said, handing him the phone. "It's ringing."

Brandon panicked because he needed to stop her from going up there to the nanny quarters.

"Vicky, babe!" he heard his agent say. "I was just about to call you. Our boy Brandon doesn't like the idea of you living in his nanny quarters, so you'll need to work on him—"

"Sorry to disappoint you," Brandon interrupted. "But it's 'your boy' on the phone and I very definitely don't want Vicky living here."

"Oh, hey, Brandon," Scott said without missing a beat. "How you doin', buddy?"

"Fine except Vicky's here to check out my nanny quarters," Brandon said, rushing to catch up to her. Damn it. She was just about to go up the steps that led to the second level of the barn.

"Terrific. I'm glad she did as I asked. When do you think she can move in?"

Brandon felt his hackles rise. "That's just it," he said, covering the phone for a second and whispering, "Vicky, wait." He spoke into the phone one more time. "I was kidding when I mentioned it to her yesterday and I think we both agree it's a bad idea."

"And I think it's terrific," Scott said.

"The space isn't habitable," Brandon said, glad to see that Vicky had stopped at the base of the steps. She stood there, arms crossed.

"No? Then why'd you invite me to stay with you before?"

Good question. "Actually," Brandon said, thinking quickly, "I was assuming you'd stay in my house."

"Oh. Okay. Well, if your nanny quarters are uninhabitable…SSI will hire someone to fix it up. You can reimburse us for the repairs later."

"Reimburse?"

"Yeah. Once you have some income rolling in.

In the interim, I'll have one of my administrative assistants look into contractors down there."

"No, Scott…that's not the point. I'm not going for it. Period."

"You sure?" Scott drawled. "Because I've got to tell you, Vicky's about the most easygoing gal I've never met. And if you have her nearby, she'll give you all the personal attention you need… and deserve, buddy. Have her look over the place. She can call later and give one of the assistants a list of what has to be done. I'll have 'em get right on it."

"But—"

"Gotta go, Brandon."

"Scott!" But Brandon heard the distinct sound of a line being cut.

Damn that man. If he didn't need his services so desperately, he'd fire the jerk.

"He can be a bit of a bully," Vicky said.

"You think?" Brandon asked. "Where's the Redial?"

"Here," Vicky said, holding out her hand to show him.

When he tried Scott's line again, it went right to voicemail.

"Let me just go look at the place," Vicky said,

holding out her hand for her phone again. "You can call him later and tell him we both decided it was a lost cause." She turned back to the barn.

"Vicky," he said. "I think the place is locked. I'll have to go back to the house to get the key."

"Go ahead," she said, walking up the steps.

"Wait. The treads are unstable."

"They look fine," she said.

"Damn it," he muttered. Maybe if he went up ahead of her, he'd have time to hide his study books. He bolted forward, saying, "Let me go first…just in case."

"Okay." But she didn't immediately follow. Her eyes were on the stable, or what was left of the barn. At one time it'd probably been nice. Wide aisles. Stall doors with tarnished brass latches that, now, were covered with cobwebs. Metal grills across the front would have kept the horses' heads from sticking out—if he'd had any.

"I always wanted a horse," he heard her mumble.

"Really?" Good. Distract her with conversation.

She nodded, beginning to climb the stairs again. "My mom thought they stank, although given how big she is on society, I'm surprised she didn't encourage me to ride to the hounds."

"Do they still do that sort of thing?"

Maybe he should distract her with another kiss, he thought.

"They do," she said. "In the country."

They reached the landing and Brandon said, "Before you go in, you should stop at the top of the stairs. There's a little porch up there with a table and chairs. You can sit down and stare out at the view while I go in and clean up a bit."

Her brows squished together. "Brandon, is there something wrong? Some reason why you don't want me to go in ahead of you?"

"I told you, the place is a mess," he said quickly.

"You're making me think you might have a drug problem, and that maybe you're manufacturing those drugs in there."

"What? No way."

She bolted past him. He tried to stop her with two more steps left to go.

"Just sit outside while I go clean up."

"Let me pass," she said, and he could see suspicion in her eyes.

"Don't you want to sit outside for a moment and enjoy the view?"

She brushed past him again.

"Guess not," he muttered.

She didn't even pause when she reached the

ten-by-ten porch. The door opened beneath her touch. She shot him a look that was laced with disappointment, then shook her head. "Where are the drugs?"

"I told you. There aren't any drugs."

She ignored the books on the table and went straight for the drawers in a nearby desk. She didn't even comment on the rooms being not so dirty after all.

"If you're abusing a substance I need to know," she said, yanking on a drawer handle.

"Hey," he said, batting her hand away.

She ignored him. There was nothing in there, at least not that he could see. Good. So then those tapes must be in the other drawer.

"I'm not on drugs," he said again, glancing at the workbook on the desktop. He tried to shove it out of the way so she couldn't read the title.

"That's what they all say," she said, pushing past him, moving toward the other drawer on the opposite side of the desk.

"No," he said. "Don't."

"This is where you're hiding it, huh?" She thrust the cassettes inside the drawer aside.

Please don't let her read the titles, he thought.

"I wouldn't be surprised if you—"

He knew by the way she suddenly went quiet that she'd read at least one.

Reading Made Easy.

He watched her gaze dart to the desktop, to the workbooks he'd tried to move aside.

Reading Made Easy: Workbook One.

He had to listen to the lessons on tape because what else could he do when he couldn't understand the learning material? The software program he owned only read back documents he scanned in. It couldn't *teach* him words.

"Oh, my gosh," she muttered. Her green gaze collided with his own. "That's what you're trying to hide. You can't read, can you?"

CHAPTER TEN

"WHAT?" BRANDON SAID. "Me not read? Don't be ridiculous. Those were left there by the previous owner." He tried to take the tape away from Vicky.

When Vicky looked into his eyes, she saw something there that gave her pause, something almost like panic. She lifted the white cassette tape out of the way so he couldn't take it.

"Seriously, Vicky. I can read just fine. And now that you're done searching for my 'paraphernalia,' maybe we can leave. I'm sure you've seen enough. This place is a mess."

That wasn't true *at all*. In fact, she'd been pleasantly surprised by how clean and spacious the place was. Stretching from one end of the barn's attic to the other, it was bigger than her shared apartment in Brooklyn. Windows dotted the wall—four on each side. They weren't that big, but they allowed light to filter through and to illuminate the dust motes that zigged and zagged in the air. At the far end sat a private room, obviously where the occupant slept. There was even a tiny kitchenette to her left.

She turned to the workbook, opened it up to a random page, and said, "Read this to me."

He batted the book away with his hand. "No."

"Because you're being an ass? Or because you can't?"

"Let's go," he said, turning away from her.

"That's why you haven't read your contract, isn't it?" she asked. "You can't review them on your own."

"I can read just fine."

"And I bet that's part of the reason why you're so sympathetic to underprivileged children. You know what it's like to live life at a disadvantage."

He was almost to the door, and ignoring her. "You can call Scott later and tell him yourself that the place is a wreck," he said.

"But it's not a wreck, is it, Brandon?" she said, rushing to catch up to him. He was already out the door and down the steps. "You can run, but you can't hide."

At last he stopped, and she could tell he

wasn't happy. "I've got nothing to hide," he said, and she could hear the venom in his words all the way from where she was standing at the top of the steps.

That gave her pause for a moment. She hadn't seen this side of him since the first day they met.

"You couldn't read my note in that meeting, could you? The notes I wrote yesterday. That's why you ignored them. Not because you were being a jerk."

He crossed his arms in front of him. They were at eye level now. Vicky stopped, liking the way he couldn't look down at her.

"It's why you turned down that television show, *Racer to Racer,* too. Not because of time constraints. Or scheduling conflicts. But because you can't read."

He turned his back to her. She darted around him, stopping him with a hand on his chest.

"I'm leaving," he said.

"No," she said. "Not until I get a straight answer. And I'll bully it out of you if I have to, Brandon. One bug in Scott's ear and you'll never hear the end of it. He'll send you straight to a reading specialist. Makes you more valuable. You'd take a gig like *Racer to Racer* if you could read." She straightened suddenly. "God, how did you get through all those years of sponsor obligations? Or shooting commercials? Didn't you have to read from a script?"

Silence settled around them.

Vicky's hand moved from his chest to his arm. "It must have been hard. I'm surprised you made it."

"Just leave me alone."

She had her confirmation then that he indeed couldn't read. He hadn't bothered to deny it. Hadn't tried to dissuade her with yet another flimsy argument. She'd seen the answer in his eyes.

And he knew it.

Brandon Burke couldn't read.

She didn't know what to say. When he walked away, she hung back. A few seconds later, she heard his front door slam.

Now what?

Leave, Vicky. You've seen the inside of the nanny quarters. Scott will be appeased. True, Brandon will undoubtedly try and get you out of his life now. By the end of the day, you'll be on your way back to New York...without having to quit because Brandon will tell Scott to send you home.

She'd be damned if she let him do it.

SHE LET HERSELF in the house.

Brandon shot up from the old kitchen table that he'd been sitting at as though she'd kicked his chair out from under him.

"Hey," he said when he rounded the short wall that separated the cooking area from his tiny family room.

"We should talk," she said, her hands in her pocket, the look on her face one of firm resolve.

"I thought I made it clear you should leave."

"Not until we talk," she said with a small shake of her head, one that caused her hair to swing to one side where it came to rest near the open collar of her button-down shirt.

"There's nothing to talk about." He crossed his arms, daring her to defy him.

She did exactly that, moving past him to the kitchen. "You want some tea?" she called over her shoulder.

"No," he said, frustrated beyond belief. Short of picking her up and bodily ejecting her from his home, there was little he could do. Maybe he should call Scott. But, no, Scott would undoubtedly approve of Vicky's high-handed tactics.

And God forbid she tell Scott about his disability.

"How about a rum and Coke?" she asked with a trace of humor.

He followed her into the kitchen, surprised to see her rooting around as if she owned the place.

"I don't drink."

"No?" she asked. "Too bad. I could use a stiff one right now."

So could he, he admitted. Vicky now knew his little secret, and damned if he knew what to do about it.

"Ah. Perfect," he heard her say. "Instant iced tea."

As she stretched up on tiptoe to reach an elusive canister, Brandon found himself watching her as she moved. Her shirt stretched across the front of her body and the pants she wore dropped low on her waist.

Vicky had a hot body.

He hadn't noticed it before—or maybe he had—when he'd pulled her up against him yesterday. But he'd never seen her in anything other than suits.

He shook his head.

He had a serious problem here, and the last thing he needed was his overactive libido rearing its ugly head.

"That might be old," he said as she popped the lid on a can of instant tea.

"Nah," she said. "Tea never goes bad."

She was awfully perky all of a sudden.

No doubt because she had the upper hand. He wasn't foolish enough to believe that she wouldn't use her newfound knowledge to blackmail him in some small way. If he'd been in her shoes, he'd have done the same thing.

She pulled a glass pitcher down from yet another cabinet. Where he'd gotten the thing, he had no idea. No doubt it had belonged to his mother, back when his world had been relatively normal. Back before his father had discovered he had a son who might have racing talent.

"Ah," she said, after mixing the brown powder with water. "Want some?"

"What I *want* to know is why you haven't left when I've asked you to."

"Isn't it obvious?" she asked. "I'm going to teach you how to read."

If she'd told him she planned to strip her clothes and dance around his kitchen naked, he couldn't have been more surprised.

But why *wouldn't* she offer such a thing? a voice asked. If she taught him how to read, then she'd increase the chances of his earning more money for the firm. Of course it was in her best interest to teach him.

The acid that filled his mouth could only be disappointment.

"You don't need to do that. I'm fully capable of doing it on my own."

"Yeah, I can see that," she said. "That book looked like it'd been thumbed through at least a hundred times. How long have you had it, Brandon?"

The tea had left a sheen of moisture above her lips. Brandon had no idea why he suddenly became fascinated by it. He turned away again. What the hell was wrong with him?

"Brandon," she called. "Wait. I want to talk about this."

"And I don't," he said, thinking she'd leave him alone if he went into his bedroom.

He was wrong.

She followed him.

"What are you doing?" he asked.

She must have taken note of where she was then. He saw her eyes widen and then narrow curiously as she glanced around—at the socks on the floor, at the damp towel he'd left hanging on the bathroom door, at the armoire against a wall across from the bed. One of the drawers was open.

"I don't know why, but I expected a water bed."

She met his gaze, a slight smile on her face.

He didn't smile back.

He just wanted her to leave. First the reading thing and now this…this invasion of his private space. It was all too much, especially since he'd started to wonder what she'd look like atop that bed….

"I think you should leave."

"Yeah," she said. "You're probably right. But I'm not leaving," she said. "I want to help you."

"Why? Because you want to make money on me?"

Her mouth parted in surprise, brows lifting. "What a horrible thing to say."

"It's why you're here, isn't it? Why you're so afraid to go against the almighty Scott. You want your cut of the take, too."

"No," she said firmly, emphatically. "That's not why I'm here at all."

"I gave you the perfect excuse to bow out gracefully, and yet you didn't," he said.

"Because I didn't want to go back to New York a failure. Because when I thought about going home, I realized I'd be taking the easy way out. I want to be an agent, Brandon. I want to be a *good* agent. I want to help you, and if that includes teaching you how to read, then so be it."

"I told you before, I don't need your help."

"But you do," she said, stepping closer to him. "You're just too proud to admit it."

"That's what you think."

"How'd you manage it?" she asked quietly. "All those years being in the limelight, fooling your sponsors, talking to the press. How'd you pull it off?"

He debated whether to answer. Frankly, it was none of her business. *None* of this was *any* of her business and yet it'd become obvious she had no intention of leaving anytime soon.

"It wasn't hard," he said, brushing past her. He needed something to drink. Something that would burn a path down his throat.

"Did you have a learning disability when you were younger? Is that what happened?" He could tell by the sound of her voice that she'd followed him to the kitchen.

"Yeah," he muttered, opening a cabinet where he kept the liquor for guests. "You could say that."

"What was it? Dyslexia? ADD?"

"No," he said, pouring a drink from a bottle with amber-colored liquid inside. He didn't even know what the liquor was; he didn't care. "My dad."

CHAPTER ELEVEN

"EXCUSE ME?" Vicky said, thinking she'd mis-heard him.

He chugged the contents of the short glass, gasping when finished. One of his hands clenched the beige counter once just before he turned to face her. A lock of hair had fallen over his fore-head, giving him a bad-boy appearance that would rival James Dean's.

"My dad," he said again.

"I don't understand."

He slammed the glass down, turned to face her fully. He leaned against the kitchen counter, am-bient light highlighting the contours of his face. Wide nose. Masculine forehead. Sexy lips. And yet…and yet…he appealed to her now more than ever because she didn't see a dangerously sexy pro-fessional athlete anymore. She looked at him now and all she saw was a man, one haunted by his past.

"Why should you learn how to read when you're going to make your living driving cars? You can't read and drive."

"Is that what he told you?"

"That was his answer for everything. From the time I drove my first go-kart, he groomed me to race cars. I was going to be a star. Racing royalty. He used to call me 'Little prince.' I was too young at the time to realize all he really wanted was a way to fill his own coffers."

"So you never went to school?"

"I was—" he lifted his hand and made quotes "—home schooled. Nobody knew my dad was the one doing all the work. When I flunked the state mandated tests, he said it didn't matter. Who cared about school when my true talent was driving? And he was right. I was talented. I had sponsors at nine. Yeah, I know. Sounds impossible. But believe me, it happens all the time. By the time I was twelve, I had a fully paid ride. When I was sixteen, I sat in my first full-size car. From there I went to Europe, where I drove for a year. Cutting my teeth, my father called it. When I won my first race over there, I knew I'd made it. It didn't matter that I couldn't read. My father was right. All that mattered was winning."

"And so you ignored the problem."

"Oh, I could never do that. Words are everywhere, Vicky. They're impossible to ignore," he said, going to the bottle and pouring himself a second shot.

He was going to get drunk if he didn't watch it, she realized. She crossed to his side and took the glass away from him.

"You shouldn't let it bother you," she said, placing a hand on his forearm. Maybe he was already drunk because his eyes grew glassy. She thought she saw him sway, a deep breath catching in her throat as he tipped toward her. But then he pulled away and Vicky wondered what had just happened.

He'd looked as if he was about to kiss her again.

But, no, that was impossible. Why would he try to kiss her again when the first kiss had been nothing more than a ploy to get her to shut up? She'd been smart enough to figure that out all on her own.

"This is ridiculous," she heard him mutter. He turned back to her. "And none of your business. You don't need to know any of this. It affects nothing. I've gone years the way I am and it's never ruined a relationship with a sponsor, or the media. There's nothing for you to worry about, nothing to report back to Scott. Eventually, I'll learn how to read, and when that happens, you'll be the first to know."

She knew how she handled herself now, how she responded to his verbal dismissal, would set the tone of their relationship from that moment on. She gently touched him again.

"Brandon," she said softly. "I'm not your dad. I'm not going to abandon your needs just so I can make an extra buck. I'm not going to neglect you as a person."

"No. You're going to walk out that door and do your job."

"Even an agent can be a friend."

"Is that what you want to be, Vicky. My friend?"

"Of course," she said. "It's what any good agent wants."

"And what if I want more?"

She felt her breath catch again. "What do you mean?"

"You know what I mean," he said softly.

"Brandon, I don't want to play games. You're not going to scare me away by pretending you want to kiss me again. I don't know why you feel the need to try and drive me away, but I should have thought by now I've proven myself an ally, not an enemy."

"Who says I'm pretending?" he asked, moving away from the counter.

"Come on, Brandon," she said, holding her ground. "We both know I'm not your type."

He stopped in front of her, and Vicky's heart was suddenly pounding. "Why don't you let me be the judge of that?"

Her voice came out low and husky when she said, "Something tells me your judgment might be impaired right now."

"Something tells me you might be right."

He kissed her.

Vicky stiffened in shock. She'd thought he'd been bluffing, and yet suddenly his lips were against her own. And suddenly she wilted toward him. She couldn't seem to stop herself. The man turned her on.

"Brandon," she protested, pulling away from him.

"Vicky, you always taste so good," he moaned, his head tipping toward her again.

"No," she said, somehow managing to find the force of will to step away. "Don't do this." She turned her back to him, having to clench her hands to keep from turning back to him and running her hands through his hair. Damn, she wanted to do that, could practically feel the silky strands beneath her finger. "I *hate it* when you do this."

He came up behind her, wrapped his arms around her front, pulled her up against his hard, masculine body.

Okay, so she'd definitely turned him on. *That* was now obvious. Also, she now knew that he found her attractive, that he wanted to do far more than kiss her.

She shivered, felt her legs go weak when his arms began a downward slide, when his head tipped toward her neck, his nose nudging aside her hair so he could find her ear.

"Brandon," she huffed, thinking that it was unfair that he could do this to her with just a touch. When his lips found the shell of her ear, she hissed his name and closed her eyes. It didn't matter that he might be kissing her for all the wrong reasons. She didn't care. All she cared about was how good it felt to have Brandon nip her earlobe.

"Oh, man," she moaned.

Now one of his hands was sliding across her waist.

"Please, Brandon, don't." She gasped, turned toward him out of self-preservation.

He immediately pulled her up against him.

"Don't do that," she said quickly.

"Do what?" he asked.

"Kiss me." Because she'd begun to realize that the fission of awareness she always felt when he came near had less to do with sexual attraction and more to do with something she sensed in him, something that drew her as surely as a hummingbird to sweet nectar. *Loneliness.* She knew all too well what being alone was like.

"Why not?" he asked.

"Because I'm your agent. Or I'm kind of your agent. Scott's still your main man. But I'm assisting him, and if you keep on kissing me, then something might happen, something we might both regret, and I don't think that'd be good because just right now you need me—"

"Vicky?"

"Yes," she said.

"Shut up."

"Brandon—"

He silenced her with another kiss, even as a part of Brandon knew she was right. This would complicate matters. But he didn't care. It was good between them…for whatever reason. Maybe it was a chemistry thing. All he knew was that every time he kissed her, every time he touched her, something went *zing* and his mind went *zap*. He couldn't get enough of her.

"Vicky," he moaned against her lips.

She kissed him back, her fingers caressing the nape of his neck.

Never, *ever* would Brandon have expected her touch would make his knees grow weak, but it did. Or maybe it was the alcohol. Maybe this was all because of the alcohol, but suddenly he wanted her. Up on the counter. Atop the kitchen table. In his bedroom…yeah, definitely in his bedroom.

He picked her up.

"Brandon," she said.

He didn't want to drop her. That would ruin a near perfect moment, but his equilibrium seemed to be just a little bit…off.

"Brandon," she said again, more sternly.

She didn't weigh much, he thought, hefting her so that she rested in the crook of his arm. She sure looked sexy with her hair all mussed up and her lips swollen from their kiss.

"Put me down," she said.

"I'm gonna," he said, having to turn sideways to fit through the kitchen doorway. Lucky, his bedroom wasn't far. One of the perks of owning a small home.

"I mean, *now,*" she said.

He glanced down at her again, then the oddest thing happened. Staring up at him the way she was now, resting in his arms, she made him feel strange. Almost like the time his crew chief handed him his brand-new baby boy, and Brandon, who'd sworn never to have children, had looked down at that soft, wiggly little boy, and he'd felt his whole world sort of tilt.

He let Vicky go.

"Hey," she cried, because he literally dropped her. He reached for her at the last moment, catching her under the arms. Unfortunately, his last-minute rescue caused them both to go down in a tangle of legs and arms.

"Nice move, Romeo," she said as he lay beneath her, groaning.

"Sorry," he moaned. She moved off of him and he slowly sat up. "You okay?" His head spun.

"Fine," she said, sitting next to him.

"You said let go."

"I didn't mean *drop* me."

"You should probably get out of here before I kiss you again," Brandon said.

"What?"

"Leave."

She must have read something on his face because her brows shot up. Those pretty eyes of hers widened. But then she scrambled up. "Right," she said quickly.

"Vicky," he called when she turned away. "You going to my race?"

That wasn't what he'd been about to say at all, but he couldn't beg her to stay.

"Scott expects me to."

That wasn't really an answer, but he let it go. She didn't leave. "Brandon, about your reading—"

"I don't want to talk about it."

"I really want to help you with your problem."

The only problem he had was the nearly irresistible urge to scoop her up in his arms again—and look into her eyes again and recapture that fluttery sensation when he held her hand one more time.

"We'll talk about it later," he said.

He needed her to leave. Now. The sooner the better. Maybe with a little distance he could sort all this out.

"All right then. Later," she said.

He watched her turn away. Only when she was gone did he get up off the floor.

"Good job, Burke."

She knows you can't read.

Yet she wanted to help him.

For a moment he allowed himself to hope that maybe, just maybe, it was possible.

But who was he trying to kid? He'd *tried* to learn, numerous times. But no matter how many hours he worked at it, the letters continued to be a jumble of symbols. The few words he did recognize were not enough that he could make sense of anything. He was beyond hope. He was probably too old to learn. Vicky wouldn't be able to help. Besides, he needed her to act as an agent, not a reading instructor.

That's what mattered, he finally decided, watching as she started her car and backed out of his gravel drive.

He needed her on a professional level, not a personal one. Personal relationships never worked. He should know. His father had screwed him out of his personal fortune. His mother had screwed him out of a personal life by not standing up to his father and insisting Brandon be allowed a normal childhood. Every relationship he'd ever tried to have had ended in disaster. Most of the women he dated were only after his money. A few were out to snag themselves a celebrity husband. Most could care less about him as a person.

What he needed more than a temporary lover...what he needed more than physical release, was someone to get his career back on track. That was it.

Even an agent could be a friend.

Wouldn't that be nice? a little voice asked. He didn't have many of those.

Hell, he didn't have a single one.

"When I've got a lot on my mind,
it helps to get in the car and drive."
　　　　　　—*Todd Peters*, race-car driver

CHAPTER TWELVE

Vicky was late.

Panic began to clog her throat as she tried to navigate Daytona's race day traffic. She turned onto Speedway Boulevard only to find it at a complete standstill. As she'd glanced at her watch, the digits moving closer toward the noon hour, she wondered what had possessed her to ask Scott when she should leave for the speedway. Scott probably hadn't been to a race in years.

She should have called Brandon.

Just recalling his name amped up the beat of her heart. That's why she couldn't call him, and why she'd tried to avoid even *thinking* about him since that day in the kitchen when he'd scooped her up in his arms. Luckily, she had a brief moment of clarity once his lips had left her own, a moment wherein she'd realized that this was it—she was going to bed with Brandon Burke. If the ensuing panic hadn't ricocheted through her body like a hollow-point bullet, well, she might have brought new meaning to the words *personal attention*.

Each minute that passed was agony. By the time it was all said and done, she arrived at the track an hour before the race was due to start. She knew that wasn't good. She'd been given specific instructions on the use of her Cold Pass, a pass which meant she'd have limited access to the garage. Had she made it to the track on time, she'd have had to vacate the garage one hour before the race started. That was now.

"Damn," she said, pulling to a stop. The track schematic she'd been overnighted along with her garage and parking pass showed her to be a good distance away. It'd take her at least ten minutes to get there. Crap.

Nagging at the back of her mind was the thought that Brandon hadn't called. It wasn't so much that she'd expected him to contact in the three days following their kiss—she wasn't that unrealistic. It was more that he hadn't phoned her this morning. She'd told him she'd see him today. Wasn't he the least bit concerned about her whereabouts?

She ran to the garage, having been pointed toward its entrance by at least a half a dozen people.

"Sorry, can't go in," said the security officer guarding the garage area. He pointed to the red light that hung atop a chain-link fence, the lens flickering as though it belonged on an ambulance.

She stood there for half a second, disappointment turning her temporarily speechless.

"But…I'm from SSI. I'm Brandon Burke's agent. I was supposed to see him before the race."

"Honey, I can't let you in. Garage is Hot."

"Look," she said. "Is there any way to get a message to him?"

"You're kidding, right?" the man said. "Forty-five minutes until the green flag drops, and you want me to go deliver a personal message to your favorite driver. Give me a break, lady." The guard motioned to someone behind her. Another person who wanted in, only *he* had the right pass. Green, she noticed, the word *Hot* emblazoned in reflective foil across the front.

"I don't mean for you to deliver it personally. Can't you use a radio or something?" Vicky asked.

He waved another person through. "Lady," he said. "If you want access to pit road, you'll have to get there like everyone else does, through the Fan Zone."

"You mean, I can still get inside with this pass?"

"Fan Zone," he said impatiently. "That'll work there. Pit road entrance is straight ahead. But you've only got fifteen more minutes before they start clearing it of Cold Passes." He pointed her toward the industrial-like complex she'd passed earlier, one with race fans streaming in and out of it. It was only a couple hundred yards away. She could make it. Perhaps flag down Brandon before he climbed into his race car....

"Thanks," she muttered.

She took off running like a champion racehorse. But once she neared the entrance, she had to slow down because a line of people wanted in, too. By the time she crossed beneath a sign proclaiming her inside the Fan Zone, she had barely five minutes left.

"Where's the entrance to pit road?" she asked someone.

"Straight ahead," a guy wearing a white T-shirt and shorts said, a camera strung around his neck.

She passed by concession stands, then a stage. "Thank god," she muttered, passing through a tunnel lined with people on both sides, cameras poised and ready in case their favorite driver walked by, autograph books held in anxious hands, many of them wearing shirts already signed by their heroes.

The speedway was at the end of the road she stood upon, a lane obviously used by the cars currently lined up nose to tail. Beyond the parked vehicles, she could see the track, the black tar seeming to glow as if it held an inch of water. Above it all rose the grandstands. Each seat seeming to be taken, the constant shifting of human bodies making it appear to undulate as if it were alive.

She glanced at her watch. Pit road was about to close and the drivers were obviously not at their cars because most of the cars were still covered. Maybe she could find Brandon hanging out with his pit crew. She'd no idea if drivers actually did that, but she had to try.

"Sorry," said a man wearing a white uniform, "you can't go out there."

Disappointment turned her stomach.

"You can only go through there with that pass." He pointed to the narrow alleyways that ran alongside the white wall that separated pit road from where the mechanics stored their tools.

"Oh…thanks," she said, and darted off, only to suddenly draw up short. She could go down the aisle to her left or right. "Do you know where Brandon Burke's pit place is?"

"Pit *stall?*"

She nodded.

"Don't have a clue."

Vicky's smile fell. "Okay, thanks," she said, turning away. Which direction to go? She chose left. How long did she have before they started to boot people out? She wondered. Did they give a sign of some sort? A warning bell? Not that she'd hear anything over the roar of the crowd. The constant drone of elevated voices, generators and aircraft overhead was so intense, she didn't know how people stood it for any length of time.

"Excuse me," someone said from behind.

She turned. A man zoomed by, expertly maneuvering the tires he pushed out in front of him around crates with car parts, spare toolboxes and rolling coolers.

"Excuse me," she said, rushing up to him.

He turned, the red uniform he wore was nearly the same shade as his sweat-streaked face. He didn't slow down.

"Do you know where Brandon Burke's pit stall is?"

He pointed with his chin back the way she'd come.

"Thank you," she gushed, spinning on her rubber soles. More colors assaulted her senses. Brightly colored plastic chains kept fans away from the mechanics area. The flicker of television screens were embedded in toolboxes. Everywhere she looked, there were crew members in multi-hued uniforms, some of them rushing to and fro, some of them doing last-minute chores, a few of them reclining on the pit wall, talking to fans.

The opening she'd come through earlier loomed ahead. She needed to cross it to get to the pit stalls on the other side. Was it time to leave? When security saw her pass would they boot her out at last? She decided to brazen her way through, hoping the NASCAR official wouldn't have time to spot her pass.

She should have known better.

"Ma'am," a man called to her as she zoomed by. "Gonna have to ask you to leave."

She pretended not to hear him.

"Ma'am," he called louder.

She noticed then that there were actually two men acting as guards. One controlled one side, the other controlled the side she'd entered.

The second man turned, blocked her path. "Sorry," he said. "Gotta leave."

"But—"

He held up his hands. "No arguing, no begging, no pleading." He pointed toward the short tunnel she'd crossed through earlier. "Cold time's over. We're clearing the pits. Leave."

Her shoulders must have sunk three inches. Vicky knew it was her own fault. She should have given herself more time to get to the track. Two hours, it would seem, was not enough time to travel twenty miles of city streets when those roads were clogged with race fans.

"Yes, sir," she said.

She was about to turn away when she looked out past the second guard. There, less than a hundred yards away, she could see Brandon's car, the car cover mimicking the black paint scheme so the white skull and crossbones on the hood was unmistakable.

Brandon stood next to it. Actually, the whole crew stood next to it, the men lining up arm to arm in a row that reached all the way to their pit stall. She understood why a split second later.

The national anthem was about to be performed.

"Lady," said the guard impatiently.

"Can I stand here and pay my respects to our flag?" Vicky asked, hoping she sounded sufficiently offended at his suggestion she should move when everyone else suddenly stood.

"Just for the song," he said, removing his black cap.

Vicky nodded, but she didn't turn toward the flag—wherever that was—instead she kept her eye on Brandon, hoping he'd look her way. Silently she begged him to glance in her direction. He didn't. She covered her heart, automatically mouthed the words to the song and wondered what the guard would do if she started to wave her other hand. Probably boot her off pit road, national anthem or not. So she stood there, staring, and the moment the music stopped, she yelled Brandon's name as loud as she could.

Several heads turned. Half of pit road looked in her direction, including the startled guard. Brandon slowly moved to the side of his car, watching as one of his crew members removed his car's cover.

"Out," the guard said. "Now."

"Fine. I'm leaving. But I'm his agent," she said. She shook her head, and it was hard to say who she was more mad at—the guard and his snarky attitude, or herself. "I screwed up by leaving too late for the racetrack. I was supposed to see Brandon before the race, only I missed him and now I'm afraid he thinks I stood him up or something."

The guard smirked. "Sure, honey."

Vicky gave up, but as she turned away, she shot Brandon one last glance. He'd begun to climb into his car, his legs inside the cockpit, his rear end on the window still. He paused for a moment, his face in profile as he scanned the lineup of cars ahead of him, and something about his expression tugged at her insides. Determination clung to his face, his lips pressed together in a flat line, eyes like an eagle that surveyed its prey. Then he slipped inside the car. He looked like a warrior off to fight another battle.

Alone.

SHE HADN'T SHOWN UP.

Brandon slid inside his car, telling himself he'd been a fool to think she would. Obviously, she'd opted to stay home rather than face him again.

Face it, Burke, you scared her away.

Why he imagined his dad's voice, he had no idea, except it irritated the hell out of him.

"Testing, one, two, three," he said after he'd

plugged in his earpieces and pulled on his helmet. "Test, test."

"We got you," Chad, his crew chief, said.

Brandon didn't acknowledge him, just pulled on his gloves. Why bother? He hadn't been exactly chummy with his NASCAR Sprint Cup Series crew. In recent years he'd come to realize it was a total waste of time to get close to anyone. Nine times out of ten, they screwed you. Why be friendly with someone who'd bail on him if they got a better offer with another team?

"Five to go," Chad said. "You'll be pushing off in five minutes."

Brandon lifted a hand before reaching for the steering wheel on the dashboard. He slid it into place, then stared straight ahead. He was starting in sixteenth place—Brandon having outqualified last season's champ, and his teammate, Todd Peters. That gave him a moment of supreme satisfaction.

There were some familiar cars in front of him, too. After starting in his first race late last season, he'd gotten to know more than a few of the drivers on a personal basis—personal as in their car's rear end kept crashing into his car's front nose. How that always happened, he had no idea, but most of the time they blamed him.

Maybe because it really is your fault.

He silenced the voice. Maybe it was, maybe it wasn't. All that mattered was that these guys knew to give him a wide berth. That was worth its weight in gold when your car carried the yellow rookie stripe.

Rookie, my ass.

"Start it up," Chad said.

Two seconds later, the car came to life around him. Red needles twitched like hyperactive Geiger counters. Fuel pressure. Check. Oil pressure. Check. Amps. Check. Everything looked good.

"They're rolling," Chad said, referring to the front of the line.

Brandon revved his motor, his hands suddenly clenching the wheel, his chest cavity reverberating from the force of his heartbeat.

Careful, Burke. Calm down.

He pressed down on the accelerator as the car in front of him—the red-and-green car of Paul Donovan—smoothly accelerated.

"Remember, Brandon, you'll be at 2,500 rpms when rolling down pit road."

"I know that, Chad," Brandon said, trying to stay calm even though he was certain his crew chief's words were meant to remind him that at his last race in Texas, he'd blown it when he'd come down pit road. He'd been chasing after Lance Cooper who'd just about wrecked him when he'd raced by him a little too close. Too bad NASCAR hadn't accepted that as an excuse. They'd clocked him doing twenty miles over the speed limit and sat him down for a lap. It'd taken Brandon half the race to catch up to Cooper. When he'd finally done it, he'd been so angry, he'd spun Cooper out without a second thought. It was probably not one of Brandon's better moments, but it'd sure felt good.

"All right, one more lap when you come to the line," Chad said. "They're calling for green with one more to go."

"Roger."

The field began to accelerate. Brandon adjusted his grip on the wheel.

Why hadn't she shown up?

Quit thinking about her.

He imagined his dad's voice again, and it pissed him off so bad, he pressed his accelerator harder than he intended. He nudged the driver in front of him. "Oops," Brandon said, but of course he didn't mean it. Truth was, he loved this part of racing. He loved the way his pulse quickened when his front bumper made contact with other cars. He thrived on the rivalry between himself and other drivers. Most of all, he loved the way he could close his mind, focusing only on the track in front of him, and forgetting the stress and hassle of day-to-day life.

Forgetting about his father.

Forgetting about Vicky.

"Looks as if we're going green," Bart, his spotter, said.

Sure enough, the field sped up even more. Turn Three loomed ahead, skid marks intersecting the smooth asphalt. The catch fence lost its gridlike appearance, seeming to turn into a solid-looking wall.

"Green, green, green," his spotter said.

Brandon ducked low.

Donovan tried to block him.

"Inside high," Bart told him.

"Bah-bye," Brandon said. He rode the yellow line, passing Donovan in mere seconds.

"Clear."

That's the way to get it done, he thought to himself. The crowd might boo him, the press might despise him, but they couldn't take away from the fact that Brandon Burke could drive.

"You're going down next, buddy," he said to the car in front of him. Tucking his front bumper snug against the guy's rear end, Brandon assessed the competition. The guy's end jumped all around. Too loose? Too tight? Or was he squirrelly because of turbulence? It was hard to tell.

"There's a car coming up on you," Bart said.

Donovan again, Brandon thought. But, no. That wasn't Donovan. That was…

Todd Peters.

Damn. Where'd he come from?

"Coming high," Bart announced.

Brandon didn't need to hear that. He'd seen Peters's bumper swoop to the right. They were in Turn Three now, and Brandon knew from practice that his car handled better in the high groove. Right where Peters now rode.

Damn. His steering wheel vibrated, a sure sign his car wasn't happy. His foot lifted off the accelerator. That was exactly what Peters had been hoping for and it pissed Brandon off.

The No. 82 on the side of his competitor's car was nothing more than a blur as Todd zoomed by. So much for gaining a spot.

"Clear high."

The moment Brandon shot up the track, clean

air settled his car like a soothing hand. Better. No one rode where he did. Everyone was lower. When he glanced at Peters, he saw he could gain on him as long as he kept the high line.

You're going down, buddy.

Teammate or not, veteran driver or no, Brandon didn't care. He knew he had the talent and skill to beat the guy. He just needed to stay in his lane.

He inched closer.

"Outside low," Bart said.

Brandon glanced to the left. His window net vibrated, obscuring his vision, but he could still see Peters down there. His car began to level out as they crossed over the black-and-white start/finish line yet again. Brandon pushed his car to go even faster.

"Take it easy out there," Chad said. "Still a lot of laps to go."

Yeah, but he might not get another chance to pass Todd. Anything could go wrong at any second. Someone could wreck. He could pop a tire. Blow an engine. He didn't want to wait when he could do it now.

"Brandon?" Chad said his name as if he wasn't sure Brandon could hear him. He could, but he ignored him. Black edged closer to red, Brandon's front bumper drawing nearer to the No. 82 car's rear end. He was just to the right of him, still following the high line, but that would change soon. Once he exited the corner, he'd move behind Peters, and with any luck, take the air off the guy's spoiler just before he dodged to the inside.

Just a little closer.

Brandon could feel his pulse pound, the foam in his helmet pressing against his temple. He seemed to chant along with the rhythm. Closer. Closer. Closer.

One second he was five feet away, the next...
BAM.

Both he and Peters began to spin.

CHAPTER THIRTEEN

BRANDON HIT THE WALL at a hundred and forty miles an hour. There was no time to react. No time to even blink. One minute he looked down the track, the next his HANS device had slammed into his shoulder. He grunted, but still clutched the steering wheel for some reason. When he opened his eyes again, he was sliding backward toward the bottom of the track.

He braced himself. Around him he could hear other cars racing past, some skidding to avoid him, others zooming by as if they hadn't even bothered to slow down, and probably they hadn't. Through it all, he waited for the inevitable BOOM of a front end T-boning him.

It never came.

He didn't know how he managed to avoid getting hit again. It sure wasn't through any skill of his own. His car was dead beneath him, like an amusement-park ride that slowly ground to a stop. He heard silence. He tried to start his engine. No such luck. He couldn't see the damage to his engine compartment—his hood was flat up against his windshield, the skull appearing to laugh at him, but he imagined it must be pretty bad. He could smell coolant, and burned oil— never a good sign.

"You okay?"

The voice came from inside his helmet, and Chad sounded concerned.

"Fine," Brandon said. Just angry. What the hell had Peters been thinking checking up like that? He'd wrecked them both because of the stupid maneuver.

"How's the car?" Chad asked.

"Done," Brandon said. He released the steering wheel, tossed it up on the dashboard. It took him a moment to unclip his safety harness, then his window net. The radio cord tangled in his hand. He jerked it free, wasting no time as he slipped out the driver's-side window, helmet and all.

"You okay?" someone else asked him.

It was the safety crew. It always amazed him how quickly they arrived. "Fine," he said with a lift of his hand, although he doubted the guy could hear him. His voice was muffled by his helmet, his words covered up by the sound of a thousand irate fans.

They booed him.

Story of his life. But as he looked up and down the track, he could sort of understand why. Peters wasn't the only one taken out by the wreck. It looked as if half the field had also been taken out. Cars were scattered everywhere. He counted maybe ten cars in all. Some of the brightest and most-loved NASCAR stars amongst the wreckage. Although some drivers already restarted their cars, it was obvious many would be hard-pressed to finish the race in their damaged state. Tires ripped up the infield grass as the cars took off.

"Sir," someone else called as Brandon slipped off his helmet. "I'm going to need you to come with me to the Infield Care Center."

"I'm coming," Brandon said with a shake of his head. He pulled the tape off his ears, stuffed the tiny speakers into his helmet.

"What the hell did you think you were doing?"

Brandon turned. Todd Peters came at him. Brandon ducked just in time.

"You could have killed us both," Todd said, swinging again.

Brandon scooted out of the way one more time. "Me?" he yelled right back. "You were the one who checked up."

"I didn't check up. You rammed your nose right up my ass."

"I did not."

"Hey!" one of the paramedics said, jumping between them. "Knock it off, you two."

"You're supposed to be my teammate," Todd yelled, his dark hair ruffled, brown eyes glaring. "Instead you took us both out."

Brandon lunged. The rescue worker caught him around the waist. By then someone else had arrived. They tackled Todd just as he lunged, too. Both drivers were swung away from each other. The paramedic whispered, "They're carrying this on live television. Is this really what you want viewers to see—you beating up Todd?"

"I don't give a damn what the viewers see."

The paramedic tightened his grip on Brandon's arm. "Get in the ambulance before NASCAR fines your sorry butt."

By now the haze of rage had begun to fade,

enough to note that the man speaking to him was older, but not necessarily wiser. He must not have had any idea of who he was dealing with.

"NASCAR's not going to fine me," Brandon said, his cheek twitching he was so mad. "They're going to come down on that jerk." He'd raised his voice so Todd could hear him. "He's the one that started it."

"Let me at 'im," he heard Todd say.

"In the ambulance," the paramedic ordered, the grip he had on Brandon's arm enough to make him wince. "Now."

THEY WOULDN'T let her see him.

Vicky wasn't that surprised. Apparently only wives and girlfriends were allowed inside the Infield Care Center. She supposed she should just be thankful her Cold Pass got her anywhere near the place at all.

She stood outside the single-story building, a growing throng of print and television reporters gathering along with her. With each new arrival, Vicky's stomach tightened. This didn't bode well. Brandon and the press had a long, thorny past. He was sure to be in a bad mood when the para- medics let him go.

The red door opened. Brandon, still in his black uniform, emerged.

"Brandon—" someone cried. "What happened out there?"

"Mr. Burke, can you comment on the wreck?"

"Brandon, why'd you take Todd Peters out of the race?"

"Mr. Burke, will not be answering questions," someone yelled, causing a momentarily lull. Vicky spotted Mrs. Parsons, Brandon's PR rep, exiting behind him. "We'll have a statement later."

"No, we won't," Brandon said.

Vicky saw Mrs. Parsons step in front of him. She gave Brandon a look that plainly said, "Keep quiet, young man."

He didn't.

Brandon spoke into the nearest microphone. "I did *not* take out Todd Peters," he said to the tall, lanky reporter who'd accused him of doing exactly that.

Vicky lurched forward, trying to intercept Brandon before he said something rash.

It was too late.

"That idiot, Todd Peters, is responsible," Brandon added.

The TV reporter scooted closer, his microphone in hand and his cameraman nearby. "Didn't look that way to me," he said.

"Watch it again."

"I will…if you'll watch it with me," the reporter replied.

"Brandon," Mrs. Parsons said in a low, urgent voice. Vicky noticed then that she looked rather harried. Some of her gray hair had escaped out of her bun. Her glasses looked askew, too.

"Don't need to see it for myself. *I* was out there. Were you?"

"Brandon," Vicky said, clutching his hand. "Let's go."

His eyes swiveled to hers. For a split second, she thought she saw relief in his blue gaze, but it disappeared quickly.

"Finally decided to show up, huh?" he said, anger once again simmering in his gaze.

Vicky looked at the reporters nervously. Mrs. Parsons shot her a look. "Mr. Burke won't be giving any more statements," Mrs. Parsons said.

"Mr. Burke can answer all the questions he wants," Brandon contradicted, turning back to the press. "And y'all can tell Todd Peters to kiss my—"

"Brandon," Vicky cried, at the same time Mrs. Parsons grabbed Brandon by the ear.

"Ouch," he yelled. "Let go of me, you uptight old biddy."

"This old biddy is spry enough to kick you in the you-know-what," she answered back.

Vicky heard laughter. "Let him go," she told Mrs. Parsons.

"Not until he learns some manners."

Brandon wrenched away, but he cried out in pain as he did so. "Damn." He clutched at his ear.

The film crew caught it all on tape.

"Knight Enterprises will no longer tolerate your outbursts, Mr. Burke," Mrs. Parsons said. "I've been given permission to do whatever I deem necessary to keep you in hand."

"Are you saying he's under a gag order?" someone asked.

Brandon swung toward the older man. Vicky tried to stay him with her hand.

"No one's gagging me," he all but snarled, pulling away from her. He faced the nearly bald man. "She can grab my other ear for all I care, but it won't stop me from saying what I want to say. Todd Peters caused the wreck. Obviously, he needs to go back to NASCAR driving school.

Either that or move over when a better driver tries to pass."

"So you're claiming that you, as a rookie, are a better driver than Todd Peters, a ten-year veteran of the circuit," the man said.

"I've been driving a long time, too," Brandon said, eyes as hard as the steel structure behind them.

"But not in the NASCAR Sprint Cup Series," the reporter said.

"What're you inferring—"

"That's it," Vicky called, sliding between Brandon and the reporter. "No more questions."

"I'm not finished," Brandon responded.

"Oh, yes, you are." She leaned toward his ear. "And if you don't shut up, your career will be over, too."

"That's all you care about, isn't it?"

If she'd been taller and less intimidated by all those cameras, she'd have grabbed him by the ear, too. Bully for Mrs. Parsons for having the courage to do exactly that. Luckily, Vicky had other weapons in her arsenal.

"If you say another word," she said in a low voice, "I will announce to the world what you've tried so hard to hide over the years."

"What's that?"

"A, b, c, d, e, f, g," she sang, the familiar song filling the space between them.

It took him a moment to catch her drift, and then he drew back. "You wouldn't dare."

She cocked her head, and said, "Try me."

He gave her a look that could have melted ice. He shot the same look at Mrs. Parsons. "Fine."

He stormed past the two of them. Reporters took off after him.

"I don't know how you can tolerate that young man," Mrs. Parsons said, arms crossed in front of her.

"There's more to him than meets the eye," Vicky replied.

"I should hope so, else I'd have to wonder why it is you defend him."

Vicky's cheeks warmed like a witness caught lying on the stand. "It's not like that."

"No?"

Vicky shook her head, looking toward Brandon. The throng of reporters had begun to draw back, clearly giving up on him.

"There are reasons why he is the way he is. You have to trust me on that."

"Perhaps so. But it remains to be seen if those

reasons can be kept in hand. Mr. Knight wants him on a very short leash."

"I know. But don't give up on him yet, Mrs. Parsons. Really. Brandon's a good guy."

"I suppose time will tell."

"Please tell Mr. Knight everything will work out. I promise."

"And if it doesn't, Miss VanCleef, what then? Because you know what we'll have to do if you can't keep him in line."

Yes, Vicky knew.

Brandon would get fired.

CHAPTER FOURTEEN

"HEY, WHY DON'T YOU TRY wrecking me, big man,"
a fan wearing a red-and-orange jersey with
Todd's car number shouted as Brandon was leaving the infield.

"Just wait till next weekend," someone else
yelled.

People were lined up against a chain-link
fence, but at least he'd ditched the media behind
him. He couldn't believe what a big deal the
press—and the fans—made out of a little bump-
ing and nudging. Now, NASCAR's irritation he
could understand. They'd called him into their
trailer for a stern lecture where he'd been told to
expect a fine. Well, so be it.

"Boo," cried a woman. "Get out of here. Go on
home."

"Yeah, go back to Indy," someone else said.

"Hey…wait up," a woman said.

Brandon recognized that voice. He glanced back just to make certain it was Vicky. Sure enough, she rushed to catch up to him.

He sped up.

But Vicky's footfalls drew closer. "Brandon," she said, right as he reached the exit. "Slow down."

"Leave me alone," he said.

"No," she said right back.

They crossed a road. Out on the track Brandon heard the sound of cars picking up speed. Going back to green. Through a maze of RVs, he glimpsed the backstretch, a long distance off, but not so far away that he couldn't make out a herd of cars. He should be out there with them. Would be, too, if not for that Todd Peters.

Up ahead loomed the entrance to the private parking area. "Mr. Burke," the security officer said. "Hup, hup," he said to Vicky. "Need to see your pass."

Here, at last, was Brandon's chance for peace and quiet. He continued walking, but heard Vicky say to security, "I'm with him."

"Sure you are, honey," the man said.

Brandon glanced back at Vicky. The look of humiliation on her face was his undoing. "She's with me," he called.

"There. See," she said to the security guy before running to catch up with him again.

He kept on walking. Maybe she wouldn't catch him. He could only hope.

"Brandon, wait."

He ducked between his black motor home and the bright blue-and-gold motor home sitting next to his. He pressed the keypad to his motor home, the buttons chiming in his wake—2-4-90. The day he'd won his first race. He'd been eight years old and it'd been one of the best times of his life.

His door hissed open with a whistle of hydraulic pressure.

"Hey," she said, diving for the door.

"Vicky, now's not a good time." He stepped back.

She squeezed her way through somehow. He stepped away in surprise. She moved fast for a petite woman.

"We need to talk."

"Not right now," he said, pulling on his uniform's Velcro catches.

"We need to come up with a statement. Something we can feed to the media that will, hopefully, forestall the headlines coming our way."

"Later," he said, jerking the uniform down his shoulder. He wore a white tank beneath.

"The sooner we do it, the better. You can bet Mrs. Parsons is speaking to Mr. Knight right now. If we beat him to the punch—Brandon!"

He'd pulled off his shirt, was in the midst of pulling the uniform off all the way, exposing his Jockey shorts beneath. Suddenly he found himself on the verge of laughing. She'd spun away so fast she looked like a flamenco dancer.

"What's the matter?" he asked. "Never seen a naked man before?"

Maybe it was good he'd let her in, after all. Nothing like a woman to keep his mind off things, and that kiss they'd shared a few days ago proved they had chemistry.

"Not in a long, *long* while," he heard her mutter.

Really? Well, he just might be in a position to remedy that situation.

"Come on," he said softly, coming up behind her. "Let's go to bed."

"Excuse me?" she said, whirling toward him.

"Don't you *want* me?"

"No!"

He reached out and touched the side of her neck. He heard her gasp. "You did the other day." He dropped his head next to her ear and whispered, "Come on, Vicky. Nobody has to know."

"*I* would know," she gasped.

His hand had drifted lower, to her collarbone. He enjoyed teasing her and for a not so nice reason—he *wanted* to drive her crazy.

"Sometimes, Vicky, doing something wrong can feel very, *very* right."

He nudged up against her, pressing himself against her body.

"Brandon," he heard her whisper. When he glanced down, she had her eyes closed. "You are one bad, bad boy," she said. Then she started to shake her head. "I can't let you seduce me."

That's right, he thought. Because to her he was just a way to make money. She was just like everyone around him. *Damn her.* She hadn't even bothered to find him before the race today. Hadn't even taken the time to wish him luck. She'd come around afterward—when it was all said and done—and he'd done something to damage his "image." Well, he'd give her a new image to remember.

He pulled her to him.

"Brandon," she gasped.

His kiss wasn't sweet. It was hard and rough and angry. He wanted to prove that she did want him. Brandon, the man…not the client.

She could have pulled back or stepped away, but she didn't. Their tongues met, slid against each other, entwined.

She was leaning into him, pressing her body against all the right places, and Brandon felt a high unlike any other because he knew then— right at that *very* moment—that if he'd wanted her, he could've had her. He could have made her beg and plead and moan and groan and she would have never, ever confused Brandon Burke the client with Brandon Burke the man.

Only he let her go.

She staggered back. Her rear made contact with the passenger seat of his motor home. She wilted against it.

"What are you doing?" she asked, her white shirt pulled from her waist, lips raw from his kiss. She had a mark on her neck, too. He'd branded her with his mouth.

"Proving something to myself."

"What's that?"

"None of your business."

He turned away, suddenly more angry than he could ever remember being. He reached down, picked up his uniform, headed for his bedroom door. "You can show yourself out."

"What?"

"There's a button to the left of the entryway. Use it."

He closed the door behind him, then leaned against it. In the mirror above the bed he could see himself standing there, the uniform held in his hands, a look of intense anger on his face.

To hell with it. To hell with her. To hell with Mr. Knight, too. He didn't need anybody. Never had. Never would. Just look at how he'd walked away from Vicky.

"Brandon."

He stiffened.

She knocked on the door. "Let me in." He heard her finger the handle.

"Vicky, no," he ordered, turning to close it.

"Oh, Brandon," she said softly. "You don't have to do this by yourself. I'm here for you. Yes, I'm your agent, but I've told you before, I also want to be your friend."

He pinched the bridge of his nose. "Just go away."

"No," she said, taking his hand. "I'm not going anywhere. You can try and scare me away. You can be cruel to me all you want. But I'm not leaving you. Not now. Not ever."

His hand dropped. "You must really need money to say something like that."

"This isn't about money. This is about being human. It's about helping someone who needs help. You, more than anyone, should understand what that's like—it's why you want to open your boys' ranch."

"I'm surprised you haven't protested about that. After all, the ranch might just take me away from other obligations, obligations that would make you and Scott more money."

"Will you stop that! It's not like that. I'm not going to take your money and run. I'm not going to abandon you if the money stops flowing, either." She closed the distance between them, cupped his left check with her hand, her fingers brushing against his sideburns. "I'm not cruel and heartless and selfish, Brandon. *I'm not your dad.*"

CHAPTER FIFTEEN

BRANDON JERKED AWAY from her. Her hand fell back to her side. She watched as he stood there, his agitation clearly evident.

"I know about the fist fight you had with him," she said. "The media portrayed it as just another story about Brandon Burke behaving badly, but I read between the lines. Knowing what I know about your father—about how hard he pushed you—I had a hunch about what he might have done to provoke you. I asked a friend to do some more digging into your background. How much did your father steal, Brandon?"

"This is *none* of your business."

"Five million? Ten?"

"You're way off base."

"He was handling your career," she said. "Managing your money. Paying your bills. Opening up bank accounts—accounts you never even knew existed."

She watched his jaw flex. Watched his cheek spasm. "You should leave," he said.

"Everyone screws you over. Your dad. Your agents. The car owners who let you go. That's why you're so committed to helping young boys. You want to be there for them in a way that nobody was ever there for you."

He turned away, reached into a drawer and grabbed some jeans. The way he jerked them out, she could tell he was furious. He stood there in his underwear, every square inch of him chiseled from hours of working out. Damn it. How could she be so desperate to get through to him and yet still...*still* have a part of her think he's hot.

"Brandon," she said, daring to place her hand on his shoulder. The muscles there were hard cords of hot tension. "I stood you up before the race."

"Doesn't matter," he grated, turning to face her at the same time as he pulled on his jeans.

"That's what you tell yourself all the time, isn't it, Brandon? That it doesn't matter? Nobody matters."

"Nobody does," he said, staring her straight in

the eye, hands on his jean-clad hips now. "Including you."

Okay, that had hurt, but she'd seen it coming. "I'm sorry I didn't get to see you before the race. I hit traffic. Left too late. A stupid move that'll never happen again, but I want you to know that every minute I sat in traffic, with every second that passed, all I thought about was you. Not whether you'd win or lose." She waved him silent because she just knew he'd been about to say some cutting remark. "*But you.* Whether you were nervous. Or worried. Or wondering where I was."

"I wasn't."

"Then why are you so mad at me? Why do you kiss me senseless and then leave me hanging."

"Is that why you won't leave? You want me to soothe your sexual needs?"

"No," she cried. "I want to help you. I want to be there for you. I want you to know you can trust me."

"Bull," he said. "You want something else. Everyone always does."

She shook her head, more frustrated than she could ever remember feeling. Why did he keep pushing her away like this?

"Do yourself a favor, Vicky. Concentrate on

being my agent. Lord knows, you'd be a waste of time in bed…at least judging by the way you kiss."

She reeled back. *Careful, Vicky. He's just trying to hurt you.*

But he'd succeeded. In spades. She'd been dumped enough times to wonder if there was something wrong with her lovemaking skills. Brandon had homed in on the weakness with the precision of a legal prosecutor.

"I can see this conversation is going nowhere," Vicky said.

"No one invited you to stick around."

"Yeah. I know. Stupid me for thinking you might need someone to talk to."

He didn't say anything.

She began to back away. Her eyes stung for some stupid, ridiculous reason. When she turned on her heel outside his bedroom door, it was all she could do to hold on to her tears.

"See you around, Vicky VanCleef," he called sarcastically.

Not if she could help it.

"Be sure and tell the press I'm not interested in releasing a statement."

"I'll forward that on to Mrs. Parsons," she mumbled through a throat clogged with tears.

She couldn't reach the door fast enough. The moment the thing hissed open, she darted outside, gasping in a breath of air only when it'd shut.

"Damn him," she muttered. She wiped at her eyes, her hands shaking with the effort it took to fight back more tears.

As she walked away, she failed to notice the curtain that moved, and the face the peered out at her, one filled, ironically enough, with desperation and longing.

SHE CALLED Scott the next morning from her hotel room in North Carolina. It'd been a short flight home, but she was still exhausted and it burned her up that Scott hadn't made it in yet. Probably sleeping in after a busy weekend partying. She left a message on his cell phone, too, and paced her room as she decided what to do. Today was the day she was to decide which apartment to rent, but if she was going back to New York there was no sense in that. Scott, of course, had been pushing her to refurbish Brandon's nanny quarters, but she'd been adamant that it was out of the question.

"Damn it. Why doesn't he call me back?" she said to her cell phone.

It was almost as if he heard her because just then the phone rang.

"Vicky," Scott drawled when she answered. "Tell me things are as bad as Mr. Knight says they are."

Mr. Knight?

"He claims our star driver has created a royal mess for him to deal with."

"You spoke to Mr. Knight?" she asked.

"Just now. The man paged me about ten times. What happened?"

It figured that Scott hadn't watched the race this weekend. "Brandon wrecked someone. He blamed it on the other driver."

"Is that all?"

Well, it was a little more than that, she wanted to say. But she didn't. She was done with it all. "Scott, look. Brandon and I aren't exactly getting along. Yesterday, he insulted me when I followed him to his motor home. He doesn't trust me. He thinks I'm only after his money. I don't know whether to be insulted or outraged."

There was silence, then a low chuckle from the other end of the phone. "Welcome to the world of being an agent, Vicky."

"Scott, I don't think you're hearing what I'm saying."

"Mr. Knight wants a meeting this morning, kiddo. You're to collect Brandon at his house and bring him to the meeting by 9:00 a.m."

"Have you asked Brandon if he'll drive himself?"

Please, god, let him drive himself.

"According to Mr. Knight, he's not answering his phone."

Vicky glanced at the clock blinking on her nightstand. Nine o'clock that was a little over an hour from now.

"No," she heard herself say. *I can't face him again.* "I quit. I'm heading back to New York. You can fire me if you want, but I quit."

"Vicky…baby—"

Baby?

"I know Brandon's a first-class jerk, but that's just the nature of the biz. That's what I'm trying to tell you. No need to get your panty hose in a twist."

"It's not just that, Scott. Brandon has…issues." Should she tell him about Brandon's illiteracy? Would Scott even care? Despite her words to the contrary, she doubted her boss would. As long as Brandon could drive, that was all that mattered—that and the paychecks.

"So what?" Scott was saying. "Who cares? Just *deal* with it."

"I can't."

"You're disappointing me, Vicky. I thought you were a real go-getter. Obviously, I was wrong."

She *was* a go-getter, just not where Brandon was concerned.

"But I'll tell you what. I'll make it worth your while to stay," her boss said.

"Scott."

"Mr. Knight expects a meeting this morning, and I know better than to upset him. You take the meeting. Just sit there for me. After that, you can come home, but I've got to warn you. I've already filled your old position. If you come home, you'll be left without a job."

What was it with men? They begged and cajoled you with one breath, then informed you that you weren't wanted with the next.

"Forget it, Scott. It's not worth it to me to have to deal with Brandon anymore."

"That's what I'm telling you," he said. "I'll make it worthwhile. Go get Brandon, bring him to the meeting and I'll give you two weeks' severance pay."

Two weeks. That might be enough to get her through the next month, and time to find a new job.

"If you get him to do whatever it is Mr. Knight wants him to do, then I'll double that."

A month's salary? Scott must really be desperate, Vicky thought.

"What, exactly, does Mr. Knight want him to do?"

"Don't know. Something with the media. Maybe it's a press conference or something. I didn't ask questions. He was pretty hot under the collar. Made it clear that unless Brandon shapes up, he'd be out on his ear."

She'd suspected that was coming.

"Just one more day, Vicky. Then you can come home. Who knows? Maybe I can find you something else to do around here."

Nice carrot, she almost told him, but in the end she held her tongue. Frankly, if she lost this job, it'd be back to Mom and Dad, and the last thing she needed was their "I told you so."

"Fine," she heard herself say. It was just a couple of hours. How hard could that be?

CHAPTER SIXTEEN

"I'M NOT HERE," Brandon called when Vicky knocked on his door."

"Brandon," she called. "Let me in."

He ignored her. He crossed to his stereo and turned it on. The music drowned out Vicky's sudden pounding. He'd study his reading workbook, he thought.

But the prospect of trying to decipher the jumbled letters only filled him with disgust.

And shame.

I want to be your friend.

Yeah, well, he'd heard that one before.

He closed his eyes, trying to tune out the sound of her fists beating on the door. But every time the music paused for a beat, he heard it…and her voice.

"Brandon."

He closed his eyes harder, as if that might somehow help his ears. Still…*still,* there it was.

In the background, faint, but still audible. Bang. Bang. Bang. Bang. And then, "Brandon!"

She wasn't going to go away. Damn it.

"Open up, or I'm coming through a window."

He turned toward the window to the left of his recliner. She wouldn't actually attempt to break in, would she? A female face peered through the glass, hands cupped so she could see inside. "Open up," she ordered, pointing toward the door just in case he missed her meaning.

"What?" he yelled, refusing to budge.

"I need to talk to you."

He knew what about, too. He'd received no less than five calls this morning. One from Mrs. Parsons. One from Mr. Knight. A couple from reporters. And one from Scott. All of them wanted something from him. Well, too bad. Today he wasn't open for business. He'd even taken the phone off the hook.

"Open. The. Door," Vicky said slowly and succinctly.

"No," he said, leaning back and crossing his arms in front of him. With any luck she'd go away soon. Then he could go back to enjoying his morning.

Suddenly it was quiet. Or, as quiet as it could be with the music blaring in the background. He strained his ears, hoping to catch the sound of an engine starting up.

Abruptly, the stereo shut off.

His eyes snapped open. Vicky stood over him.

"What the hell?"

"Get up."

"How the hell did you get in?"

"Doggie door."

"What?"

"I used to crawl through them all the time when I was a kid. Glad to find I could still fit. Get up," she said again, crossing her arms in front of her. "I'm in no mood for your shenanigans, Brandon Burke, so you'd best do as I ask."

"You leave," he said, sitting up.

"I'm *not* leaving. At least not without you. We have a meeting to go to."

He purposely leaned back in his chair again, sliding his arms behind his neck in a show of bravado. "Not going," he said. "Feel free to attend without me."

She looked ready to grab his ears in the same way Mrs. Parsons had. Instead she leaned toward him. "I've had it with you," she said in a low voice. "This morning I was all set to go back to New York. Yes," she said, obviously seeing the way his eyes widened in surprise before he could stop them. "I quit SSI, Brandon. Because of you. I'd be on a plane right now except Scott begged me to do one last thing—drag you to a meeting at KEM. I didn't want to do it. Almost turned around half a dozen times on my way here. But you know what, Brandon? Damned if you'll make me slink off like some terrified young pup. I'm a full-grown woman, and I've worked hard to get to where I am. Finally I had to ask myself just why the hell I was letting you push me around."

She leaned even closer to him.

"And you know what, Brandon?" she asked.

What, Brandon resisted the urge to ask. That wasn't the only thing he resisted doing. He clutched the arms of his chair. The closer she got, the more her scent filled his nostrils. Sweet. Flowery. Womanly. She looked furious, more angry than he could ever recall seeing—and for some twisted reason it turned him on.

What the hell was wrong *with him?*

"You know what," she said again, even more softly this time. "I realized that I didn't have to let you push me around. I have the power to control you."

"No one controls me."

"Oh, I do, Brandon," she said, her hair loose and floating around her shoulder, the morning light turning the brown strands the color of caramel. "I do."

She leaned back suddenly. Brandon felt his hands loosen.

"It occurred to me on the way over here that since you refuse to believe I want to be your friend, that I should just go ahead and be the mean, manipulative woman you expect me to be. Actually, that's what I think you *want* me to be. Therefore, Brandon, I no longer want to be your friend. In fact, I feel the distinct urge to treat you like an enemy. You will go to that meeting with me at KEM or I will shout from the rooftops that you're the first illiterate driver in NASCAR."

It took a second for her words to penetrate. "You wouldn't dare," he said, his heart pounding.

"Oh, trust me, Brandon. After what you've put me through, I would."

"If you do that, you'll only end up hurting my career."

"Hah," she scoffed. "As if you haven't done that already on your own. As if you won't continue to do it," she added. "I'm tired of it. I'm tired of watching you self-destruct. Because that's what you're doing. You're sabotaging your own career. It's almost as if you don't want to succeed, but that's not possible—"

She stopped suddenly. Brandon's heart pounded in his ears.

"Or is it?" she asked quietly. "Oh, my lord, that is what you want, isn't it?"

"What?" he asked, suddenly darting up from his chair. "What the hell are you talking about?"

"You don't really want to succeed."

"Of course I do," he said. "Or haven't you looked around you? I'm broke, Vicky, but I don't intend to stay that way forever."

"That's what you tell yourself, Brandon, but I don't think it's really true. I think deep down inside you're still mad at your father. So angry, in fact, that you want to show him what a screw-up you can really be."

His lip curled. "What is this? Pop Psychology 101?"

"It's true," she said. "I read about it in college. There are a ton of books on the subject. Well, most of them deal more with underachievement in academics, but the principle is the same, at least as it applies to you. The issue at hand is self-worth and low self-esteem, something that occurs when a child is raised by a controlling and dominant parent."

"This is ridiculous."

"I don't know why I didn't think of it before."

"I'm *not* going to the meeting."

"Wow," she said, running a hand through her hair. "Who would have thought those psychology classes would come in handy?" She placed her hands on her hips again. "Not that it makes any difference. I'm tired of your attitude so either you come to the meeting with me today, or I spill the beans about everything."

"I don't like being threatened, Vicky."

"And I don't like threatening you," she said softly. "Contrary to what you might think, I'm a decent person. But you need a wake-up call, Brandon, and I've decided I'm just the one to dial your number. You'll listen to me, if only for a day. Someday you'll look back and realize I had your best interest at heart."

BY SOME SMALL MIRACLE, her blackmail worked, although she had to pretend to call Scott—she actually dialed his number—and then pretended to ask to speak to her boss—she'd gotten his voicemail. She'd loudly pronounced, "Scott, I have something to tell you," before Brandon had stomped over to her and demanded she hang up, which she had.

He'd insisted on taking his own car and he insisted on wearing a ratty pair of jeans with a hole in one knee and an equally tattered T-shirt. When she'd suggested he change, he'd glared at her. She'd decided not to push the matter.

They arrived just in time for the meeting. They were shown to the same small conference room as before. Vicky had a feeling that this meeting would be every bit as uncomfortable as the first.

Mathew Knight arrived with the ear-tugging Mrs. Parsons in tow. They didn't even bother to sit down, the two of them stared down at Brandon like a judge and his bailiff.

"These are driving directions to our PR firm in downtown Charlotte." Mr. Knight tossed a piece of paper at them both. Brandon didn't even bother to swing it toward him from his position at the end of the table. Vicky did it for him.

"The name of the firm is Adopholus & Sons. You'll report there on Thursday for an all-day session where you'll learn how to handle yourself in front of television cameras and reporters."

They wanted him to do media training, Vicky thought. Brilliant.

She glanced over at Brandon. His face looked as hard as the table they sat at.

"Here's Thursday's itinerary," Mrs. Parsons said, her eyes as cold as glass, too. "And just so you know, Mr. Burke, I'll be there, too."

"I'm not going," Brandon retorted.

"You'll go, and you'll go happily," Mr. Knight said, crossing his arms in front of him.

"Brandon—" Vicky said. "Do I have to call Scott?"

He shot her a look. She warned him with her eyes. His lashes lowered. "Fine. I'll go. But not without *her.*"

"What?" Vicky exclaimed, snapping her gaze on Brandon again. "I don't need to go. I can't go. I'm quitting. Remember?"

"You're quitting?" Mr. Knight said. "You mean, you're no longer Brandon's agent?"

"Well, yeah, I guess you could say that."

"I'm not going without her," Brandon said again.

"Brandon, I can't go," she said. "And you know why."

"Then I suggest you call Scott," Mr. Knight said.

"Scott will fly down and be with you," she said

to Brandon, pasting a politely professional smile on her face.

"Fine," Mr. Knight said. "I don't care who goes, as long as *he's* there," he said, wagging a finger at his driver.

"Whatever," Brandon said, leaning back in his seat and crossing his own arms.

Why did he have to make things so difficult?

Because he hated authority, a voice answered. Because he couldn't stand being told what to do. Because, ultimately, Brandon sought to control his own life by forcing his will on others.

Much as she'd forced her will on him—and so now he did it back to her.

She almost groaned.

"You'll need to memorize these before you arrive," Mrs. Parsons said, laying another sheet of paper out before Brandon. "They're phrases we'd like you to use when dealing with media. Phrases like 'no comment' and 'my media spokesperson will issue a statement shortly.'"

Vicky caught Brandon's eye, but not by word or deed did he let it be known that he might have a bit of a problem memorizing said phrases. That, she realized, was how adept he'd become at keeping his little secret all these years.

"You'll be filmed using these new phrases," Mrs. Parsons added. She straightened, tapped the ends of the folder that'd been holding her papers on the edge of the table. "You'll also be taught how to use the media to your advantage, *not* your disadvantage. How to smile into the camera. And, most importantly, how to be polite...to everyone. There's also some other information we expect you to memorize. You'll need to be at Adopholus & Sons an hour early so we can go over what you've learned, you and—" she shot a look at Vicky "—whoever."

Brandon's jaw jutted out. He spun the paper around. Vicky wondered if he realized it was upside-down. She had a feeling Mr. Knight did, and that he interpreted the gesture as Brandon's disinterest in what had been put before him. She saw the car owner's eyes narrow.

"See that you're there," Mr. Knight snapped out before storming from the conference room, Mrs. Parsons in his wake.

"At least she didn't grab your ear and pull you from the room," Vicky said.

He stared at the table blankly.

"So, what are you going to do about the reading thing?"

He got up from his chair. "The same thing I always do."

She stepped in front of him before he could dash out of the room. His cheek was twitching again, something she knew from experience was never a good sign. "I'm sorry I blackmailed you, but you really shouldn't try to get even with me by insisting I stick around to do media training."

"Who says I'm trying to get even?" he asked.

"Aren't you?"

He scooted close to her. "Maybe I want you there."

That was his other defense mechanism, she realized. Whenever he was feeling particularly threatened he made a pass at her. But it wasn't going to work this time. She'd started to develop an immunity. Well, all right, maybe only a little one because she still got that strange feeling in the pit of her stomach whenever he stared down at her the way he did, but it wasn't as bad as before—or so she told herself.

"Brandon, look. I really am sorry I strong-armed you into coming here. It was unprofessional, but you had me up against a wall."

He leaned close to her, his eyes clearly saying, *I'd like to press* you *up against a wall.*

"Stop it," she said. "Stop giving me that look. I know you're not really interested in me. You're just trying to throw me off guard. To…to get back some of your own confidence by making me grow weak at the knees. And you do, all right," she said, deciding honesty was the best policy. "I desire you for some *insane* reason. I don't know why, but you do. You're rude and obstinate, but you know what? My body doesn't care. There. It's out in the open. So you can just stop making those smoky eyes at me. I'm onto you. What's more, I'm not going to that meeting with you. I quit. The only reason why I dragged you to this meeting today was because Scott threw me a bone. He promised to find me another job within SSI, and so I just might be able to escape this debacle of an assignment with my dignity intact or a nice reference instead of none at all. Either way, I'm gone. You did what you set out to do. You drove me away. Congratulations. You now have nobody in the world who gives a damn about you. Not your stupid career. Not how much money you make. But *you*."

She tried to read his expression, but his eyes told her nothing. They were as blank as the walls around them.

"I did care," she said. "No matter what you might think, I did."

Still, he said nothing.

She shook her head, fed up with the situation. As she left the room, she said, "Good luck with your career."

She had a feeling he'd need it.

CHAPTER SEVENTEEN

GOOD LUCK WITH YOUR CAREER.

Brandon clutched the paper in front of him. Damn it. Why the hell did he feel so...so scared? Was it the thought of trying to decipher the pages in front of him? That shouldn't be a problem. It was a simple matter of scanning them into the computer and having the software program read it back to him. He'd gotten good at memorizing text quickly, as long as it was read back to him.

Maybe his fears stemmed from the coming media-training session and the pitfalls and perils of keeping his disability a secret. What the hell would he do if he was given cue cards to read? When he'd filmed things in the past, he'd always insisted he was given a copy of the script ahead of time. But that wasn't possible this time.

"Damn," he said, turning to the door.

Vicky found him attractive. Well, he'd known

that. No woman would kiss a man back the way she did unless that man turned her on. The question was, what the hell was he going to do about it?

Above him fluorescent lights buzzed. Beyond the conference-room walls he could hear muted voices. The receptionist's phone rang. He caught the buzz of an incoming call. Business as usual at KEM.

And he was about to lose Vicky.

"Damn," he said, exiting the conference room and walking to the main lobby. Through the glass walls he could see Vicky stomping down the sidewalk that intersected the courtyard.

"Vicky," he called.

She glanced over her shoulder. She'd nearly made it to guest parking, her rental car's bumper nudged up against the concrete sidewalk. When she saw it was him, she flicked her head up, something he'd begun to realize she did whenever she felt confronted or threatened.

He raced to catch up to her, footfalls echoing off the walls of the building.

"Well?" she asked when all he did was stare at her.

He took a deep breath, opened his mouth, and when nothing came out, shook his head.

"See ya," she said, opening the door.

"Wait," he quickly called. Damn. Why was this so hard? And just what, exactly, *was* hard? What the hell did he want from her?

"Look," he said, taking a deep breath before plunging into…what? "I'm sorry."

An apology, he realized. All this angst was over a simple "I'm sorry." He'd really hit a low point in his life if he couldn't say two simple words.

"Apology accepted," she said, beginning to slide into her car.

"Wait," he said, edging up to her driver's-side door. "Look," he said again. "I know I've been an ass, and I know I have no right to ask this, but do you think…" He shook his head, tried to put words to his thoughts, something that seemed damned hard to do lately. "Do you think you could maybe…stay?"

Her jaw dropped. No, that wasn't exactly true. Her whole head lowered, her left ear turning toward him a bit as if she thought she hadn't heard him. "Stay?" she asked again.

"Yeah, stay," he said.

She didn't say anything for a long moment. But then she leaned back, her shoulder blades resting against her doorjamb. "Why should I?"

He should have known she wouldn't make it easy. Then again, did he blame her? He hadn't exactly been nice to her, especially kissing her as he had the other day, then leaving her hanging. He wouldn't have blamed her if she laughed in his face.

"I need you," he admitted. "Not to teach me how to read," he said quickly because her eyes had narrowed. "I don't need you that way. Well, maybe I do. I don't know. I just don't think…" He shook his head, taking another deep breath while he tried to wrap his mind around what he was trying to say. "I just don't think I can do this without you."

She crossed her arms in front of her. He had to admit, a part of him admired the way she held firm. On the heels of that thought he realized that if she'd truly been sticking it out as his agent just so she could make some money off of him, then she'd have been shaking his hand by now. Instead she stood there, her green eyes never wavering, her brown hair flitting about her shoulders. She'd left it down. Her glasses were nowhere in sight, either. She had such wide, expressive eyes. A person would always know where they stood with Vicky because everything she thought shone right through that gaze.

She was trying to decide if she wanted to kill him or forgive him. He could tell.

He ran a hand through his hair, trying to hide his nervousness.

Nervousness?

Yes, damn it, he was nervous, because he hadn't realized until exactly that moment how much he needed someone like her in his life. Someone who couldn't be intimidated by him. Someone who gave him as good as she got. Someone who cared.

"If it makes any difference," he said. "I never asked Scott to fire you. I don't know why he told you otherwise, except maybe to make himself look better, but I swear, the word *fire* never crossed my lips."

She narrowed her eyes and pursed her lips. And yet, still…still, she didn't look convinced.

"And you were right. I was mad as hell that you stood me up at the racetrack. I didn't realize until you never showed how much I was counting on you to be there."

Her lips began to relax, but her eyes were still narrow slits.

"And I kissed you afterward because of that anger. It was a lousy thing to do and I'm sorry."

She tipped her head sideways, and Brandon thought that for the first time in his life, he was facing a woman he *liked*. Really, truly liked.

"All right, fine," she said, pressing away from the side of her car and slipping inside. "I'll see you on Thursday." She began to close her car door.

"Hey, wait, whoa, whoa, whoa," he said, stopping her. "What about all that stuff I have to learn?"

It was the wrong thing to say. Brandon recognized that instantly. It completely negated everything he'd just said because he could tell Vicky thought his speech was just another in a long line of ploys he used to get his way.

Damn it.

That wasn't the case. That wasn't the case at all.

"I'm sure you'll manage," she said. "You always do." She slammed the door.

"Wait," he said again.

But she started the car's engine and backed out of her spot without sparing him another glance.

"Damn it," he said, wincing when her tires squealed. She was pissed. She might even change her mind about sticking it out as his agent. "Damn, damn, damn."

Now what?

CHAPTER EIGHTEEN

Sucker.

Schmo.

Sap.

These were the words Vicky called herself the whole way back to her hotel. Just what the hell had possessed her to allow that no-good, smooth-tongued jerk to talk her into sticking around for a little bit longer as his agent. She must have *chump* stamped on her forehead or something. Either that or she was just desperate for a job. Probably a combination of both.

And now he knew.

He *knew* about the attraction she fought. Crap. Why the hell had she admitted to that?

Because you'd thought you were quitting, she told herself.

Only she wasn't. And now she'd spend the next few days wondering what Brandon would do with the knowledge that she wanted to sleep with him. Probably nothing. Yeah, he'd kissed her a couple times, but that'd all been for show. He didn't really find her attractive.

When she got into her room she noticed her phone blinked. She had a message from Scott. "Hey, I just heard from Brandon that you're sticking it out. Way to go, Vicky. Glad to hear it. Call me and tell me how the meeting went with KEM."

There was no "Goodbye." No "Thanks." No "How are you?" It was typical Scott. What'd she expect? A bouquet of roses and a band playing in her room?

She sat down on the edge of the bed. Well, wilted was more like it, her upper body sagging forward so that she was forced to hold her head up with her hands.

"You, Vicky, are a total schmuck."

SHE SPENT THE REST of the day finalizing the details on an apartment near the outskirts of Huntersville. She only signed a month-to-month lease because she had no idea how long she'd be forced to play babysitter to Brandon. Hopefully, not long.

She never called Scott back. It was a rash act of rebellion that felt pretty good. To be honest, she expected to hear from Brandon, but she didn't. The only person who called was Mrs. Parsons and she phoned the next day. Vicky was surprised to hear another meeting at KEM had been called. Terrific. Just what she needed. More worrying about what Brandon would say. More fears that this time, whatever inflammatory remark he spewed would result in his firing. More concern that she should have left North Carolina before *she* was fired. She didn't bother to see if Brandon needed a ride, or if he planned to show up. If he wasn't there, he wasn't there. She was tired of roping him in.

So when she pulled into a spot outside the familiar office complex, she didn't search for his car. To be honest, she probably wouldn't have found it even if she *were* looking. There appeared to be some kind of company event going on. A corporate affair that, judging by the numerous three-sided tents set up around the courtyard, was meant to be enjoyed by employees. Game booths, their white facades glaringly bright beneath the early-morning sun, held colorful stuffed animals and balloons and even fishbowls. An inflatable slide, the kind normally found at carnivals, sat to the left of the booths, children merrily climbing up and then sliding down it with gleeful whoops of joy. Out in the parking lot, in the spots reserved for guests and their vehicles, a miniature roller coaster had been erected, the ride painted to look like a green dragon. She spotted a white-and-blue news van, too, the camera crew unloading equipment from the back of open double doors.

Wow.

What would it be like to work for a company like KEM, one that did such cool things for its employees that it attracted media attention? She spotted a popcorn stand and a cotton-candy booth near the entrance to the giant courtyard between KEM's U-shaped building. When she got out of her car, she could smell grilled meat and hear the clank-clank-clank of the roller coaster climbing the rails.

What she wouldn't give to be strolling around, too.

The sound of raised voices and the squeals of excited children only increased her longing. She wanted to hang in the courtyard, to watch people at play. Alas, she had that damn meeting. But maybe after. She wasn't doing much now that she'd gotten the condo situation under control. In fact, she'd been kind of wondering if she should call Scott and ask him if he wanted her to do some actual work while she was "on the job."

"What's going on outside?" she asked the receptionist.

"Annual Employee Appreciation Day," the woman said, sliding her a clipboard so Vicky could sign in. "You're Brandon Burke's agent, aren't you?"

Vicky felt her stomach drop as though she was outside on that ride. "Yes." How'd she know that?

What did Brandon do now? she wondered.

She could tell by the look on the receptionist's face that something was up. The woman could barely contain her smile as she gazed up at Vicky

"Perfect," she said. "We've been waiting for you."

"Oh, yeah?" Vicky asked. "Am I late or something?"

"Oh, no," the woman said, punching a button. In a low voice she said, "She's here," to someone on the other end of the phone. "Mrs. Knight will be right with you," the receptionist said to Vicky.

"Excuse me," Vicky said. "I don't think I'm supposed to be meeting with her." Or was she? Mrs. Parsons hadn't told her exactly what they were supposed to be doing today.

"Oh, your meeting's with her, all right," the receptionist said. "And a few other people." Then the woman began to choke, but not before Vicky had heard the laughter she tried to hide.

What the heck was going on? And where was Brandon? She was half tempted to ask if he'd arrived, but something about the way the woman was acting made Vicky turn away.

"Vicky?" a woman asked a few minutes later.

Vicky turned toward the voice, surprised to see such a warm smile on Mrs. Knight's face. She didn't know what she'd been expecting Mrs. Knight to look like, but this wasn't it. Small of stature with a slight limp, the blond-haired woman looked more like a PTA mom than the svelte, überglamorous woman she would have thought Mathew Knight would be married to. In her beige slacks and dark blue shirt—one with KEM's logo on the left pocket—she looked more like an employee than the wife of one of America's richest men.

"Hi," she said. "I'm Kristen Knight." The hand Vicky clasped had a firm grip, and short nails. Not a manicure in sight. "So glad you could make it," she added.

"Um, me, too," Vicky said. "But I'm a bit confused as to what this is all about. I thought I was meeting with your husband and Mrs. Parsons again, but now I'm not so sure."

"Oh, you'll be seeing them soon. But first, I wanted to have a little chitchat."

Kristen Knight wanted to "chat"? This got stranger and stranger by the minute.

"Have you been shown around the shop?"

"No. Um. Not yet. I've been kind of…busy when I've had meetings here in the past."

"Oh, good. Then I'll do it."

"Oh, no, that's really not necessary. I'd rather just start the meeting. Or is Brandon not here yet?" Vicky asked, concerned.

"Oh, no. He's here," Kristen said, the same sort of smile as the receptionist's lighting her eyes. "He can wait."

"Oh, but I—"

"Or don't you want a look around?"

"I'd *love* a look around," Vicky quickly said. "It's just that…"

I'm confused as hell as to what's going on because it was plain as day something *was up.*

"I just thought we were pressed for time," Vicky said.

"Nope," Kristen said. "Follow me. It's actually

a pretty neat setup. The NASCAR Sprint Cup Series car shop on the right side of the building, the NASCAR Nationwide Series car operation on the left."

What followed was a tour that took nearly an hour. Vicky was shown through both car shops and the whole time she kept peeking glances at her watch, her heart rate increasing in direct proportion to each passing minute. It was one of those uncomfortable situations where she didn't know how to behave. She kept wanting to interrupt Kristen, to point out that they had to hurry up, but the woman was Mathew Knight's wife. Surely she knew when, how and where the meeting was, and if it was important that they hurry up and arrive. That thought was confirmed when, unbelievably enough, she learned that Kristen was one of KEM's top engineers, and that not only was she good at her job, but she was a well-liked and well-respected member of the team. At least judging by the warm smiles they received everywhere they went. Granted, the vast majority of employees were outside, but there could be no mistaking the affection she saw in everyone's eyes.

"Look," Vicky said. "I really think I should

get going. I don't want Brandon to think I've stood him up." Lord knows it was never pretty when that happened.

"Oh, don't worry about it," Kristen said. "He knows you're here."

"He does?"

"Sure. He's been with my husband. Man talk," Kristen said. "Actually, I'm pleased they're sitting down and hashing things out."

Without her. Oh, crap. Brandon would be furious that she'd been waylaid, even if it was by his boss's wife.

"But… I'm supposed to be in there with him."

"Not yet," Kristen said. "In a few." She must have seen the panic in Vicky's eyes so she added, "Don't worry. It'll be fine. *Trust* me."

Vicky didn't know Kristen well enough to trust her, damn it.

"So," Kristen asked in a very obvious attempt at changing the subject. "How long have you known Brandon?"

They were waiting to take an elevator upstairs to the administrative offices. Kristen wanted to show Vicky around, even though as she'd explained earlier, most of the administrative offices would be empty desks.

"Only a couple weeks," Vicky answered with another quick glance at her watch.

"Do you enjoy working with him?"

Vicky hesitated. "Um, sure," she answered.

"Uh-oh," Kristen said. "I recognize that tone of voice."

"What tone?"

"I've been in your shoes before," Kristen said. "It isn't easy being a woman in a man's world, or dealing with male egos or starting a new job. You are new at this, aren't you?"

"I am."

"That's what I thought. You've done well then. I respect that you've toughed it out this long."

"Yeah, well, we'll see how much longer I last." If she didn't get to Brandon soon, she had a feeling she'd have a fight on her hands.

"Oh, I think you'll be around for a little while longer yet."

"What makes you say that?"

Kristen's phone trilled. "Oops. Probably my husband." She fished a tiny black cell phone out of her pocket. "Hey," she answered after pressing the talk button.

"We're ready," replied a masculine voice Vicky

had only ever heard from across the expanse of a conference table.

"We are? Great."

"There's at least twenty people in line already."

"Only twenty?" Kristen asked with a wry grin in Vicky's direction. "I'd have thought it'd be longer than that."

"I'm sure it will be, once word gets around. By the way, Todd's first in line."

"Why am I not surprised?" Kristen said. "We're on our way." She snapped the phone closed, stuffed it in her pocket right as the elevator pinged. Kristen ignored it and they turned away.

They didn't head toward the conference room that Vicky expected to be taken to. Instead they headed back toward the reception desk.

"Where are we going?" Vicky asked.

"You'll see," Kristen said.

What was going on? Vicky wondered as they exited the building.

Outside the festivities were in full swing. The booths were set up around the perimeter of the courtyard so she had an unobstructed view of everything. There seemed to be one booth in particular that had more people around it than the others. But it wasn't really a booth, she noticed. It was more of a dunk tank.

She felt her brow wrinkle in confusion. Had that been there before? She certainly hadn't noticed it. She saw why the moment they drew closer. It'd been covered up. But now it was exposed. It looked as if someone was inside already, and that people were lined up to try their hand at plunging him into the water. Whoever that unfortunate person was, he wouldn't be dry for long, at least judging by the determination that glinted from the first participant's eyes.

Wait a second.

That was Todd Peters.

Was this where she and Kristen were supposed to meet Mathew Knight? If that were true, then where was Brandon? She eyed the glass cube.

He sat on the perch above the water. "What is *he* doing in there?" Vicky asked.

Kristen had a delighted smile on her face. "Humiliating himself."

CHAPTER NINETEEN

BRANDON KNEW Vicky had seen him.

Boom.

He jumped, not having seen Todd fling the ball at the booth's bull's-eye. A collective gasp filled the air. Brandon, miraculously, still retained his perch.

He glanced around at the crowd. All right, maybe, just maybe, this idea had been over the top, although to be honest it wasn't really his idea. Kristen Knight had told him about the Employee Appreciation Day, and that if he really wanted to make amends to all the KEM people he'd insulted, he'd volunteer himself for target practice. Of course, it was Vicky he really wanted to prove himself to, but if this was one way to get her attention, he'd volunteer to be dunked.

"Go, go, go," someone chanted, others taking up the call. Brandon braced himself. Todd had been handed another ball. He'd learned from

Mathew Knight that each person had three tries to bring the dunkee down. Todd looked ready to do exactly that.

"Hoo, boy," Brandon groaned. It was eerily quiet inside the glass box. Water sloshed against the sides thanks to his legs that dangled into the frigid water.

"You're going down," he thought he heard Todd cry, although Brandon supposed he might have read the man's lips.

He braced himself.

The ball was flung. Brandon winced.

Bam.

One minute he was sitting, the next he was falling into the coldest damn water he'd ever felt.

"Crap."

When he came back up a split second later, it was in time to hear the crowd's raucous cheers.

Well, all righty then. Mission accomplished. He'd completely humiliated himself in front of KEM's employees, not to mention Vicky and the media. This ought to make front-page news, at least in the sports section.

"Come on out," someone called from above him.

Brandon looked up. Mathew Knight stared down at him, the biggest grin Brandon had ever seen stretching from cheek to cheek.

"I'm ready," Brandon said, unable to resist smiling back. He and his boss had had a heart-to-heart earlier in the day, and he had to admit, Mathew Knight wasn't the jerk Brandon had thought him to be. "A little wet, but ready."

He thought the man might have chuckled, but it was hard to tell with the water sloshing along the sides of the tank. There was a ladder to his right. He began to climb, and to his surprise, Mathew held out a hand.

"Thanks," Brandon said.

"Your hand is *cold*," his boss said.

"I was freezing my you-know-what off in there," he said. Despite the fact that it was easily eighty degrees outside and sunny, the water had chilled him. "Probably because I'm half-naked."

"Yeah," Mathew said. "Your fans should see you now."

Actually, there was only one person he sought out, and she met his gaze instantly.

"Hey, there," he called. "Glad you could make it."

Someone handed him a towel. Brandon sat on the edge of the tank and slid his legs out, his gaze never leaving Vicky's. She stood near Kristen Knight. He felt a drop of water drip down his neck. It lingered for a moment near his collarbone then dripped down his chest. He couldn't tell for sure, but he thought he saw Vicky's gaze follow its trail.

I'm attracted to you.

Her words rang out in his head. If he were honest with himself, he could admit he was fiercely attracted to her, too. Surprisingly attracted. She wasn't his type. Sure, he'd kissed her a time or two, but that'd just been a way of shutting her up, or at least that's what he'd told himself. But as he stood there watching her, he admitted that he'd liked the way she looked at him. He wasn't a trophy to her. He could see that in her eyes. She wanted him for him. In a physical way. She might not like it. She might fight it. But she felt it.

That turned him on.

Man, did it ever turn him on.

"Todd, you're next," Mathew said as Brandon climbed down. It was time to see if watching him play Dunk the Driver had softened Vicky's attitude at all.

"I'm not going in there," Brandon heard Todd say.

Brandon paused by the edge of the tank, still

toweling himself off. He smiled at Vicky, telling her without a word that he'd be right over.

"What?" he said. "You can dunk me, but I can't do it to you?"

Todd squared off, his wide shoulders flexing as he crossed his arms. "I didn't say that," Todd said. "I'm just afraid if you throw balls anything like you drive, I might be in for a bumpy ride."

The words weren't said in anger. They weren't muttered in a snide tone. Brandon realized in that instant that he was being teased by his rival. Two weeks ago he might have jumped down Todd's throat. Two weeks ago he might have said something back. Today he just smiled.

"You got that right."

A few people laughed. Someone said, "Get in there, Peters. I want a turn."

Brandon looked around. It was Todd's crew chief who'd spoken.

"I'm next," someone else said.

Chad, Brandon's own crew chief, said, "I'm just disappointed I didn't get *my* turn to dunk him."

"Don't worry," Brandon said. "I'll give you another shot in a minute."

"Right on," Chad said, a grin just about splitting his face in half.

"Just as long as I can take a few pitches at you," Brandon added.

Chad came forward. He held out his hand. "You got it, buddy."

Brandon admitted in that moment that he'd never, not once, felt this much camaraderie with a team as he currently felt with this one. Maybe back in the early days, when he'd started his career and all he had was his dad and a few friends. But never since.

He turned to Vicky.

She was smiling, actually *smiling* at him.

He'd have sat in twenty dunk tanks if he'd known that's all it would take. Warm North Carolina air clung to his skin. It felt good. His bare feet scuffed the rough surface of the concrete. The soothing warmth sent a chill up his spine.

"Cold?" she asked.

He gazed down at her. She'd worn her hair down today. He liked it like that. She'd left her glasses behind, too, and so he had a clear view of her eyes. They were as green as the rolling hills that surrounded his home, and as usual, they met his gaze head-on.

"I can't believe you just did that," she said.

"I can't believe I did it, too." He glanced back

toward the tank. Todd was stripping down to his skivvies, his head obscured by the T-shirt he pulled off. "But I'm glad I did," Brandon added, turning back to her.

"Are you?"

He nodded. "When Kristen suggested I do this as a way of showing people my human side, I thought she was nuts." Actually it was only Vicky that he'd wanted to prove something to, but she didn't need to know what. "She was convinced it might help smooth things over between me and the rest of the team." *And me and you.* "So I did it."

"Well, whatever your reasons, it was a good thing to do."

"You think?"

He saw her glance down, then immediately look away. Brandon thought she might have blushed, but it was hard to tell with her standing beneath the bright Carolina sun. "I'm certain of it," she mumbled.

Water ran down his back. He swung his towel so that it hung around the back of his neck. Only when he continued to play with the ends did he admit that he was nervous for some strange reason.

"So, ah…I guess you've figured out that this was the meeting I needed you to attend."

"Was it? Kristen Knight mentioned you had a meeting with Mr. Knight earlier. How'd that go?"

"Good," he said with a nod. "Really good." He turned away. Todd was climbing into the dunk tank, much to the delight of his crew. The good-natured ribbing brought a smile to Brandon's face. "I think this is going to work out," he heard himself say.

"Do you?" she asked, and when he faced her again, her eyes were intense. "Do you really? Because I've got to tell you. It'd make my job a heck of a lot easier."

"I do," Brandon said. The time for games was over, he realized. Not just with Vicky, but with his career, too. She'd helped him see that. "I'm sorry for all the grief I've put you through."

He didn't think she'd accept his apology. Frankly, he wouldn't have blamed her. But to his surprise, she looked him in the eyes and said, "That's okay. I understand why you feel the way you do."

"Uh-oh," he teased. "Not more psychoanalysis."

"No," she said. Then she smiled again and he felt something strange happen. It forced him to look away. "I promise none of that anymore."

"Actually, I don't think I minded it."

"No?"

He shook his head. "You made me take a good, hard look at myself. I didn't like what I saw."

"But you saw it," she said softly. "A lot of people look in mirrors and never see their faults. You did, and you took steps to make things right. I respect that."

"You do?" he asked.

She nodded.

"Good. I'm glad."

She refused to meet his gaze. Even when he shifted a little so that he stepped directly into her line of sight. She couldn't lift her head, she seemed to be afraid to.

"About that other little problem I have," he heard himself say.

Her eyes lifted, snapped to his for a second, but only a split second, and when she looked away, he saw her gaze catch on his bare chest again.

She swallowed.

He could see her do it. Could see the tense brackets around her mouth. He saw her blink afterward, and then blink again, as if she fought to erase the image of him half-naked from her mind's eye.

"What problem?" she asked.

"Look," he said, lowering his voice, leaning toward her.

The brackets around her mouth deepened.

"I really need help," he said softly. "I'm tired of having to use a software program to decipher what a document says."

"Is that how you do it?" she asked.

He nodded. "I just scan stuff into the computer and it reads it back to me. But I'm sick of it. I want to learn to read on my own."

"We can hire someone."

"I want *you*." This time when her gaze caught his own, she held it.

"You offered yourself to me once before, but I was too much of a fool to take you up on it."

"No, Brandon. I can't."

"Yes, you can," he said, stepping closer to her, watching her chest rise and fall and feeling her breath waft across his bare chest.

"You can," he said again, "and it'll be good."

He wasn't referring to his reading. She had to have picked up on that, at least judging by the way her breathing suddenly grew irregular.

"I'll look into hiring someone," she said, stepping back and pulling her hand out of his grasp.

"I only want you," he said.

Once again, their gazes met.

What was it about her that had him feeling out

of breath, too? Why did he suddenly find himself noticing things about her that he'd never noticed before? Like the way the sun caught strands of her hair and turned it nearly blond. Or how her teeth raked her bottom lip whenever she was uncomfortable…like now. Or how adorable her nose was, small with just the tiniest little tilt at the end.

Adorable?

Yeah, he admitted. *Adorable.*

"Look, Brandon. I'm more than happy to help."

He saw her take a deep breath, saw her square her shoulders by hiking them up and pulling them back. "But I can't do it myself."

"Yes," he said. "You can. Tonight. We'll get started tonight."

"No," she said.

He was already backing away, already turning back to the dunk tank. "Six," he called out. "We'll get an early start."

"Brandon—"

"I'll see you then," he said. "Unless you're going to stick around and watch me dunk Peters here."

"Brandon—"

"See you tonight," he said, cutting her off.

He didn't give her time to say his name again, and even if she had, he would have ignored her.

He almost laughed when he took a quick glance over his shoulder. Vicky looked so thoroughly frustrated, so adorably piqued that he almost took pity on her. Almost.

She won't show.

What will you do if she does show?

He smiled. Oh, he had a pretty good idea about what he'd *like* to do. He just doubted he'd be given the opportunity.

"You back for more?" Mathew Knight asked, still perched atop the dunk tank, albeit with Todd Peters inside now.

Brandon nodded. "But not before I dunk him."

Todd must have heard because he said challengingly, "Good luck with that."

"I don't need luck," Brandon said. "I make my own luck."

"Go get in line," Mathew Knight said with a laugh.

Brandon nodded, but then his own smile faded. "Hey, Mr. Knight," he asked in a voice low enough that only his boss could hear. "Can I talk to you about something in a bit?"

The space between Mr. Knight's brows crinkled. "What about?"

"It's personal," he admitted, looking around

them so that the man understood he didn't want to be overheard. "Something I think you should know about me."

His boss just nodded his head and said, "Then let's go chat right now."

Suddenly Brandon knew he'd made the right choice. Vicky might be right. It was time to start trusting again. God knows, it wouldn't be easy. He had enough baggage to fill an airport, but he had to at least try. If not, he didn't stand a chance at this whole NASCAR thing. Or having a normal life. But most of all, he didn't stand a chance with Vicky.

"You can have the fastest car in the world, but if a driver doesn't have the heart to pilot it, you might as well just park it."

— *Lance Cooper*, race-car driver

Dunking and Doughnuts
By Rick Stevenson, Sports Editor

I've seen some strange things in this industry, but I didn't think I'd ever see anything as bizarre as *The Variety Show*—that strange talent competition Sanders Racing held a couple years back.

I was wrong.

Dunkin' Drivers, folks. That's what Knight Enterprises called it. A competition held at today's Employee Appreciation Day wherein said employees got a shot at dunking their favorite driver—or their *least* favorite driver as the case may be. Rumor has it the line to dunk Brandon Burke was about a mile long. Rumor also has it that Todd Peters was first to do the honors.

What a concept.

Wouldn't it be nice if, after each NASCAR

Sprint Cup Series race, it was *required* that drivers who were, shall we say, less than nice were marched directly to the dunk tank? Okay, maybe not a dunk tank. Maybe one of those beanbag things. The kind where a person puts their head through a hole and people take aim. Now that'd be a way to settle differences. A few well-aimed shots and then—*bam*—that "nudge" is all forgiven.

But what surprised me most about that whole thing was that Mr. Burke returned for a second round. And so maybe, just maybe, there's hope for good ole Brandon Burke.

Maybe.

CHAPTER TWENTY

HER CELL PHONE RANG at exactly a quarter to five.

Vicky knew who it was. One glance at her caller ID confirmed her suspicions. And she wasn't going to answer, either. No way.

Just the thought of Brandon standing half-naked with water dripping down his chest had her shivering.

She'd have fantasies about that for weeks. Some really, really hot fantasies because that was all she'd allow herself where Brandon was concerned. No way would she be swayed by the wicked glint in his eyes. Reading lessons weren't the only lessons he wanted to work with her on.

Why? she thought, jerking off her clothes so she could get into some comfy jeans. Why was he giving her those suggestive leers? Did he think it would help his cause if he pretended to be interested in her? Little did he know. She was wise to that trick. During her sophomore year, one of the university's star athletes had done the same thing. Unfortunately, she'd realized too late he was just using her to pass contract law, and she had felt like a major fool when she'd tried to kiss him late one night.

Never again would she let a man make a fool out of her.

She tugged on a T-shirt. Tomorrow her stuff would arrive, one of her roommates in New York having graciously agreed to pack up her stuff. The furniture SSI had rented on her behalf would be at her new place, too, and so all in all it was shaping up to be a busy week....

The hotel phone rang.

It was Brandon. She was certain of it. Calling to make sure she'd be at his house for his "lessons."

Not going to happen.

But when her cell phone rang again and then, two minutes later, the hotel extension, she decided drastic measures were in order. She took the hotel phone off the hook and shut off her cell phone.

Now she could prep for tomorrow's media training. Lord knows, that promised to be a lot of fun.

An hour into her review of the documents Mrs. Parsons had given both her and Brandon, she was startled by yet another sound—this time a knock on her door.

Uh-oh.

A glance at the clock revealed it was close to six. Surely that couldn't be Brandon. He wouldn't be so bold as to hunt her down, would he?

She took a glance out the room's peephole and she realized he would.

"Go away," she called through the door.

"Vicky," he called back. "I need to talk to you."

"No," she said, raising her voice so it could be heard through the door. "I'm…not dressed."

Why the heck had she gone and said that?

"I mean, I just got out of the shower."

What the heck was wrong with her? The door must be getting warm from the heat radiating off her face.

"I'm…I'm…in a robe."

Well. That was at least a little better.

But to her surprise, he didn't say anything sarcastic in return. All he said was, "Please. I really need to talk to you now."

"Tomorrow would be better." In a public place. Not now. Not in, good lord, her hotel room where there was a bed not five feet away.

"But I need your help tonight," he said.

What was *with* the man? Couldn't he take no for an answer? She didn't want to be alone with him. Especially when the memory of his half-naked body was still firmly implanted in her mind.

"If it's about your learning to read, go ask your computer for help. Or better yet, hire someone."

"Vicky," a deep voice said, a voice that did not belong to Brandon.

She jammed her eyes against the peephole.

Damn.

She jumped back from the door. That was Mr. Knight standing out there in a pristine dark gray business suit, his formidable green eyes trained on the door.

"We need to talk to you," he said.

It took three deep breaths and some fanning of her hand against her overheated face before she opened the door, and when she did, Brandon peered back at her, arms crossed, a supremely smug smile on his face.

"Mr. Knight," she said breathlessly, covering her chest with her hand. "My goodness. I didn't know you were here, too." On the heels of that thought came the realization that he'd overheard every word she'd said, including her comment about Brandon learning to read.

Oh, crap!

"I see you've gotten dressed," Brandon said, and the way he drawled the words, she knew he was onto her.

She blushed all over again, noting that in an off-white polo shirt and tan slacks, it was much easier to stare at him than when he was bare chested.

"I just now pulled on some clothes," she lied. "While we were were, uh, talking. They were on my bed," she added quickly.

She thought she heard Brandon choke back a laugh. Mr. Knight just stared back at her, one brow lifted.

"Come on in," she said, pulling the door wide, and wishing she'd never taken off her business suit. Somehow she felt better prepped for battle when wearing office attire.

"Your hair's not wet," Brandon quickly whispered as he walked by.

"Shower cap," she hissed back.

"Vicky," Mr. Knight said, the man oblivious to their conversation. "We tried calling earlier."

She glanced over at the phone on the end table next to her bed. It was off the hook. "I, uh, didn't want to be disturbed."

"While you showered?" Brandon asked.

"Whatever the case, I'm glad we caught up with you," Mr. Knight said.

"Um…yeah. What can I do for you?" she asked Mr. Knight, her palms suddenly sweaty because he had overheard her conversation with Brandon. What would he do? Confront them both about Brandon not knowing how to read? Although, she realized with a quick look at Brandon, he didn't look the least bit worried.

Odd.

"Actually," Mr. Knight said. "I have a favor to ask."

Vicky glanced at Brandon again, trying to discern if *he* knew what the heck was going on. But Brandon just returned her stare, an odd little half smile on his face.

"Brandon and I talked after you left," Mr. Knight said.

"Oh, yes?"

"He told me about his problem."

"What problem?" Vicky asked. "As you've no doubt noticed, he has many."

"Yes," Mr. Knight said with a small smirk. "I'm aware of that. But this is a problem that you mentioned earlier. A problem that has to do with reading."

"Oh. But I was just teasing about that, Mr. Knight. Brandon here isn't exactly the fastest reader in the world, but he manages to review everything you've sent him."

"Vicky," Brandon said. "There's no need to cover for me. Mr. Knight knows."

She looked into Brandon's boss's eyes. "Frankly," he said, "at first I was a bit taken aback that this wasn't revealed to me from the outset."

"And then I explained to him that nobody knew about it until that night you figured it all out," Brandon quickly added.

"Which made me feel marginally better, although it would have been nice if you'd informed me of the situation the moment you became aware of it."

Vicky gleaned in that instant how Mr. Knight had managed to maintain his success throughout the years. He had a way of looking at you. One of those all-encompassing sweeps of the eyes that made you feel as if you'd somehow let him down.

"I'm sorry about that, Mr. Knight. Frankly, I didn't know what to do about it myself."

"Yes, well, be that as it may, we now have an opportunity to remedy the situation."

Vicky knew she wouldn't like what was coming next.

"Brandon here tells me he's asked for your help. He also told me you're rather reluctant." Mr. Knight gave her a tight smile. "Given what I just overheard, I would have to agree with that assessment."

"I just don't feel I'm qualified," she lied, because she just couldn't imagine having to work closely with him. Every time she was near the man, she lost about half her brain cells. Even now she found herself wondering what the heck kind of cologne he wore. He smelled like leather again. But also like the inside of a cedar chest. However those two scents managed to combine, it did something to her insides.

"For the moment, I don't feel we have any choice," Mr. Knight said. "I'd rather keep his little problem under wraps. If we go outside our immediate circle, there's the chance that Brandon's situation might be leaked to the press. I'd rather that not happen. At least for now. However, that said, Brandon has agreed that when the time is right we'll make an announcement about his disability. Frankly, he's in a position to help others with the same problem. KEM will support his efforts to help enlighten the public about adult illiteracy. But for now, he needs your help in over-coming it."

"Of course I'll do my part," she heard herself say.

"That's the ticket," Mr. Knight said, a smile coming to his face. "I knew we could count on you. Brandon, did you bring your study material?"

"It's out in the car."

"Excellent," Mr. Knight said. "You can begin your lessons tonight."

"Oh, but—"

"*Tonight,* Ms. VanCleef. He needs your help with tomorrow's press training."

"Yes, sir." Man, the guy was good. No wonder he'd built his empire into one of the most prof-itable in the world. The guy intimidated the crap out of her.

"Good. I'll just leave you two to it, but I'll ex-pect a full report at tomorrow's media training."

"Will you be there?" Vicky asked.

"I'll be dropping by, but Mrs. Parsons will han-dle the bulk of it."

"I see," Vicky said. When she peeked at Brandon, she realized, he would be alone with her. In her hotel room. Just the two of them.

The grin he shot her made her want to run to the door.

CHAPTER TWENTY-ONE

SHE DIDN'T WANT to be alone with him.

Brandon nearly chuckled as he went to retrieve his study material. Poor Vicky. She probably sat up there in that room, waiting, fuming and trying her damndest to think of a way to get out of the coming task.

But she couldn't.

He'd made sure of that. It'd been a stroke of genius on his part to confide in Mathew Knight about his learning-disability situation. Sure, he'd been leery of coming clean. Actually, he'd been terrified. But when Brandon had broken the news about his handicap, his boss had reacted with such an outpouring of understanding and compassion that Brandon was immediately suspicious. About two-point-nine seconds after he'd had that thought, he'd realized that was he was being foolish.

Vicky had been right. He had trust issues, and he would start dealing with them right now.

He adjusted the duffel bag slung over one shoulder. Inside were the workbooks that Vicky had caught sight of what seemed like an eternity ago, but was really less than two weeks ago. Damn. It was strange how he felt as if he'd known Vicky his entire life. Hard to believe she'd only been a part of it for such a short time.

When he pushed the up button for the elevator, he realized his hands shook. Nerves, he admitted, but anxiety over what? Being alone with Vicky? Or the supposed lessons she was about to give him?

To be honest, he didn't know which.

"Damn, Burke," he muttered inside an empty elevator. "You're acting as nervous as a rookie at his first race."

That wasn't like him. That wasn't like him at all.

His mouth had gone dry by the time he knocked on her door. The bag felt as heavy as an engine block hanging off his shoulder. His heart beat as hard as it did when rounding Turn Four, just before he zoomed beneath the checkered flag—although that hadn't happened in a long, long time.

"What took you so long?" Vicky asked.

She didn't look pleased. In fact, she looked distinctly hostile as she stepped back from the door, the thick framed glasses she favored firmly in place. Her room was small, but not overly cramped. Typical hotel room. Bathroom to his right. Bed on the same side. Windows straight ahead. She had the drapes pulled back, the Charlotte skyline drenched in sunshine.

Still, he felt the presence of the beige painted walls as if they were about to close in on him.

"Afraid I wasn't going to come back?" he teased.

"No. More like hoping you *wouldn't* come back." She'd crossed to a small, faux cherry table nudged into a corner, and jerked back the matching armchair so quickly she almost tipped it over. "Take a seat," she said, motioning to a second chair across from the first.

"Vicky," he said. "I know you're upset about having to do this for me."

"Upset?" she asked, taking a seat. "Who's upset?"

"You are," he said, walking toward her.

Her gaze darted away. That always happened whenever he got too close to her and he knew the reason why, too. He could have sensed her discomfort from a mile away. She was attracted to him, and if she'd been like any of the women he'd been involved with before, he would have jumped her.

Oddly enough, he held back.

"Look," he said softly, taking a seat opposite her. That seemed to help her relax, a little bit. "I know it wasn't particularly nice of me to involve Mr. Knight."

She snorted. "What'd you tell him? 'Order Vicky to be my tutor and I'll win you a race'?"

"No. I just told him the truth," he said, setting his bag of books down on the floor. "I told him I need you."

She met his gaze, quickly, nervously, as if she didn't quite believe that his words could be true.

"I do," he said. "I know you have a hard time believing that, but I can't do this without you." He leaned across the table and reached for her hands. He saw her try to draw away, but he was too quick. In a flash he had her fingers entwined with his own.

Suddenly everything changed.

He froze for a second, his gaze catching his masculine fingers resting against her feminine ones.

He let her go.

"I brought all the books we'll need." This time it was Brandon who looked away. "We can start at the beginning. To be honest, I haven't absorbed as much as I should."

"Brandon," she said softly.

He looked up at her. "I don't think I can do this."

"No?" he asked back, dumbly.

"You know why."

"Do I?"

She nodded.

He did. He could feel the sexual tension crackling between them, too.

"Please," she said. "Don't tempt me."

But that was just it. He couldn't seem to make himself leave. He didn't know what this was between them, yet he had a feeling it was something far more than physical attraction. He wanted to explore it. He felt *compelled* to investigate her feelings, too.

"It's not me who's doing the tempting," he admitted. "It's you."

"Don't be ridiculous," she said.

"It *is* true." It took every ounce of his willpower to keep sitting there when all he wanted to do was kiss her. That was all. Just kiss her.

"Said like a man who's used to saying whatever he needs to get his way."

"Yeah, well, maybe I learned that from you."

"Excuse me?"

"Or was that someone else who all but black-mailed me into behaving when we first met?"

"Desperate times," she said. "Back then I would have done whatever it took to get you to conform."

"And now?" he asked.

"Now I just want to get this over with," she said.

"Vicky." He said her name softly, as if he quietly pleaded with her to meet his gaze. But she couldn't do that, because if she did, he would see the truth. That she didn't really despise him. That what she felt for him was more like admiration. She liked that he strove to improve himself, not because he needed to, but because he *wanted* to.

She heard him shift. Her heart began to beat like a sprinter at a marathon.

"Help me," he said gently, kneeling down next to her. "Help me to better myself."

Oh, lord. How did he know exactly what to say to her?

"I'm afraid."

Crap, Vicky. Now, why the heck did you go and say that?

"Of what?" he asked gently.

The time for half-truths was over. *That* was why she'd admitted her fear. "Of getting hurt."

"I'm not going to hurt you."

"After we sleep together you might."

She saw his eyes widen. His body went still. His gaze took on an intensity she'd never seen before.

"That's one thing I admire about you, Vicky. You're never afraid to take the bull by the horns."

"I'm right, aren't I?"

"That we're going to sleep together? Yes."

She warmed. No, that wasn't true. She *combusted*. Hearing him say that…*whew.* It turned her inside out.

It turned her *on.*

"But not right now," he said softly. "Later."

"No," she said. "Not later. Now."

She heard a breath gush out of him, knew he wanted her, too. Lord knows why. She didn't particularly want to explore that right now. All she wanted to do was kiss him—and touch him.

"Vicky," he said again. "If we do this, things will change."

"I know," she said. "But maybe if we do this, I'll get you out of my system."

He drew back. "That's not a very nice thing to say."

"It's true," she said. Now that how she felt was all out in the open, she could meet his eyes. "I don't want you to mistake the matter, Brandon. All I want from you is sex. Nothing more. You're an itch that needs to be scratched. Hopefully once I've done that, I'll be over it."

He stood.

Vicky followed him up. "Don't look at me like that."

He ran a hand through his hair. "How the hell am I supposed to look at you? You think I'm flattered that all you want from me is some sort of physical satisfaction? Vicky, you're as bad as everyone else."

She'd blown it. She could see that now. Damn it. But what else was she supposed to say? That she liked him? That she—yeah, right—*loved* him? That wasn't what this was. Frankly, she'd have thought he'd be pleased by her honesty. "Most men would love to meet a woman who only wants to be bedded."

"I'm not most men."

"No?"

She saw him narrow his eyes. He came toward her. Vicky's breath caught in her throat. There was such a look of lust in his eyes, and such a look of outraged dignity, that she knew he'd taken everything the wrong way and that now he was determined to prove he could tame her, make her want him.

He jerked her to him. Her held breath gushed out.

Oh, yeah. He was mad. She could tell the minute he kissed her. Mad and turned on. She was turned on, too. He knew how to kiss and he kissed her hard. She felt something hot against her lips, realized it was his tongue, then she opened her mouth to meet his assault.

Yes, she thought. Yes, yes, yes. This was what she wanted. To be with him—no matter what the consequences.

"You want sex," he said. "Fine. I'll give you sex."

Something about the look in his eyes, something about the way his jaw clenched and unclenched had her slowing down. She lifted a hand to her face, slowly, deliberately removing her glasses, and then she gently placed them on the table. After that she began to pull her shirt over her head. She was just woman enough to want to make him sweat a bit, so she took her time as she pulled the fabric free.

His eyes narrowed even further.

"I want you to touch me," she said softly. "I want you to do things to me that I've only ever dreamed about. I want to remember this night for the rest of my life."

Was that her sounding like a sex kitten?

She didn't care. Her striptease was working. His hands clenched and unclenched now.

She wanted him to know that she wasn't seducing him because of who he was. She wasn't in this for the glory of bedding an athlete. She was doing this because she wanted him. *Him.* Not Brandon Burke, the race-car driver, but Brandon Burke the man.

And why is that important to you?

"Vicky," she heard him groan.

Suddenly he was there, up against her, and she knew, she just knew that her striptease was over.

He spun her around, then kissed her hard.

Oh, yeah.

This would, indeed, be a night to remember.

CHAPTER TWENTY-TWO

WHEN BRANDON WOKE UP, Vicky was gone.

He rolled over in bed, feeling around for her. But she wasn't there. A glance at the clock revealed it was six in the morning. Holy crap, he thought, sitting up. Where'd she go?

"Good morning," said a cheerful voice from the corner of the room. "I'm glad you're up. We have a lot of work to do before our meeting at ten."

He swiveled toward the voice. In the corner of the room, looking spry and chipper despite the ghoulish glow cast by her computer monitor, sat the woman he'd spent hours and hours making love to.

"I've found some great articles on how to teach people to read," she said. "I just love the Internet."

He didn't know what to do. He didn't know what to say. He'd never woken up from a night of pleasure with the woman he'd pleased off in some corner acting as if nothing had happened.

"Did you make coffee?" he asked, sniffing the air.

She nodded. "Yup. There's a pot in the bathroom. Help yourself. There are towels in there, too, in case you want to shower."

What the hell was this? Wham, bam, thank you ma'am?

"Vicky."

She looked up from her computer monitor, the frown clearing from her forehead as she looked away from whatever she'd been studying. "What?"

"Don't you want to come back to bed?"

The irony was, he'd heard those same words a few dozen times, only they'd been spoken to him by other women.

"Actually, no," she said, her eyes refocusing on her screen. "I really think it's important that we get to work. We didn't exactly have a productive evening last night and we need to review the phrases you have to memorize for the meeting today."

Productive evening? What the hell?

He slipped out of bed. She looked away. He padded over to her, folded her monitor closed. "Come back to bed," he ordered, hands on hip.

"No," she said.

"Vicky, I'm not going to beg."

"And I told you once we slept together that it would be over. *Finito.* Through. You may as well get dressed. I want to be able to tell Mr. Knight that we made some progress with your reading, too, today."

He sat there, speechless. Damn it. What was with her? She hadn't really meant it when she'd told him all she wanted was a one-night stand. Right? He'd heard women say that before, although he'd never had one demand sex quite the way Vicky had. But whenever a woman claimed to want him for a night, it was usually just an act, a way of making herself sound different. The next morning they always got pouty when he hopped out of bed and acted as if nothing big had happened. But last night something big had happened.

"Fine," he said, because he could wait. If she wanted to play the all-it-was-was-sex game, then she'd met her match. "But first let me go shower."

"Great," she said with a flick of her head. "I'll pull out your workbooks."

Yeah. Workbooks. They'd do some work, all right. He'd work on seducing her…when the time was right. But for now he could wait. Give her a taste of her own medicine because if there was one thing he knew, it was that Vicky wasn't as immune to him as she seemed. No woman could do the things she'd done last night and feel nothing come morning.

No woman.

"SO WHAT YOU NEED TO DO," Mrs. Parsons said, "is appear relaxed and confident. Confident, but not cocky. Approachable, but not too friendly."

They were in a downtown high-rise, four other people in the room with Vicky and Brandon. Who they were, Vicky didn't know. And what their names were…well, she couldn't remember that, either. The only familiar face was Mrs. Parsons, the venerable lady looking the quintessential schoolmarm today in her ruffled white blouse, which covered her neck, of course; her dark gray skirt, to her ankles; and her serviceable black pumps. The view outside was mostly the same as the one outside her hotel-room window.

Thinking of her hotel made her think of tangled sheets and hot, incredible sex.

"Don't you think?" Brandon said, interrupting her thoughts.

Vicky pushed her glasses back up her nose and

stared around the table. Five sets of eyes stared back at her, and they each gazed at her as if they expected her to say something.

"What was that?" she asked. Brandon sat next to her, but him she ignored because if she met his gaze, more memories would pop into her head.

"He was saying," Mrs. Parsons said, "that he thinks you should receive some training, too."

Concentrate, Vicky! "Oh. I, ah… I should, *what?*"

She heard someone chuckle. It was Brandon, the rumbling from his chest a low baritone that made her teeth grind together.

"Wow," Brandon said, and she knew he leaned closer to her because she could see his reflection in the glass surface of the table. "Someone had a late night."

Yeah, she thought to herself. *Because of you.*

"Actually," she said. "It was a late meeting." She picked up a pencil that sat by the documents in front of her.

"So did I," Brandon whispered. "And it was a very…*very good* meeting."

Had anyone else heard the words? She glanced around the table. The other women in the room were staring at the two of them as if wondering just exactly what kind of meeting they'd had. After a second or two, Mrs. Parsons looked ready to breathe fire. The two men kept their eyes on the papers in front of them as if embarrassed to look up.

Vicky almost groaned.

Damn Brandon. Why'd he have to do this? He might as well climb the light fixtures above the table, beat his chest and crow like Tarzan.

Me bed woman last night. It good.

"Yes, well," Mrs. Parsons said, picking up some papers and tapping them on the table. She looked ready to fling them at them both if they didn't start to behave. "I think Mr. Burke might have a point. If you'll be representing him at the track, then you should receive training, too."

"I'm not planning to go to any more races."

"Be that as it may," Mrs. Parsons said, "you might be called to speak on his behalf. In that event, it would be good for you to receive the same schooling as Brandon."

Brandon leaned in close. She could smell his cedarlike scent. "You're going to the track with me this weekend."

"No, I'm not."

He reached under the table and squeezed her leg. She dropped the pencil that she'd been holding. "Brandon," she whispered fiercely, noticing there were nail marks in the wood where she'd stabbed her fingers into it.

Brandon let go and said, "I totally agree. Especially since I expect Vicky to come to *all* my races."

She could feel her skin prickle where he'd touched her. "No," she all but growled. "I don't need to go to the track. That's what you have Mrs. Parsons for. Besides, I'm the type of person who likes to *type* up statements, not actually talk to the media in person."

"Now, now, now," he said, glancing around the table with a smile. "Vicky's just being modest. She actually loves being in the spotlight. Why, you should have seen her last—"

She kicked him under the table.

"—week," he finished after a long silence that seemed to raise the eyebrows of everyone in the room, including the men who were now staring avidly at the two of them. "She jumped right in front of the cameras at Daytona and told everyone we'd issue a statement later. It was great."

Mrs. Parsons stared at them with what could only be called a disapproving frown.

She knew.

Damn it all. Once the woman found out from

her boss that Brandon and Vicky had been together in her hotel room last night, she'd put two and two together. No doubt everyone at KEM would find out then. In a matter of days they'd all know she'd slept with Brandon Burke.

"Well," Mrs. Parsons huffed. "I'm glad to hear your agent is such a team player."

Vicky almost groaned. Oh, yeah, that'd been a dig. The emphasis on the words *team player* combined with the scowl on the woman's face couldn't be mistaken.

"And," Mrs. Parsons continued, "since I feel Mr. Burke has a point, we'll add you to the schedule, too."

Terrific. Just what she wanted. To be given faux interviews in front of a television camera so her performance could be replayed and everyone in the room could tell her how badly she'd messed up. She *hated* being put on display like that.

"Well, if there's nothing further, let's go over our key messages," Mrs. Parsons said, nodding to one of the men in the room. He got up, went to the giant whiteboard and began to write. Vicky tried to pay attention, she truly did, but it was hard with Brandon's hand sliding onto her thigh from time to time, and Mrs. Parsons shooting them looks that clearly indicated she knew what was going on. Vicky felt like a teen in high school.

"Would you stop it?" she said the moment they were alone. They were standing by a row of windows, sunlight casting checkerboard patterns on the buff-colored floor beneath them—both of them waiting for a crew of technicians to finish adjusting the cameras and sound. Mrs. Parsons and company were gathered in a corner, reviewing their notes.

"Maybe I don't want to stop," he said.

"You should," she snapped back. "Because if those people over there haven't guessed by now that you and I have been intimate, I'll eat my glasses."

"Oh, now, don't do that," he said softly. "You look so adorable in them."

"I'm serious, Brandon. You've got to stop."

"No," he said, his words bringing her back to reality. "Last night was the first of many nights you and I will spend together."

Damn him, his words had her warming up all over again.

"I'm not going to let you walk away. What happened between us wasn't meaningless. *You* know it and I know it."

"I know nothing of the sort," she said, slipping her glasses back up her nose.

"Yes, you do," he said softly. "I can see it in your eyes. Tell me, was one night enough? Did you—how did you put it?—get me out of your system?"

No. Not by a long shot. If anything, her craving for him had grown worse. He was like a spot of poison oak. You knew you shouldn't scratch it because once you did, it'd only itch worse. And that's exactly what had happened. She wanted him again. Wanted him to do the things to her that he had last night. Wanted him to make her moan and sigh and cry out in pleasure.

No, she screamed inside. No, no, no. It wasn't going to happen again. This time she would be the one to do the dumping.

"Look," she said, turning to him. "I don't know what kind of woman you think I am, but I am definitely not the type to engage in affairs with men like you. No. Way."

"Men like me?" he said. "What the hell is that supposed to mean?"

"Big star athlete. I used to see them prance around campus back in college. Always with a girl on their arm. I don't like men like that. I like men that can give me tit for tat. That can hold up their end of the conversation."

"And you think because I can't read I'm not your intellectual equal."

"No," she said, grabbing him by the forearm. "I do not think that. Don't you ever think I think that," she said, releasing him only when the spark of anger she'd seen in his eyes faded away. "I'm saying you and I have nothing in common. You race cars for a living. I might have a career in law if being an agent doesn't work out." After last night, that was a distinct possibility.

"You must know something about racing if you wanted to be an agent. You must know something about sports. You must like it, too. Why else would you want to do this for a living?"

Why, indeed? She couldn't tell him about her parents. How living with her mom and dad— or rather, *step*mom—had been like living with strangers. They were so different, so into wealth and power and prestige. She'd never felt that way. She'd refused to work in the family law firm. She wanted to do something different with her degree. Sure it'd been an act of rebellion, but so what? Sure her stepmother called her just about every other day to ask if she'd changed her mind, but that was to be expected. They hated sports—and she'd gone and decided she wanted to spend her life dealing with athletes.

"Because I love sports," she admitted. "I'm a jock inside, even though I've never been talented at anything even remotely athletic. The closest I've come to racing was trying to outpace the woman on the treadmill next to me. But that doesn't mean I don't love the roar of a crowd. I get excited when someone I'm rooting for does well, race-car driver, tennis player or basketball star—it doesn't matter. I love it. And I want to be on the inside. Or at least I think I do. I don't know yet. The jury's still out."

"So you want to live vicariously through your clients?"

"Maybe something like that," she said. "I'm not going to let you blow it for me, either. So back off, Burke. If you don't, I'll quit."

"You won't do that," he said softly.

"Oh, yes, I will."

"No, you won't," he said with a shake of his head. "It's like you said. You love sports. You're a competitor at heart. You don't want to lose, and walking away from me would be a loss. That's why you haven't quit before now."

"I haven't quit because I need to make ends meet."

He shook his head again. "Nah. I don't buy it. You're not being honest, Vicky VanCleef. We *do* have something in common. We both like to win, and when it comes to you and I, I'll tell you right now, you're going to lose."

She let out an exasperated breath. "I give up."

"And I'll tell you something else, too. You're going to be at my race this next weekend."

"No, I'm not."

"You will because you want me to do well. That whole vicarious winning thing."

She snorted. "Don't flatter yourself."

"Of course, you'll also have to go because I'm going to tell Scott I want you there. He won't refuse me."

"Blackmail again?" she asked with a lifted brow.

"Whatever it takes."

"It won't work."

"That's what you think," he said softly, leaning toward her. "You've become a challenge to me, and like I said earlier, I hate, absolutely *hate* to lose."

CHAPTER TWENTY-THREE

JUST AS BRANDON had predicted, Scott had ordered Vicky to be at the race.

But that didn't necessarily mean she'd listen to him, Brandon mused as he stared at the people milling about beneath him. He was up on top of the race-car hauler, looking down into the garage.

Vicky had given him "lessons" twice more, but the woman had him outfoxed. She'd demanded they meet in public places, something he couldn't exactly say no to since he was certain Mr. Knight would see right through him if Brandon demanded they meet in her hotel room. So she'd shown up at restaurants, always busy ones, yet not so busy that they couldn't find a secluded spot away from prying eyes. He hadn't been able to do much more than make suggestive comments.

He watched as, down below, someone pushed a tire car toward the garage. The man's colorful shirt proclaimed him to be with one of NASCAR's newest manufacturers, a Japanese company that had created quite a stir when they'd entered the racing league's ranks. A few of his fellow crew members were lounging near a pit stall. It was an hour before qualifying so most cars had already passed through tech inspection. Cars were lined up out on pit road in preparation for qualifying. The scene below him was different from the one before Indy qualifying. If this had been an Indy race, the cars out in pit road would have been hooked up to million-dollar computers, not a two-thousand-dollar generator whose sole purpose was to keep fans blowing and the oil inside the engine warm. The hauler he stood upon would have been parked a million miles away, too.

"She's here."

His phone had chirped and he hadn't even heard it. Yet another sign that he was seriously distracted.

"Where?" Brandon asked after pushing the answer button.

It was Chad, his crew chief, doing the talking. He'd embroiled him in his affairs, albeit, reluctantly, but it'd turned out to be a good move. Obviously, he'd figured out what was going on, but

Brandon didn't care if Chad knew he was having an affair. Maybe that'd keep the other guys away.

"I think that's her down by the No. 86 garage," Chad said.

Brandon changed positions, the hauler rocking beneath him. Sure enough, Vicky came toward them, her lips firmly pressed together, her hair loose and streaming out behind her.

She looked pissed.

"That's her," Brandon said. "Thanks, buddy."

"My pleasure," Chad said. From down in the garage, his crew chief waved. A few members of his crew turned to follow Chad's gaze. They waved, too. A week ago, Brandon would never have expected such a gesture, but today he returned those waves.

He went straight down the first level of steps, the ones that allowed him access to a platform that hung off the back of the hauler. It was actually the tailgate of the semi that yawned open like an elevated drawbridge, but it worked well as a metal canopy, too, even if it was a hassle to get up and down the ladder chained to its side.

When his feet hit solid ground, Vicky was just stepping beneath the square patch of shade cast by the platform he'd just been standing on.

"Hi, there," he said, giving her his best smile.

She gave him a glare in return.

"Where can I put my briefcase?" she asked, holding up the same bag she'd carried that day at the drag race track.

"In there," he said, pointing over his shoulder to the "office" area of the race-car transporter, the sliding-glass doors off the back reflecting their images and that of the garages behind them.

"Great," she said, and behind the lenses of her glasses he caught a brittle I-wish-you'd-drop-dead glare.

This might be a long day.

His supposition seemed confirmed when she just about jerked the sliding-glass door off its track because she pulled on it so hard. And when she slammed it closed, Brandon was certain people five haulers over heard the impact.

"Man," someone said. "She sure looks mad."

He turned. A little boy peered up at him and Brandon wondered who the kid was. He sat on one of three director's chairs someone had placed beneath the shade of the elevated tailgate.

"You know, I think you're right."

The boy smiled and Brandon recognized him then. "You're Benjamin Koch."

"Cool," the kid said, his whole face lighting up. "I've been recognized by a famous race-car driver."

Of course he had. The kid was famous at Knight Enterprises Motorsports. They'd all met him through Miracles, a charity organization that fulfilled the wishes of terminally ill children. Benjamin had been battling leukemia at the time, but, thankfully, the kid's cancer was in remission right now. He looked as healthy as a horse, or so Brandon thought. Well, he still had peach fuzz for brown hair, but he didn't look nearly as sick as he used to.

"What are you doing here?" Brandon asked. "Not that you're not welcome," he quickly added at the crushed look on the boy's face. "I just know you and Todd are pretty tight."

"Are you kidding? You have no idea what a zoo it is over there. I got tired of being asked to move. Now that I'm no longer in a wheelchair, people don't give me any respect. Not that I want to be back in that wheelchair or anything."

"I bet not," Brandon said. He knew "over there" referred to the other side of the garage. The teams were lined up in order of last year's points. That's the way it would be until the first few races were over. Then the teams would line up based on the current year's points standing. Since Brandon was new, that meant he was out in the south forty. Todd's hauler was clear on the other side of the garage, next to all the other NASCAR hotshots.

"Does your mom know you're here?" he asked, looking for the familiar blond woman.

"Yeah. She knows. But she's trying to get some rest in Todd's lounge. She's pregnant."

Someone opened the glass doors. Not Vicky. She appeared to be hiding.

"With Todd's child," Benjamin added.

"Oh, yeah?" Brandon asked, trying to see inside the hauler. Where'd Vicky go?

"She's only a couple months along, but she said at her age, it feels more like she's ten months along. She said it's all Todd's fault. Babies born on his side of the family have all been whoppers."

Finally, the kid's words sank in. "Wait," he said, shifting his gaze back to the boy. "You mean, your mom's pregnant with Todd's kid?"

"Uh-huh," Benjamin said with a wide grin.

"Does his wife know?"

"Indi?" Benjamin asked. "Of course she knows. It's her baby, too."

"Wait, wait, wait," Brandon said, sitting down. The chair squeaked, the wood frame protesting his weight. "How can your mom be pregnant with Todd and Indi's child?"

"She's a surrogate."

Brandon drew back in surprise. "Well, I'll be damned. I didn't even know that kind of stuff still went on."

Some fans stopped near a row of tires that were parked about twenty feet off the back of the hauler. He waved them over, signing an autograph or two with a practiced smile. These days, he was grateful for anyone who wanted his signature.

"My mom says there's big business in being a surrogate. Some women make up to sixty thousand a year."

"Really? Wow."

"But she's doing it for free."

"That's nice of her."

"Yup," Benjamin said with a proud smile.

"Do they know what it is yet? Oh, wait. Of course not. Too early to tell, isn't it?"

"Yup," Benjamin said. "But they asked for a boy and I guess there's a way they can make that happen." He shrugged. "I don't know."

"Crazy."

"And if it *is* a boy," he said, "they're going to name it after *me*." He stabbed himself in his chest with his thumb.

"Wow."

The sliding-glass door opened again. It was Vicky. Brandon leaned toward Benjamin. "Is she carrying a knife?"

Benjamin shook his head.

"Holding a gun?"

"No."

"Pitchfork, stun gun or any other implements of torture?"

Benjamin giggled. "Nope."

"Then I guess I'm okay," Brandon said. "See ya, kid," he said, rubbing his palm against the peach fuzz.

"What are you doing?" Vicky asked when he stepped in front of her.

"Showing you around." Brandon glanced back at the boy. "If you don't mind me leaving you alone," he said to Benjamin.

"Of course not," the child said. "Beats the craziness over at Todd's hauler."

Brandon took Vicky's hand. She jerked away.

"What are you doing?" she asked in a near growl.

"Staking my claim," he said with a wide smile.

"Staking your claim on what?"

"You," he said.

"Oh, no, you're not."

"Come on," he said, placing a hand against the small of her back. "You need to have a look around if you want to do a good job representing me."

"Oh, yeah? How so?"

"How the heck are you going to know what I'm talking about if you don't know what the heck everything is?"

"Give me a break," she said, crossing her arms in front of her.

"All right. Tell me what a spotter is and you can stand here all day long."

"It's someone who helps a driver navigate through race traffic. An eye in the sky, if you will."

"Lucky guess," he said, taking her arm. "What's a track bar?"

"Something that goes on the rear of a car to help give tires traction."

"Wow," Benjamin said, overhearing their conversation. "She knows a lot."

"Yeah, but has she ever *seen* track bars before?"

Vicky didn't say anything. "Aha. Got you there."

Her eyes narrowed.

"Just humor me," he said. "I've got to qualify

in less than an hour so it's not as if we'll go far. Just have a look around the garage. Now's a good time what with most of the cars out on pit road."

She looked as though she might balk again.

"We'll just be right over there," he said, pointing.

She moved away from him, but Brandon was relieved it was toward the garage. "She's secretly in love with me," Brandon murmured to Benjamin.

"Sounds like it," the boy said with a giggle.

Brandon smiled and quickly followed after Vicky. As he did so, he found himself thinking it seemed surreal to be chasing her. Usually when he brought a woman to the garage she was trying to keep *him* entertained, or at least interested. Vicky seemed content to walk in silence, the scowl on her face clearly visible.

"It's actually pretty interesting," he said, catching up to her. "Stock cars might not look high-tech, but just as much money goes into designing and engineering one as they spend on open wheel cars. You should see some of the equipment we've got in there."

"I can't wait."

She was just trying to get him riled. Brandon understood that. "Chad," he called to his crew chief once they were inside the garage. "Have you met Vicky VanCleef, my agent?"

"No," he said, walking forward. "I haven't, but I think I spotted her recently somewhere."

"The Employee Appreciation Day," Vicky provided, quickly offering her hand.

She didn't jerk away from *his* touch, Brandon noticed.

"She was there," Brandon said. "She was hoping to arrive early enough to throw some balls, but Todd beat her to it. I think she's hoping for a second chance, though. You don't happen to have something she could throw at me, do you?"

"You mean, she doesn't like you?" Chad asked with a mock look of horror. "Imagine that."

Brandon noticed a slight smile had come to her face. He couldn't decide if he was relieved or perturbed that it was Chad who'd put it there.

"You want to give her the dime-store tour?" he said. "I need to get changed into my uniform." Maybe that would impress her, he thought. God knows, he needed something to give him an edge.

"Sure," Chad said, motioning Vicky toward the engine compartment. Brandon noticed she didn't hesitate to follow his crew chief.

"Okay, well, have fun," Brandon called out.

She didn't even spare him a glance, just stopped by a toolbox where a TV monitor played.

"Don't worry," Chad said. "I'll take care of her."

Another member of his crew, one carrying a plate of food, said, "And if he doesn't look out for her, I'll do it."

There were choruses of "Me, too" around the garage. Brandon just shook his head. He'd walk Vicky around once she'd calmed down. Then she'd get to see what it was like to be the girlfriend of a driver. How, even though so many fans professed to hate him, they'd still ask him for his autograph—and hers, too, sometimes. The women would flirt. The men would gawk. And Vicky could stand back and watch.

Stupid of you to want to try and impress her in such an obvious way.

Yeah, well, so what? He didn't have any other choice. Besides, he really did want her to see what his life was like.

Why?

Well, now *that* thought he refused to examine. At least not right now.

"Where'd Benjamin go?" Brandon asked another one of his crew guys. The engine specialist was sitting in the chair next to where Benjamin had been sitting, a plate of food in his lap.

"I think he went back to the eight-two camp," he said over a mouthful of food. "Something about watching qualifying from atop the hauler."

"He could have done that here."

"Guess the view's better from there," the guy said. "Oh, and hey, you've got a visitor in there."

"In where?"

"In the lounge."

"Who?"

The guy shrugged again. "Some old man. I don't know. He walked in like he owned the place. Wouldn't answer my questions. Since he had a hard card, I just figured you knew him."

A "hard card" being a NASCAR season credential. Maybe it was a reporter.

"Said you and he had some unfinished business. Something about Florida."

"Thanks," Brandon said, reaching for the metal handle on the sliding-glass door. Once inside the hauler, he focused his gaze on the door at the end of the long aisleway, or more specifically, the two steps at the end of it that led to the hauler's twenty-by-twenty lounge. He hesitated a moment outside.

Calm down. It's no big deal if it *is* him. But his hand still shook as he let himself inside.

It was just as he feared. His worst nightmare faced him.

CHAPTER TWENTY-FOUR

"SON," HIS FATHER SAID, getting up from the chair he'd been sitting in. Harold Burke looked the same. His cheeks were tinged red from alcohol and they were still just as round as ever. His hair was still just as gray. His belly still just as wide.

Apparently, Harold was eating good…thanks to Brandon.

"Dad," he said, going to the cabinet to the right and pulling out his uniform.

Be cool. The man doesn't have any power over you. Not anymore.

"What the hell are you doing here?" he asked, setting the red-and-orange suit down. Yellow writing with the words *Snappy Lube* sprawled across the chest, the *Snappy* on one side of the Velcro, *Lube* on the other.

"What else would I be doing here?" his father asked in the same, scruffy-toned baritone voice

Brandon remembered so well. "I'm here to straighten you out."

He'd been in the midst of pulling his shirt off, but Brandon paused. "Straighten me out?"

"Yeah," Harold said. "I don't think I need to tell you that your driving hasn't exactly been up to par."

Brandon whirled. "I'm still learning how these cars handle—"

But then he cut himself off. What the hell was he explaining himself for? He didn't owe the old man anything. Damn him.

"I know I'm struggling," he forced himself to say—and to calm down. "But you know what, Dad? I'm having a good time learning. For the first time in my life, I'm driving for an owner who really seems to care, a crew that wants to help me be my best, and an agent who doesn't just want a cut of the money—she cares about *me*."

"Sleeping with her, are you?" his father asked.

"No," he said. *Not at the moment.* "And even if I was, she's the type of agent who'd lay down her life for a client she represents. She might not like the athlete she represents, but that wouldn't stop her from doing a good job. She has *ethics*."

Unlike some people in the room.

"Wow," his father drawled. "I'm happy for you, son. I really am."

Yeah, right.

"Sounds as if you're in a real good place. Too bad it doesn't show up in your driving. But we can work on that."

"*We* aren't doing anything," he said. "Or did you expect me to forget about all the money you stole? All the fraudulent bank accounts. The credit cards in my name that weren't really mine. The cars and boats—everything you bought for yourself."

"I told you in Florida, I bought that for us," his father said, taking a step toward him.

"Yeah, right," Brandon said. "And when the money dried up, when I lost my ride, where was the us?" His cheek began to twitch. Brandon told himself to calm down. He shouldn't let his father rile him up, not anymore, and *especially* not just before qualifying. "I can't believe you," Brandon said. "I can't believe you actually have the nerve to come here as if nothing had happened."

"I came because I'm your father," Harold said.

"I lost my dad years ago," Brandon said, refusing to back down. "I lost him when I made my first million and my dad went on a gambling

binge in Las Vegas. But you know what? I probably lost him before that. Back when I was
thirteen and I begged you to get me a tutor
because I wanted to learn how to read. You said
no. Do you remember that, *Dad?* You told me I
didn't need to learn that stuff. That I was going
to be a famous race-car driver and all drivers
needed to do was learn to go fast. I *begged* you
to get me some help, and when I wouldn't shut
up, what did you do?"

He waited for his father to answer. He wondered if he'd have the guts.

He didn't.

"You beat me black-and-blue," Brandon said.

His father's eyes went hard.

"And that wasn't the first time, either. The first
time was when I didn't make that race down in
South Carolina. Do you remember that? And the
time after that was when I snuck off to go fishing
with a friend. Remember? And throughout the
years, I took it. Oh, I tried to fight back—once—
but you were bigger than me. By the time I was
old enough to match your size, I was so beaten
down I wouldn't have fought you over the last
drop of water on earth."

Brandon steeled himself, took a step toward

him. "Not anymore." Despite his words to the contrary, he braced himself for his father's fist. "I'm through with you, Dad. When my career started to nosedive and you took off to find greener pastures, it was the best thing that ever happened to me. I'm on my own now. I like it that way. So you can just show yourself out."

He turned, jerked off his shirt, then waited for his father to leave. The whole time, the entire damn time, his flesh tingled in anticipation of the blow that in times past, he'd have most certainly received.

"You'll fail," his father said in a voice that was almost a snicker. "You'll fail at this just like you failed driving an Indy car."

"You know what, Dad?" he asked softly. "That may be. I may be the worst driver NASCAR has ever seen. But at least I'll fail on my own. At least I won't have to put up with you stomping on my self-esteem. I'm done with that. Look at the money you stole as a parting gift. I never pressed charges because I'd hoped you'd just stay away, but I should have known better. Frankly, I'm surprised it's taken you this long to track me down." He jerked his shirt back on. He could change in the damn public restrooms.

"Where are you going?" Harold asked.

Brandon paused by the door he'd headed toward. His father's voice could still cause his heart to pound. Still caused him to flinch—albeit, inwardly. "I'm leaving," he said with a tight smile. "Without you."

He stormed out—and nearly ran Vicky down.

"We're not through yet," hollered a voice behind him.

"Oh, yes, you are," Vicky told his father as she stepped around Brandon.

When Brandon turned, his father was standing in the doorway. He looked taller than he actually was thanks to the steps leading up to the lounge.

"I won't let you push him around, either, and if you don't leave, I'll have garage security remove you," Vicky countered.

"Who the hell are you?"

"I'm his agent," Vicky said, hands on hips by now.

Suddenly Brandon's anger faded as he stood back and watched the woman he loved—

Whoa! *Loved?*

Yes, he admitted, pride filling him as she tapped his father on the chest. "But I'm also his friend," she said. "Which is more than you ever were. You're through messing with his head. Messing with his life. If you have an ounce of sense, you'd get out while the going's good."

That was when Brandon noticed something else. Behind him, lining both sides of the hauler's aisle, was his team, each man facing his father as if they'd knock his father senseless if Harold so much as flinched.

"I think you might want to leave," Chad said, his gaze firmly fixed on Brandon's father.

Brandon felt his eyes burn.

He took a deep breath, tried to stifle the emotions rolling through him.

"Leave," he heard Vicky say.

When he turned back to his father, the man was breathing harshly. His eyes darted around as if analyzing his chances of successfully bullying his way back into Brandon's life.

"This isn't over," Harold replied.

"Oh, yes, it is," Vicky said, leaning to the right. There was a door there, a back entrance to the hauler that Brandon oftentimes used to get in and out. "Go," Vicky ordered again, pointing.

With one last glare in Brandon's direction, his father finally left.

WHEN VICKY TURNED AROUND, Brandon was gone. No, she realized, he wasn't gone. He was at the end of the hauler, his body disappearing between the glass so quickly, she wondered if he might bump into his father outside.

"Thanks, guys," she said to his crew.

"No problem," Chad murmured.

"I had no idea he'd been through so much," someone else said.

She'd suspected. The moment she'd seen Brandon's father—a man she recognized from press clips—slip through the hauler's glass doors, Brandon apparently oblivious to his presence, she'd quickly collected Chad and anyone else she could gather. She'd known this confrontation between father and son wouldn't be pretty. However, she stayed them all with a hand when she'd heard Brandon defend himself valiantly.

"You think I should follow him?" Chad said.

"No," Vicky said. "I think he needs some space. How long till he has to qualify?"

"Twenty minutes."

"Can you buy him some time?"

Chad shook his head.

"Then I guess I'll go after him."

"Are you sure that's wise?"

"No," Vicky said. "But I'm his agent. That's what I do."

"He's lucky to have you," Chad said.

"Yeah, well, I'm not so sure he knows that."

Brandon's team let her pass, but only as she stepped outside did Vicky realize she had no idea where Brandon might have gone. He'd been carrying his uniform, so maybe he'd gone to change. If so, where?

"Did you see Brandon Burke pass through here?" she asked a crew member from one of the other teams.

"Went that way," he said, pointing.

"Thanks," she muttered, taking off.

Fortunately, the track's layout made it easy to get around. Both Daytona and Fontana had garages that faced each other—the buildings a giant equal sign—so it was a simple matter of going up one row and down the next, hoping to spot him coming out of a restroom or something.

Fifteen minutes later she was ready to give up. But then she spotted Brandon in his uniform, standing by Todd Peters's garage. Actually, he was inside of it, talking to the driver himself, a group of fans lurking outside, cameras poised to catch a picture of last season's NASCAR Sprint Cup Series champion.

She almost didn't go up to him. What would she say? Sorry about your dad, but you've really got to go qualify? To her surprise, she didn't have to say anything at all. Once Brandon spotted her, he gave her a tight smile, then waved her over.

"Excuse me," she said, brushing by the fans.

"Have you met Todd?" Brandon asked, motioning to the other driver.

"Ah, no," she said, baffled. She'd expected Brandon to be a wreck. To maybe excuse himself so they could go chat about what had just happened. Instead he politely introduced her to the other driver, the dark-haired, dark-eyed stranger greeting her with a warm smile.

"Todd's married, but he just knocked up some other woman."

"Hey," the driver said, smacking Brandon in the arm. "Don't say it like that. She's going to think I'm a total jerk."

"It's true," Brandon said with a teasing grin.

"My wife and I can't have children on our own, but we've been lucky enough to find a surrogate," Todd explained.

"I see," Vicky said, with a glance between the two. "Ah, when's the baby due?" she asked when she realized both men stared at her.

"September thirteenth."

"Wow. Great," Vicky said. "Congratulations."

"Hey, guys," someone named Dan said, a giant pair of blue headphones resting on his shoulders "We'll be pushing off in just a few minutes."

Brandon gave Vicky a smile. "Guess that's my cue to get a move on."

"Chad would probably appreciate that."

"Walk with me?" Brandon said.

She stared at the hand he held out, debated whether or not to take it. In the end, something made her reach out, made her clasp his fingers.

Suddenly she knew. She just *knew* that she was starting to fall in love.

CHAPTER TWENTY-FIVE

HE FELT TEN FEET TALL.

Brandon walked back to his garage, the occasional fan stopping him. He took their pens, scrawled his name across pieces of paper. Through it all, he held the hand of the only woman in his life to steal his heart.

"Brandon," she said when they had a moment alone. "About what just happened—"

"You mean, Todd?" he said, trying to be deliberately obtuse. "I'm sure he doesn't mind me telling you about their surrogate."

"No," she said, looking exasperated. "That's not what I meant, and you know it."

"I know," he said, giving her fingers a squeeze. "I just don't want to talk about it. I want to enjoy the moment. Revel in the scent of carburetor cleaner. Absorb the warmth of asphalt whose ambient temperature is a hundred degrees. Perhaps quaff a sports drink before I attempt to qualify."

"Did you just say quaff?"

He gave her a big smile. "Impressive, huh? I've been studying. On my laptop. I can't read words yet on my own, but I can memorize them."

She nodded, looking away. She seemed shy all of a sudden, as if she had something to say but didn't know quite how to say it.

"You going to watch me qualify from atop the hauler?" he asked.

"Is that where I'm supposed to go?"

"Yeah," he said. "Either that or in the lounge."

They'd made it to pit road by then. Chad was standing near the side of his car, an anxious look on his face as he scoured faces for Brandon's.

"Looking for me," Brandon said, coming up nearly behind him.

"There you are," his crew chief said in relief. "I was about to call Vicky on her cell phone."

"Did you think I wasn't going to show?"

Chad looked at Vicky, eyebrows raised. "I wasn't sure *what* to expect," he said.

"Relax," Brandon said. "I'm fine. Let's get the show on the road."

Chad nodded, followed Brandon to the side of

his car. His helmet, Brandon was glad to see, lay atop the roof, its reflection casting a glow over the red paint scheme. He reached inside the car and pulled the pin securing the steering wheel. He laid it next to his helmet.

"We made those changes we talked about," Chad said. "Don't know that messing with the aero is going to help as much as you'd like, but I guess we'll see."

Brandon nodded, waiting for the safety net on the driver's-side window to be dropped.

Brandon glanced over at Vicky. She looked terrified. "Relax," he said. Then he did something he'd never done before. He closed the distance between them, lifted his hands to her cheeks and bent down to place a gentle, tender kiss on her lips. "I'll be fine."

Behind the lenses of her glasses, he thought he saw surprise and then fear followed by acceptance. She reached up and clutched one of his hands. "Take care of yourself."

His hands dropped to her shoulders. He pulled her to him, the tension draining from him even more with her in his arms.

"Uh, Brandon," Chad said, clipboard tucked between his arm and his side. "I hate to break up such a tender moment, but we've really got to go."

"Ten-four, buddy," Brandon said, kissing Vicky on the cheek before he let her go. She didn't protest. She didn't pull away. Didn't offer some sarcastic comment.

Suddenly Brandon felt hope.

"I'll see you in a moment."

VICKY CLIMBED UP on top of the hauler. It was a perilous journey up a rickety aluminum ladder that shook and rattled beneath her feet. Next she had to climb over a rubber-coated chain, one that appeared to help support the metal platform she stood upon. A short journey up four more steps, and she'd made it to the top.

She was not alone.

"Hi," Kristen Knight said, her dark blue shirt in stark contrast to the red roofs that covered the buildings around them. She leaned against one corner of the railing, her clipboard sitting on a small, triangular-shaped table that stretched between the two corners of the railing. A computer monitor sat above the desk—if one wanted to call it that—a metal shield shading it from the sun. She could see a bar of light, one that highlighted the car number of the team currently trying to qualify, the sound of his engine echoing over the infield.

"Mrs. Knight. Hello."

"How are you, Vicky? And I told you to call me Kristen."

Yes, she had. However Brandon was Vicky's client and one day Vicky and this woman could end up across from each other at a negotiation table, or at the very least, she'd end up across from her husband. Best not to get too chummy.

"I didn't know you were here," Vicky said, having to fight not to call her Kristen for some reason. She was just so nice.

"I come to every race," she said. "Part of my job."

Vicky squinted against the glare beamed up by the aluminum floor they stood upon. Behind them, in the grandstands that ran along the front stretch, fans were milling about. It wasn't a full house up there, but it would be come race day.

"Did you have a nice flight?" the woman asked with a slight Southern drawl.

Vicky had flown out on the team plane which KEM had purchased to ferry people from track to track. Brandon hadn't been onboard. He'd come in on an earlier flight.

"It was great, thanks," Vicky said. "Everyone treated me like one of the gang."

"Yeah," Kristen said with a smile. "We have a great group of employees at KEM."

"I can tell," Vicky responded.

"Are you hungry?" Kristen asked. "If you are, we have a catering truck out by the other hauler."

Only then did Vicky realize she'd clutched her stomach. It was tingling. "Oh, ah. No. Not really. Just nervous."

She was nervous for Brandon, and he wasn't due to go out for several more minutes yet. He'd gotten a lower draw, something Chad, his crew chief, seemed to be happy about. Later meant cooler track temperatures and more rubber laid down for traction, or so she'd been told.

"Relax," Kristen said. "He'll be okay. Brandon's an old pro."

"Oh, no," Vicky said. "It's not like that," she lied because she didn't want Kristen Knight to think she and Brandon were anything more than client and agent. Anything else would look totally wrong.

"Vicky, Brandon told me he's dating you."

"He *what?*" she said, turning her head so fast, her glasses just about slipped off.

"Okay, not really dating you. He *wants* to date you. Last weekend he called me out of the blue and asked my opinion on a way to get back into your good graces. I told him nothing less than getting on his knees would make up for the way he'd treated you, *and* everyone else at the shop."

"Yeah, but he doesn't like me like *that,*" Vicky said. "He just really wanted to keep me as his agent."

"Yeah, right," Kristen said. "I was in your shoes not too long ago. I know the signs. You've fallen in love with him."

"I have not," Vicky immediately countered. "Good lord, we've only known each other a few weeks."

"That's all it takes sometimes."

"And he's been miserable to me for half that time."

"Well, you know what they say about love being the other side of the coin."

"Yeah, but that's not Brandon and I."

Vicky couldn't hold the woman's gaze. She heard a sound, used that as an excuse for turning away. The car out on the track had cut its engine and a new vehicle zoomed off pit road. She glanced up at the score tower. The last car had been fast. Its number glowed from the top. Of course, only six people had gone so far.

"Look," Kristen said. "I realize I don't know you all that well, and I may be way out of line here to tell you what I think, but someone once did something nice for Mathew and I, something that changed the course of my life, so maybe I can do the same for you. Brandon's changed since he met you. I don't know what it is, but the difference is remarkable. The Brandon of old would never have subjugated himself to a dunk tank. He would never have gone up to Todd and asked for his advice on how best to qualify like he just did today. Most of all, I've never seen him look at another woman like he looks at you."

"Yeah, but you hardly know him," Vicky said.

"I know *of* him. And he's been with our team for four months now. He's changed, Vicky, and the only thing different about his life is you."

The car on the track entered the backstretch, the sound of its engine suddenly louder somehow. Vicky watched the top of it zoom by. The banking was so steep it appeared as if it'd been turned on its side.

"Brandon doesn't know *how* to care about someone," she found herself saying. "If he *was* interested in me, then it'd only be because I'm the most convenient female around."

"You're wrong, Vicky. Like I said, Brandon's been with us for four months. I've seen him with other women. They were nothing to him. But the way he looks at you…"

Vicky clutched the rail.

"I think he really likes you," Kristen said. "Really, *really* likes you. What's more, Brandon *needs* someone like you. You're a smart, vivacious woman who's going to give him the love and support he needs. I can tell. So I hope that if Brandon tells you how he feels—and I suspect he will—that you're smart enough to see the man my husband and I saw all those months ago. A man who could be so amazing—both personally and professionally—if shown a little love."

"You saw that?" Vicky asked incredulously.

"We did. It's why we hired him. We know about his background. My husband is nothing else if not thorough. Or at least his security chief, Rob, is," she said derisively. But then she immediately sobered. "We know Brandon's father took off. We know Brandon is hurting for money, no doubt thanks to his dad. We didn't know about the illiteracy, but we suspected there was something else he was hiding. His psychological profile hinted at some deep-seated issues."

"You had him take a psych profile?"

"Yes. Even though he balked at doing it. He

insisted someone read him the questions so he could answer out loud. At the time we thought it was just Brandon being difficult. Now we know better. But I'm glad we gave in to his demands. I probably shouldn't be telling you this, but Brandon's profile confirmed what we'd suspected. He's an intelligent man with fierce loyalty to those he loves—not that he's had anyone to love in recent years. He can't abide liars and wants to be surrounded by people he can trust. What he wants—or needs—is someone like you."

"No," Vicky said with a shake of her head. "I'm not—" She almost said "ready for this." "I'm not so certain that's true."

"Have a little faith in yourself," Kristen said, but then she straightened suddenly. "Oops," she said, pointing to her headset. "I've got to go. Todd's about to qualify."

Vicky watched as she slipped her headphones into place, turned to the tiny desk and adjusted the computer monitor.

Vicky needed to think. Had she really made such a huge difference in Brandon's life? Already? Could the man she'd so callously pushed away actually care for her? She recalled the look in his eyes after he'd kissed her.

I'll be right back.

To see *her,* she realized. He'd be right back to see her.

Her hands had begun to sweat, and it wasn't because of the intense sunlight beating down on her head. Her heart was pounding, too. Brandon wasn't even driving yet and she already felt close to a panic attack.

Because she felt herself falling…falling toward a future that scared the hell out of her. Life with a race-car driver meant constant media attention as a result of that connection. The constant fear that maybe one day he'd spot someone in the crowd, a woman. One that was gorgeous and who might tempt him—

"I'll be right back," she told Kristen, although she wasn't certain the woman could hear her with her headset on.

The climb down from the hauler was every bit as perilous as the climb up, but Vicky barely noticed. When her feet hit the asphalt she began to walk…and walk…and walk. Only when she heard Brandon's name called did she stop, and it was odd, too, because she didn't even realize she'd been listening for it.

When she looked around, she realized she was

lost. She'd walked herself out of the garage and into an RV park of some sort. Numerous white-sided vacation vehicles were parked side by side, the smell of barbecue hanging in the air. From where she stood she could see a group of people sitting in aluminum lounge chairs watching TV—probably qualifying. She all but ran up to them. In a special compartment near the middle of the bus sat a TV. "I hope you don't mind," she told the crowd.

"We charge rent," someone quipped, an older man with gray hair and a wide, friendly smile.

"Yeah," said someone else, a younger man who sat to the older gentleman's right. "I'll take that Hot Pass of your off your hands."

Vicky smiled. "Sorry," she said. "I'll need it later."

Everyone smiled, including the other two—both women, one younger and one older. They stared at her curiously before turning their attention back to the TV.

In the middle of the tiny screen she saw Brandon's car, its orange, yellow and red paint scheme hard to miss.

"I wonder how he's going to do," the older man mused.

"Well," drawled the younger man, his hand stroking his chin, "I'll say one thing about Brandon Burke. He knows how to qualify."

"Yeah," said the younger woman. "It's just too bad he's such a jerk on race day."

"Did you see that woman drag him off by the ear the other day?" the gray-haired man said.

"Yeah," said the younger woman. "That was hysterical."

Turn Two loomed ahead on the TV screen. At the bottom of the monitor, a qualifying meter allowed Vicky to see how Brandon's time stacked up against the other drivers. If he was fast, a tiny arrow would zoom toward the word *Pole*. If he was slow, it'd levitate over the numbers that represented various starting positions.

"He'll be taking the green flag this time around," the commentator said. "Let's see if team KEM can put another car in the front row."

"I doubt he'll have an easy time matching Todd Peters's time," said a second announcer. "That lap just about put blisters in the pavement."

"I don't know," said the first guy. "Both cars use the same engine builder. And both cars are engineered pretty close to the same. He just might give his teammate a run for his money, but we'll see in just a moment...."

"C'mon," Vicky murmured. "You can do it."

On-screen the arrow raced toward the word *Pole*. Her breath caught. Brandon rounded Turn Two.

The rear of his car began to slide. She gasped.

The arrow on-screen flew in the other direction, but Brandon held it together.

The arrow dashed toward *Pole* again. The orange, red and yellow car flew down the backstretch, heading hell-bent-for-leather toward Turn Three. She couldn't look. He was going too fast. Surely he was about to drive straight into the wall. But, no. The arrow was still pegged toward *Pole*. He turned, smoothly, expertly.

"Go," she screamed.

A second later, he crossed over the Start/Finish line as, above him, someone waved a white flag.

"Wow," the announcer said. "If he hadn't bobbled that turn, he'd have bumped Todd Peters off the pole."

"Yeah," said the second guy. "Maybe he can hold on to it this time around."

"C'mon," Vicky said, pain shooting through her hands. Her nails dug into her palms.

One more lap.

He had one more chance to get it right. The arrow was still jammed up by *Pole*. Brandon seemed to fling his car around Turn One. She held her breath as he zoomed around the corner.

Would his back end break free? she wondered.

It didn't.

"Yes!" she hissed. "Go, Brandon, go!"

And he did. She knew he was flying. The qualifying meter confirmed it. Around Turn Three he went, his car sinking toward the bottom at first, then smoothly sliding up the track, only to fall back down toward the bottom again.

"I think he's got it," one of the announcers said.

The arrow never left *Pole*.

"He's almost there," the other announcer said.

The checkered flag waved.

"Yes," she hissed. "Yes, yes, yes." She was jumping up and down. "That's it, honey. That's the way to drive." She had tears in her eyes. How stupid. It was just qualifying. There were still more cars left to qualify. But she was so proud. So damn proud.

"Are you okay?" one of the women asked—the younger woman.

"No," she said, her hands shaking as she wiped away tears. "I think I'm going to pass out."

"Wow," the older woman said. "You're a big Brandon Burke fan."

Vicky almost laughed. "You could say that," she said. And then she did laugh. Why the hell not? After what had just happened with his father. After everything they'd gone through in the previous weeks. To brush it all off and put his car on the pole...

"He deserves this," she said, her eyes misting up all over again. "He really, really deserves this."

"Do you know him?" the younger guy asked.

"Yeah," she said. And then she lifted her head. "He's my boyfriend."

CHAPTER TWENTY-SIX

HE'D JUST PUT HIS CAR on the pole and all he could think about was parking it so he could look into Vicky's eyes.

Would she be impressed?

Was it juvenile to wonder such a thing? But that's exactly what he felt as he pulled into the postqualifying tech inspection line.

"Great job," Chad said, letting down the window net. "I can't believe you've got the pole."

Brandon slid his helmet through the mishmash of metal bars that made up his roll cage, setting it down on the sheet metal that covered the area where a passenger would sit. "Yeah, but there's still a lot of cars left to go."

"Give me a break," Chad said, helping him out. "No one's left to qualify who's worth a damn. You've got it, buddy. No doubt about it."

Vicky wasn't around, Brandon noticed. Then

again, he thought, she probably didn't realize his car wasn't allowed back in the garage—not until NASCAR had a look at it.

"Thanks for giving me a great car," he said, turning his attention back to Chad.

"You're welcome," his crew chief said, clapping him on the back. "Now, if we could just do as well on race day."

"I'm going to try."

Brandon waved at the crew members who'd arrived to help push his car through the tech line, a process that'd take a good half hour. Someone tried to flag him down as he headed back to his hauler, but Brandon staved them off with a hand. Not now. He wanted to get back to his hauler.

But Vicky wasn't there.

"Hey, rookie," someone said.

Brandon turned. Todd Peters walked up to him, a wide smile on his face. "Last time I give you tips on how to run this track."

Brandon took the hand Todd extended, shaking it and clapping his teammate on the back. "Thanks," he said, but the whole time his eyes scanned the garage. Was Vicky inside? Maybe waiting for him in the lounge. "Now, if I could only get NASCAR to approve you being my co-pilot on race day, we'd be all set."

"Hah. Like I said, I'm done helping you. I've got a feeling you're about to give me a run for my money."

Brandon chuckled a bit, an emotion coursing through him that took him a moment to identify.

Happiness.

"Hey, I'll catch you later," he said to Todd because once he had Vicky in his arms, he'd be even happier.

Suddenly he saw her.

She was dashing toward him from the far side of the garage. She spotted him and stopped. Brandon stood there, people giving him curious looks as he simply waited—for what, he didn't know. All he knew was he was helpless to look away.

She moved toward him again, more slowly this time, and with every step she took, something melted inside.

"You did it," she said.

He didn't move, the realization that'd hit him earlier—the knowledge that he loved her—made him suddenly awkward.

"I did it," he said, his arm tensing, almost lifting, only to fall back to his side.

She seemed nervous, too, glanced around as if half-worried they might get run over standing there in the middle of the road. "I, ah. I was watching from outside."

"Outside?"

"In the infield."

"What were you doing out there?"

She held his gaze, and Brandon knew something had changed. "I couldn't stand still," she said. "I was up on top of your hauler half-afraid I'd pass out from nervousness so I went walking. Met up with some race fans who overlooked the fact that I was Brandon Burke's girlfriend while I watched you run your laps."

"What did you say?"

"I went walking."

"Not that," he said softly.

She stared up at him with a mixture of amusement and tenderness. "I told them I was your girlfriend."

"Vicky." He started to pull her into his arms.

She stepped back before he could do much more than lift his hands. "No, Brandon. Not here. There needs to be some ground rules. I don't want everyone to know we're boyfriend and girlfriend. I'm afraid of giving people the impression that

I—you know—that I sleep around. And I'm not going to travel with you to every race. I can't do that. I have a job, one that I have a feeling is going to take me away from North Carolina pretty soon what with you winning poles and all. Scott will realize soon that he doesn't need me here. He'll think my work is done."

She gave him a proud smile and, damn it, he wanted to hug her.

"I want to give this…thing time…whatever this is between us. I'm not going to rush into anything."

"Okay. I understand."

"Are you sure? Because I have a feeling this won't be easy. Once I acquire more new clients, I'll be jetting around the country, too. There might be weeks when we don't see each other."

Why did he feel as if he were in the middle of a business negotiation?

"My job is important to me," she added. "I've worked hard to get to this point and I'm not the type of woman to—"

"Shut up," he said, grabbing her by the arms.

"What did you say?"

"I said shut up," he repeated with a smile. "To hell with your damn rules. We'll just take it one day at a time."

"Brandon—"

He kissed the words off her lips. Whatever she'd been about to say—probably more damn rules—she must have forgotten. He knew how she felt. He forgot everything when their lips connected, too.

"Eeeyow," someone yelled.

Vicky pulled back. "Hey," she cried, her eyes wide and full of outrage. "I told you. No kissing me in the garage."

"And you should know by now, I've never been good at listening."

"That's what I'm afraid of."

"Funny," he said, taking her hand. "I'm not scared at all."

CHAPTER TWENTY-SEVEN

HE DIDN'T END UP winning the race, but he came in fifth and Vicky admitted that was good enough. What's more, during postrace interviews, Brandon handled himself with a professionalism that impressed even Mrs. Parsons.

When they flew home that Sunday evening, Brandon sat next to her, and Vicky had a hard time remembering why exactly she'd been so afraid to get involved with him. What's more, from the smoky looks he kept giving her, she had a feeling this would be a very, *very* long night.

"Your place or mine?" he asked after they'd landed.

"Mine," she said. She lived closer, her apartment just north of town.

He drove the darkened North Carolina streets. It was well after midnight, their trip back home having gotten off to a late start thanks to the two

KEM teams who'd had to pack everything onto the haulers before they could leave, a process that'd taken well over an hour. Then there'd been traffic. Then the five-hour flight home. And yet, through it all, Vicky had felt giddy, maybe even a little drunk. She should be exhausted and so should Brandon. He'd actually driven in a race that day, something that many people considered nonphysical, but that actually took a lot of strength and stamina. When he'd gotten out of his car he'd been hot and sweaty in a way that brought to mind smoky, passionate kisses....

She shivered.

"Cold?" he asked, the lights from the dash casting an iridescent glow over his face.

No. *On fire.* "I'm fine," she said.

She could tell by the look in his eyes that he knew what was on her mind. It was on his mind, too. There was an electrical hum in the air, the kind that preceded chaotic weather and that made her fidget and wiggle and made the hair on her arms stand on end.

They couldn't get to her apartment fast enough. Her single-story apartment was dark. It was actually an old blue house converted into two units, one with gingerbread windows and a low-pitched roof. Just to the right of the driveway, a single lamppost oozed milky light onto the cement walkway. More light leaked out from one of the windows of her apartment. She had the unit on the left and Vicky's hands shook as she unlocked the front door.

The door swung open.

"Victoria," someone said from inside.

Vicky dropped her keys.

"Well, I must say," the same voice said. "It's about time."

"*Mom,*" Vicky cried. "What are *you* doing here?"

Her mother stood up from her seat on the couch. "I've come to bring you home," she said.

"No," Vicky cried, momentarily at a loss for words.

From behind her, Brandon cleared his throat. Vicky half turned. "Um, Mom. This is my friend, Brandon."

Her mother gave Brandon a slow once-over, and the expression on her face was one of thinly veiled animosity. She didn't even bother to hold out her hand, just eyed him up and down. She knew Brandon was more than a "friend." Why else would a man be at her doorstep at such a late hour? But her mother didn't have to be so rude. Vicky felt her cheeks burn even more.

"How'd you get in here?" she asked, closing the door behind them both.

"A man let me in. I believe he owns this hovel you call home."

"How'd you convince him to do that?"

"I told him I was your mother. And that I was here to deliver some unfortunate news."

"And he believed you?"

"Why wouldn't he?"

Why wouldn't he, indeed? Elaina VanCleef had an air about her that commanded respect. Not only was she strikingly beautiful with her sleek black hair and stunningly big blue eyes, but she knew how to dress to impress. Today, if Vicky didn't miss her guess, she wore an Armani suit, Dolce & Gabbana shoes and enough jewelry to sink the *Titanic*. Her landlord probably figured Elaina couldn't possibly steal anything more valuable than the stuff around her neck.

"Mom, seriously," Vicky said. "You didn't come all the way down here just to bring me home, did you?"

"I met your boss, Scott, the other day," she said, her earrings catching the light and sparking like miniature stars. "I was *not* impressed. You should be grateful your father wasn't with me."

"Where's Dad?"

"Working. But I told him all about your boss and where you live," Elaina said with a look around her, her upper lip all but curling. "I told him I'm taking you back to New York in the morning."

"I'm not going," Vicky said. "I'm staying right here."

"Why?" her mother said.

"Mom, please…can't we discuss this later?" *When we're alone and Brandon isn't listening to every word?* Damn it. Why did Elaina always have to humiliate her like this?

"We gave you a first-class education, Victoria," Elaina said, ignoring her question. "You were top of your class. Your father and I thought this whole 'I want to be an agent' thing would pass. Only it hasn't, and my—*our*—patience is at end. You can take one of the family apartments. Your father has an opening at the firm. You don't have to start right away. You can begin in a week or so…or even a month. Take some time off. But give this—" she motioned around the room "—up."

Was it Vicky's imagination or had her mother's gaze settled on Brandon?

"I'm not giving anything up," Vicky said. "I've told you two at least a million times before. I'm sorry you don't like my job, but *I* do." She glanced at Brandon, tried to apologize with her eyes. "I'm not leaving. I'm not leaving *any* of it."

"Then we'll cut you off. The trust fund, your inheritance. You won't receive a dime of it."

Vicky felt the breath leave her. She should have expected this move. No wonder her father had elected to stay behind. He'd always hated confrontations. Even in his law practice, he'd always left the litigating to the attorneys he'd hired.

"If that's what you feel you need to do."

"We don't want to do it, Victoria," Elaina cried. "But it's for your own good."

"And you know I've never touched a penny of that trust fund, not since I graduated college."

Elaina huffed out a laugh. "And it's been, what, six months that you've been out on your own? Give it another six months. You'll grow tired of supporting yourself."

"How would you know, Elaina? You might make good money as a lawyer, but you haven't had to support yourself since you married my dad."

Elaina stood even more rigid. She knew when Vicky called her by her first name that her step-daughter was mad. It'd been the same way when they'd argued about which college Vicky should attend. Vicky hadn't wanted to go to Harvard as her father had. She wanted to go someplace close to home because, despite her differences with her parents, she still loved her childhood home.

A home she might not see anymore.

Well, then, so be it. Her parents needed to understand, she didn't want to live life under their control. She wanted her *own* life.

"Victoria, this is your last chance," Elaina said. "I'm not going to ask you again. Come with me now. You can call your boss in the morning and tell him you quit."

"No," Vicky said.

Elaina tossed her chin. She might look twenty years younger than she actually was, but her blue eyes could turn as hard as ancient rock. "Very well. I'll tell your father of your decision."

"That might be a good idea since it's *his* money."

"You know I've never cared about the money."

Vicky almost laughed. Given how quickly Elaina had chased down her dad after her mother had died, she doubted that was true.

"Tell my father I love him," Vicky said, opening the door. She didn't bother to say goodbye.

This confrontation had been brewing between them for years—ever since Vicky had entered her teens. Elaina had wanted Vicky to be a debutante. To dress like a lady. Attend New York balls and parties. Vicky had refused and nothing had ever been the same between them since.

"Goodbye, Victoria," her stepmother said by the door. "I do hope you change your mind."

To Vicky's shock, Elaina leaned over and kissed her cheek.

"I wouldn't count on it," Vicky replied.

Elaina left then. Vicky watched her go, a part of her hoping she'd turn back. She didn't and Vicky sighed.

"Wow," Brandon said, once the door had closed.

"I'm sorry about that, Brandon."

"She's, ah…something else, your stepmom."

"Yeah," Vicky said. "She is."

"And she looks as if she could be your sister."

"I know." To be honest, it was part of the reason why Vicky never worried about makeup and expensive haircuts. Why bother when nobody would give her a second glance? It'd taken years for Vicky to be comfortable in her own skin. Thank the lord she wasn't the type to be jealous.

"Hey," Brandon said gently, pulling her into

his arms, "don't look so sad." He gave her that wide smile. "At least you still have me."

For now. She hated to think that, but she was realistic about her chances of a relationship with Brandon. Everything was so new and just a little bit frightening. One minute she'd been lusting after him and the next—*whew*—she didn't know what to think.

"And we have something in common. We're both disowned by our parents."

Maybe. Maybe not, Vicky thought. In the morning she'd call her dad. Maybe she could patch things up through him.

"Makes you wish you could choose your own parents, huh?" he asked.

"Or your own stepmother," she muttered. He was rubbing her arms, and it was starting to feel good. Oh, who the hell was she kidding. Anytime Brandon touched her it felt good.

"Now you know why I don't want to have kids. Geesh. Scenes like that one with your stepmother and the one with my father make you wonder if the apple's going to fall far from the tree. No, thanks, man. I don't need to mess some poor kid up thanks to my unhappy upbringing. I bet you feel the same way, too."

Vicky leaned back and stared up at him. "You don't want to have kids?"

He tipped his head sideways, staring at her curiously. "No, I don't. I think that's why I want to do the boys' ranch. I can help other people's children in between focusing on my career. Just like you."

"What do you mean 'just like me'?"

His hands fell to his sides. "What you said. Back at the track. You said you didn't want anything interfering with your career. I thought that'd meant…"

That she didn't want kids, either. She could read the words in his blue eyes.

She shook her head. "I never meant that," she said softly. "I mean, I'm not saying I definitely *want* kids."

God, how could she just be discovering this now?

Calm down, Vicky. It's a little early to be freaking out. The man hasn't even said he loves you yet.

She almost huffed out an involuntary laugh. As if he would ever do that. He didn't love her. He might be temporarily fascinated by her, but that was all. *She* was the one who'd started to fall head over heels for some ridiculous reason. But it was hard not to wonder what he was thinking when he was looking at her like that.

"Let's just talk about this later," he said softly. "All I really want to do right now is kiss you."

She wanted that, too. To heck with Elaina. To heck with his father. To heck with everything.

He caught her lips with his own, and as his kiss deepened, Vicky found herself thinking she'd do anything for this man. Yes, even give up the future she'd always planned.

CHAPTER TWENTY-EIGHT

IT WAS EASY TO FORGET her troubles…for a night.

But the next morning all her fears and insecurities came back to haunt her, even with Brandon asleep by her side.

"Can I speak to Randolph VanCleef?" she whispered into the phone, careful to keep her voice down lest she wake Brandon. It wasn't even six yet, but someone already manned the VanCleef & VanCleef phones thanks to their overseas clients. "This is his daughter."

"One moment please," the woman said as Vicky sank down on her secondhand couch. Her father would be in his office now—he always was at this hour.

"What is it, Victoria?" he said without even the courtesy of a hello.

Vicky opened her mouth, so many words wanting to tumble out. *I miss you, Dad. I love you, Dad. Can I throttle Elaina, please?*

"My stepmother was here last night." She winced. Her father hated it when she called Elaina her stepmother. Was she trying to blow this thing? she wondered.

The silence on the other end of the phone told her she might already have.

"Dad," she said, "she wasn't really serious, was she? You two aren't really going to cut me off, are you?"

More silence on the other end of the phone.

"I mean," she added after a dry-throated swallow, "that's a little extreme, isn't it?"

"We're worried about you, Victoria."

Vicky clutched the cordless phone a little tighter. "I know that. I understand that. But I'm fine. Where I live now is no worse than where I lived during college."

"That's exactly the point, Victoria. You knew we despised that…place."

"It was a sorority house, Dad. A school-subsidized building where dozens of other women lived."

"We told each other it was a phase," came her

father's voice. "Something you'd grow out of. We humored you, Victoria, but it's time you grew up."

"I *am* grown-up," she yelled, but then she winced and peered into the bedroom. "I am grown-up," she repeated a little lower. "That's the point. I'm an adult now. On my own. I don't need your help, or the help of my trust fund. You should be proud of that fact."

"I'm your father, Victoria. I'll be the judge of when you're mature enough to manage your life."

"*Manage* my *life*," she hissed. "Who says I'm not managing it now?"

"I investigated that firm you work for. SSI, I believe it's called," her father said.

Vicky's breath caught. "What about it?"

"You told me the firm had an excellent reputation."

So she'd fudged the truth a little. "Look, Dad. I realize a few of the agents there have been known to do unethical things—"

"What *kind* of unethical things?" her father asked immediately.

Poach clients away from other agencies. Sign contracts with exorbitant commission fees. Make it nearly impossible to break contract once the athlete realizes what's going on. "Oh, this and that," she fudged. "But it really doesn't matter. It's my first job out of college. Better offers will come along once I gain some experience."

"You can gain that experience here in New York, while living with your mother and I."

"No."

"We've been very patient. This is your final warning. Come home. Come work for me. Come work for one of our friends' firms. I don't care what you do, as long as you come back to New York and use the degree you earned in a more respectable manner."

"No," she said again, though it was one of the hardest things she'd ever had to do. "Dad, this is what I want to do. I love being an agent. I get to live an exciting life—"

He hung up on her.

"Son of a—"

She shot up from the couch.

"I can't believe—"

She sank back down.

What the heck was it with her parents? Why couldn't they be like other parents? The type that supported their child and encouraged their independence. Why did her mom and dad want to control her? It drove her *nuts*.

Well, they'd soon learn she couldn't be bossed around. Not by them. Not by Brandon. Not by anybody.

Brandon.

Just thinking his name made her heart go soft. She turned and padded back into the bedroom. Brandon lay sprawled in bed, the sheets tangled around his legs and torso.

"My, my, my," she whispered. He was glorious, his blond hair tousled, his chin dotted with razor stubble.

And he was hers.

Yeah, but for how long? Men like him didn't, as a rule, find women like her attractive. Nor did they stick around. She wasn't flashy enough. She didn't have enough *va-voom* to her walk.

Brandon opened his eyes. "Hey, there," he said softly, and Vicky's heart turned end over end, especially when he smiled.

"Hey, there," she said back.

"What you doing?"

"Nothing," she lied.

"Coming back to bed?" he asked in a low, sexy

and very suggestive voice. The look in his eyes
sent tingles up her spine.

"Oh, yeah," she said softly.

His smile grew bigger. "Come on."

Who needed a trust fund? she thought, sliding
in next to him. She'd live on bread and water if it
meant daily doses of this.

He pulled her against his hard body. She
gasped. Oh, yeah. She'd made the right choice.

THEY SETTLED INTO A ROUTINE. Brandon stayed with
her through the week, Vicky helping him with his
reading each night. On the weekends, the two of
them would head off to a race. Sometimes Vicky
would leave with Brandon, sometimes not. It
depended on Vicky's workload because Scott had
given her another client now that Brandon was on
his best behavior, this time a football star in his
first year of the NFL. Vicky had flown to Denver
to meet the guy. When she'd come home, Brandon had greeted her with a warmth that made her
think maybe, just maybe this thing between them
might work out.

But she knew their comfortable routine would
soon come to an end.

And then one day, it did.

Scott called her early one afternoon. "Viiiicky," he drawled in that singsong voice that drove her nuts. "How's my girl?"

She only recently become "his girl" and it boded ill—Vicky could just tell. "I'm great, Scott. Everything's great."

"Vicky, darlin', I'm thinking maybe it's time you came back to New York."

There it was. The words she'd been expecting to hear for at least a couple weeks now.

"Is that so?" she asked, trying hard to keep her voice even. She'd known this was going to happen, so why'd it feel as if she'd been kicked in the teeth when it finally did.

"Our boy Brandon's been acting like a saint. Those people at KEM couldn't be happier. I'm thinking when you come back to New York I'll hand over a few more clients. I'm telling you, Vicky, you're doing a great job."

"Uh, gee. Thanks, Scott. But, um, it's going to take a few days to pack up."

"I know. I know. But I figure since your lease is on a month-to-month basis you can take until next week to wrap things up. That way you're back here before the first of the month. I'll let you break the news to our boy Brandon. I'm sure he'll be sorry to see you go, but he has to know you can't hold on to his hand forever."

As memory served Vicky, it was Scott who'd wanted her to hold Brandon's hand. However, she didn't argue the point. "I'll tell him," she said.

"Great!" Scott said. "We'll see you before the first of next month."

Vicky hung up the phone without even noticing. How the heck was she going to do this? How was she supposed to deal with a future of living apart from Brandon?

She was supposed to meet him for dinner that night. Brandon was in town filming a commercial, and Vicky found herself leaving for the shoot early. She couldn't stand to sit around and wait for the inevitable.

The commercial was actually a public-service announcement shot in a studio just outside of Charlotte. Other drivers would be there, too, as would other celebrities. The commercial was for Miracles, a charity organization dedicated to granting the wishes of terminally ill children. KEM was one of Miracles' main sponsors so she wasn't surprised to see Mathew Knight standing around the perimeter of the set. She waved, her gaze settling on Brandon. He was in his red uniform and he had to be roasting beneath the giant lights that lit the set. He also probably couldn't see her thanks to those bulbs. But Vicky could see him—and the woman he stood next to: Jessica James, aka Jessie James, an up-and-coming country music star whose songs everyone loved, including Brandon.

"Okay, everybody. Quiet on the set," someone said. "Jessie, whenever you're ready."

On set, a woman half the men in America were in lust with, draped an arm around *her* man. Vicky's skin grew cold.

"Hi, I'm Jessie James," the woman said with a million-dollar smile, her long, blond hair brushing Brandon's shoulder.

"And I'm Brandon Burke, NASCAR driver."

"And we're here to ask *you* to help others," Jessie said.

There was a camera nearby, one with a tiny screen visible above it. Vicky moved toward it, peering up at the image of Brandon and the blond goddess.

It was Brandon's turn to talk. "Every day, children around the world wage a battle for their lives."

"It could be a battle with cancer, or MS or some other incurable disease," Jessie said.

"Fighting those battles steals the joy from their lives," Brandon said.

"We're asking you to help give them some of that joy back," Jessie said, her arm snaking through Brandon's. Was she *supposed* to do that? That wasn't part of the script. Vicky had scanned the damn thing at least ten times. Nowhere had she read that Jessie was supposed to hang all over Brandon.

"Support your local Miracles foundation," Brandon said.

"Help bring a miracle to a child's life," Jessie said.

"Help Miracles," they both said together, an earnestly imploring look emanating from Jessie's eyes.

"Cut!" someone yelled. "Okay. That was great. Let's take a look at what we've got. Hang tight."

"Brandon," Vicky called, the moment others on set began to talk.

Brandon squinted in her direction.

"That was great," she heard Jessie say. "I think we finally said the words together."

"I think you're right."

Someone came forward, handed Brandon a little white towel. He wiped his face as he walked forward, still trying to peer through the light. She could tell the moment he spotted her because he straightened suddenly. "Vicky," he said, the smile he gave her doing a lot to battle back the green-eyed monster.

"Hey, Brandon," she said, slipping into his arms. They were long past the point of trying to hide their relationship. "How's it going?" she asked, resisting the urge to peer in Jessie's direction.

"Horrible," Brandon said, and then he lowered his voice. "The director keeps on changing the script around. One minute it says this. The next it says that. Thank God I've been working with you for the past few weeks. If not, I'd have been lost." He wiped the sweat from his forehead, shook his head. "Sorry to vent," he said, his arm dropping back to his side. "What's up?"

She meant to break the news slowly, had meant to tell him when they were outside, in private, but watching him with Jessie had done something to her insides, something not particularly nice. "I'm going back to New York," she said.

The towel slipped from his hands.

"What?"

"I have to pack up this week. Scott called this morning. He said it's time I stopped holding your hand. That I'm needed back at SSI."

Maybe Jessie will hold it for you now?

Stop it, she told herself.

"So you're going to go?" he asked, his body completely still.

"What do you mean, am I going to go? Of course I am. Working for Scott is my *job.*"

Brandon glanced toward Jessica. Vicky followed his gaze.

"Maybe she can keep you company when I'm gone," she said.

Had she just said that?

Brandon's eyes narrowed as he turned on her.

"You know I'm not interested in her."

No, she didn't know that. She didn't know anything. All she knew was that she had to leave and it was tearing her apart. That's why she was being such a bitch. Damn it. Couldn't he see that?

"I know," she said, wiping a hand through her hair. "I'm just…" She shook her head, blinked back a sudden burning in her eyes. "I'm just jealous," she admitted. "She gets to stay while I have to—"

He pulled her into his arms and, man, it took every ounce of self-control not to burst into tears. She didn't want to leave. She wanted to live in North Carolina. Wanted things to remain the way they were forever. But that wasn't going to happen. It'd never been part of the plan.

"You don't have to go," Brandon said softly.

"I know," she said. God help her, she knew. But what kind of hypocrite would she be if she gave up her job after everything she'd been through to convince her parents that this was what she wanted to do with her life? What kind of grown-up, mature thing to do was that? "I have to."

He drew back. "No, you don't," he said, more sternly now.

"Brandon, don't," she said. "Don't make this harder than it already is."

"You don't need your job, Vicky. *I* can support you. I'm making good money now," he said. "You can move in with me. Decorate the house or something. There's plenty to keep you busy here."

"Keep me busy?" she asked. "I want a *career*. I told you that."

"Then open a sports agency here."

She snorted. "Yeah, right. Who's going to hire me to represent them."

"I would."

"That's not the same."

He was rubbing her arms now. "Come on, Vicky. At least promise me you'll think about it."

"Just like you'll 'think' about having children?"

Good lord, what was wrong with her? Why was she being so confrontational?

"That's not fair," he said, glancing around them as if afraid someone had overheard.

"We're clearing the air here, Brandon. Might as well get all the issues out on the table. If I were to stay, what about us? Would you marry me?"

He glanced over at Jessica.

It was the *wrong* thing to do and she jerked away from him.

"Hey. Wait a second. What'd I do?"

She headed for the door. It was unseasonably warm outside, and the bright sunlight nearly blinded her.

"Vicky, wait."

But she didn't slow down. They were in an industrial complex, one of those low-slung buildings right next to identical low-slung buildings, grass and shrubs growing in the front. Her rental car was parked across the asphalt, a sidewalk between her and a busy street.

"Vicky," he said again, catching her right as she was about to step onto the blacktop. "What the hell are you so mad about?"

"Oh, I don't know," she said, still walking.

"Maybe the fact that I've been asked to go back to New York and instead of trying to comfort me you ask me to give up my career so *your* life can stay status quo and I can stand back and watch you make googly eyes at that woman inside. Come on, Brandon. The blond bombshell has been hanging all over you."

His expression cleared. And then his eyebrows lifted. "You're jealous."

"I am *not* jealous," she lied. "I'm stressed that I have to leave."

Suddenly, she just wanted to cry. She had to fight not to sit down on the edge of the walkway and do exactly that. She'd known this was coming. They'd both known one day soon she'd have to go back home. And yet they never really talked about it.

"Look," he said gently, his hand moving to her shoulder, "I know you're upset. But there's no reason to be jealous."

But you haven't answered my question, she wanted to yell. Would *you marry me?*

"Jessica was just doing what the director told her to do. It didn't mean anything."

Yes, but do I mean anything to you?

"And it's a little early to be talking marriage,

don't you think? We've only known each other for, what? A few weeks?"

Five weeks, three days and seventeen hours. But who was counting? she thought.

"You're right," she said softly. "It *is* too early. Too early for me to give up my job to come live with you."

He didn't say anything. For some reason, that hurt even more.

"I'm going back to New York," she said. "I've given up a lot to get to where I am today. I'm not going to walk away from it now."

He crossed his arms in front of him. "So it's back to daddy."

She wanted to kill him, she really did. At the very least, she wanted to throttle him. "Goodbye, Brandon," she said. "I guess I'll see you around."

Damn it, she thought, turning away. This wasn't how she wanted to end it.

Was it over?

It sure felt like it. She tensed as she headed toward her rented vehicle, waiting for him to call her back. To say he was sorry. To say anything.

He didn't.

When she reached her car's door, she paused for a moment, ostensibly to sort out her keys. He still didn't say anything. Her hands shook as she slipped inside. When she started the engine, she peered at him through her rearview mirror. He stood by the building's door, watching her.

And still, she waited.

But then he turned, gripped the door and went inside. Vicky rested her head on her steering wheel and cried.

CHAPTER TWENTY-NINE

HE WOULD CALL.

He *better* call.

The words repeated themselves for a good twenty-four hours. It was just a fight. Their first spat. He would call because he'd realize, as she had, that they'd both been upset over the news. That was all. She didn't really expect him to marry her. Not really... Okay, maybe a little.

But he didn't call.

When, a week later, the day came for her to leave North Carolina, she sat in her apartment and stared at the phone—as if she was a soap opera star playing out one last, dramatic scene. How ridiculous was that because she had a cell phone. If he needed to get a hold of her, he could reach her that way.

But he didn't phone her.

At the airport she hung outside the terminal.

Her breath caught every time she spied a red vehicle. And then, when it became obvious he wasn't going to pull into the airport in a desperate, last-minute attempt to stop her from leaving, she felt like crying.

She fought back tears as she boarded the plane. What a fool she'd been to think he cared for her enough to come after her. She'd made sure he'd known she was leaving. Mrs. Parsons had been asked to relay the news…in a discreet and non-obvious way. So she kept her cell phone on until the very last minute.

But her cell never rang.

She was, miraculously enough, in a row of seats all by herself. It made it easier to cry. Made it easier to hide her pain. And her humiliation. Because Vicky admitted then that she had fallen in love. That, against all better judgment, she'd gotten involved with a man known to have no heart. God help her, she'd thought she'd touched that heart. What a bitter lesson to learn she hadn't.

BRANDON POUNDED the steering wheel of his car.

"Come on out of there, buddy," Chad said, his voice filling Brandon's left ear.

It was on the tip of Brandon's tongue to tell his crew chief to go blow. That his car stunk. That there was no way he'd ever be able to drive such a piece of crap. That's what he wanted to say.

Instead he jerked off his helmet, all but tossed the removable steering wheel aside and climbed out.

"It won't turn," was all he said.

Chad gave him a look that clearly asked, who won't turn? The car? Or the driver.

Brandon didn't answer. He *couldn't* answer, not without letting loose a string of words that would get him into trouble, and more than likely hurt Chad's feelings, and that he didn't need. Thank god practice was over. He didn't think he could take much more of this.

"Brandon, wait up," Mathew Knight said.

Brandon stopped, tipped his head back and groaned. Just what he needed—a chewing-out from his team owner. Terrific, he thought, tearing open his uniform. Could this day get any worse?

"Tough practice," Mr. Knight said, his green eyes full of sympathy.

"Yeah," Brandon said, the man's kindness causing him to look away.

"Walk with me a moment?" his boss asked.

Brandon didn't think he really had a choice.

They headed toward his hauler. They were in Phoenix, which meant within seconds Brandon had cooled off. He didn't know why it was always so cold in the desert this time of year. Around two-thirds of the track stretched barren mountains, the plant life so sparse it looked like the surface of Mars. All right, maybe not that sparse. But it was desolate-looking, cactus and low-lying scrub dotting the hillside around them.

"Been tough for you the last couple of weeks," Mr. Knight said, the man holding up his hand to stave off fans.

"Yes, sir, it has," Brandon said, wondering why he felt as if he spoke to his father. His boss was about a million years younger than his good-for-nothing dad.

"You have any idea why?"

Vicky. Her name automatically hovered on his lips, but he couldn't admit to his boss that he was off his game because of a *woman*.

"I have an idea," he said instead.

"My wife thinks she knows why, too."

"Oh, yeah?" Brandon asked, stopping.

Mathew nodded. "She says you're broken-hearted."

"Me, nah," he brazened out.

But in truth, he was. Kind of ironic, too, because usually he was the one that did the heart-breaking. Not so this time. Vicky hadn't called him the entire week she'd been packing up. When she'd left town without telling him goodbye, he'd gotten the message loud and clear. Their relationship was over.

"I'll be back on track soon," he said, trying to interject as much confidence as he could muster.

But to his surprise, Mr. Knight just stared at him. "You know," he said, "I was once in your shoes."

"You drove race cars?"

Mr. Knight huffed. "No," he said. "Once upon a time, Kristen left me, too."

"She did?" Brandon asked because he'd have thought it impossible that a man as wealthy as Mr. Knight would ever suffer through a woman leaving him. His boss might not be a driver, but he was every bit as famous as one—perhaps more so.

"I almost lost her, too. Likely would have if not for the interference of a friend."

Against his better judgment Brandon asked, "What'd you do?"

"Cornered her," he said. "Told her how I felt. I'm told that if the woman loves you, it'll work every time."

If she loved him. That, Brandon admitted, was the million-dollar question.

Would you marry me? Her words rang in his ears.

At the time he hadn't known the answer. He loved her, yes. After all these weeks, he knew what he felt was real.

But marriage?

Frankly, it scared the hell out of him.

CHAPTER THIRTY

SHE WAS SUMMONED.

Vicky had been expecting the call for several weeks now, but when she heard her dad's demanding baritone on her voicemail, "Victoria, we'll expect you in the Hamptons this weekend," she almost pressed the delete button.

"We'll expect you in the Hamptons," she mimicked.

Of course, she could ignore the summons, but she wouldn't do that. She hated the silence between her and her parents. Elaina might only be her stepmother, but once upon a time they'd been friends. And her father... Well, he was the only family she had.

So she put on a gauzy, floral-print sundress that hung down to her ankles and that she knew Elaina would approve of, and packed up her car for the drive.

Still, there was no call from Brandon.

But she should have expected that. In the end, athletes were all the same. Women were easy to replace when every weekend you had a half dozen throwing themselves at you.

But it still hurt.

They'd been friends. *Lovers.* The two of them sharing a bond that she'd thought… Well, she supposed it didn't matter what she thought.

The drive to the Hamptons was beautiful. By the time Vicky arrived at her family's twenty-acre estate, she should have been relaxed, but she wasn't. How could she be, she thought, tensing as the iron gates opened wide. Her life was in a shambles. Well, that wasn't exactly true. Scott had welcomed her back with open arms. He'd even given her two more clients to manage. She'd be able to hold her head high when she told her father that she'd managed to succeed *without* the VanCleef family fortune.

"They're waiting for you in the study," Rudy, the butler, said as he opened her door.

Vicky slipped out, giving Rudy a brave smile. Did he know she'd been disowned? More than likely. The staff always seemed to know everything.

She took a deep breath and looked around.

Around her stood evidence of her family's vast wealth. The VanCleefs weren't just well off, they were *old money*. Indeed, her father laughed whenever people bragged that their family lines traced back to the *Mayflower. Mayflower.* Hah. The Van-Cleefs would never own to being descended from such common stock. Their ancestors were dukes and earls and, on the Dutch side, the royal family. They had been wealthy not just for decades, but for *centuries*.

The proof of that power and prestige surrounded her—acres and acres of manicured lawn, oak trees sprouting up whose trunks were at least three feet wide and a hundred years old. A mansion whose facade had been carved from European stone stretched up three stories tall. Original, beveled glass twinkled beneath a clear blue sky. A roof— its patina as green as turquoise—made the manse seem as if it'd sprouted up from the ground. Leading to a massive double door, a stone walkway curved elegantly, the glass in the front doors having been handblown in France.

So different from North Carolina.

So different from Brandon's home. But she liked that. She didn't need all this. Who really did?

"Good morning, Miss Victoria," Jane, their

maid-of-all-work, said as she opened the door. Jane had worked for the VanCleefs practically her entire life. Just as Jane's mother, and Jane's great-grandmother had worked for Vicky's grandmother and great-grandmother.

"Is it bad in there?" Vicky asked, motioning toward the study a few doors down, her footfalls echoing off the polished hardwood floor that was cleaned with beeswax imported from Italy.

Jane shook her head and shot her a sympathetic smile. When Vicky had been a child, she'd often asked the same question whenever she suspected she might be in trouble. Late for dinner because she'd lost track of time out in the park. Staying out past her curfew the night of the prom. Jane had been witness to all her youthful transgressions. Now it appeared as if they would continue through her being an adult.

"Is he alone, or is Elaina in there?" Vicky asked.

"Alone, miss," Jane said.

Well, there was that to be grateful for, she supposed.

"Thank you," she said, feeling more like a child than a woman as she approached the door.

"Come in," her father said after Vicky's light knock.

Still, Vicky paused for a moment outside the door, the brass knob cold in her grasp.

Buck up, Vicky old girl, she heard in her head— her grandmother's voice. *It won't be all bad.*

Inside, the study was just as dimly lit as it always was. Lead-paned windows to her left were framed on either side by lush foliage. She'd always thought it should be trimmed back—to allow more light—but her father seemed to like it. This was his domain. He stood, his palms lightly resting on the polished cherrywood desk.

"Hello, Dad," she said softly.

Her father simply stared, and she grew a little uncomfortable beneath that perusal. Her father— when he chose—could be a commanding figure. Two hundred years ago, he might have been an admiral, one whose portrait might have been painted against a backdrop of warring ships.

"Victoria," he said at last, slowly sinking into his chair.

She sat, too, the movement setting her heart to pounding. Or maybe that was just nerves.

Time to take the bull by the horns.

"What did you want to talk to me about, Dad?"

"I believe you know very well what," he said, his fingers a steeple in front of him.

"Dad," she said quickly, "it's not as if I'm out dealing drugs or something. It's a good job. Sure, my boss is a jerk, but I like being an agent. It's fun, and exciting, and…different." Far better than being a clerk at her father's firm, not that *he* had to work. But their long history as lawyers had a great deal to do with the VanCleefs hanging on to the family fortune.

Never be afraid to roll up your sleeves and work. That's what her grandfather had always said. It was practically the family creed.

"That's not what I wish to speak to you about."

Vicky sat up suddenly.

"I wish to speak to you of another matter."

"What?" Vicky asked.

"Brandon Burke."

Her heart stopped.

"Ah…" She coughed to clear her throat. "What about him?"

"He was with you that night you saw Elaina."

She nodded. "We were…seeing each other."

"How serious is it between the two of you?" he asked.

So this was why she'd been summoned, she realized. To be chastened for involving herself with Brandon. She should have known. "*Very* serious," she lied because she would not be dictated to about her choice in men—any more than she would be told what to do with her life.

"I received a letter from him."

"What?"

"The man has horrid penmanship."

"Oh, Daddy," she said softly. "If you only knew."

She saw his eyes flicker for a second, realized in an instant that she'd used the word *daddy*. She hadn't called him that in a long, long time.

He cleared his throat, sat up a little taller. "Do you love him?"

"I did," she admitted, realizing nothing but the truth would do. "I still do, I suppose," she quickly amended. Something was different about her father this morning, and it wasn't just the tension between them. "But we, ah, we broke up," she added, although why she did that, she had no idea.

"So the letter stated," he said.

Then why was her father questioning her on the matter?

"Why did you two part company?" he asked.

She debated how best to answer. "I was going back to New York," she finally admitted. "He wanted me to stay with him. I refused."

"So you left."

"It was a mutual decision," she said.

He stared at her for a second longer, eyes the exact same color as her own never blinking. "I see." He shifted in his chair, gave her his profile. "Do you realize, Victoria, that ever since your mother passed away I've worried about you incessantly?" He shook his head. "When you developed the sniffles, I would fret. If you had a fever, I would stay by your bedside until it broke. And god forbid you scrape your knee, or break a bone or otherwise suffer an injury because when you did—" he met her gaze "—I hurt with you."

Her eyes stung suddenly. She swallowed tears back, nodded her head. "I know."

"*Do* you know?" he asked quietly. "Do you know how much I love you? Not just me, but Elaina, too? I realize we're hard on you, Victoria… that *I'm* hard on you. I was the one who insisted on cutting you off. I know you thought Elaina responsible for that, but she wasn't. I wanted you to realize all that you'd give up by being so…independent. But it didn't frighten you, did it?"

"No," she admitted after a long moment of silence.

"You would even give up the man you love if it meant giving up your career."

Yes, she thought. That's exactly what she'd done. Only why did that suddenly feel like such a selfish thing? Surely they could have compromised.

"He's here, you know."

"Who?"

"Your boyfriend." Seeing her look of confusion, her father added, "The man who wrote the letter."

"Here?" she asked in shock.

"He came to ask me for your hand in marriage."

She clapped a hand over her mouth, her heart suddenly beating so hard she grew light-headed.

"That's why he wrote to me. He wanted to tell me how he felt about you. How much he loved you. How much he hoped to marry you. To say I was shocked to receive such a missive would be an understatement. So many people fail to understand the importance of the written word. In this day and age it's all about instant messages or e-mail or texting one another."

Vicky understood why he'd written. It was a message to her: *I haven't given up.*

Why had she? she wondered.

She clenched the arms of her chair.

He'd asked for her hand in marriage.

Her vision began to blur. She blinked, tried to bring her father into focus.

"I'll admit, Victoria, that I've been hard on you."

She wiped at her eyes, rested her palms in her lap. Brandon was here. *Here.*

"When Elaina told me she'd delivered our ultimatum, I thought I'd won. That you'd capitulate. But a week went by, and then two, and still, you didn't give in to our demands. It was then that I admitted that I might have lost my daughter. That I'd pushed too hard. Perhaps even driven you away."

When he faced her, Vicky realized he was crying. Her strong, indomitable dad was crying. Not sobbing. Not bawling. He didn't need to do that. To her father a single tear was tantamount to a bucket of them.

"I don't want to lose my daughter," he said softly.

She got up. She wasn't sure he'd noticed, especially when she crossed to him and he looked up, wide-eyed. "You haven't lost me," she said hoarsely. "I'm right here."

He inhaled sharply. "Yes, I know…I know—"

She cut off his words with a hug. He was stiff at first, but then he softened, slowly he stood. His suddenly harsh embrace took her breath away, but she didn't care. He was her father and she was so grateful—so very, very relieved—that their feud was over.

"Now," he said, drawing back. He looked older, she realized. Somehow, her father had aged without her noticing. "About that young man."

BRANDON THOUGHT he might throw up. Not since the time he'd started his first race had he felt so nervous.

Vicky was here, he thought, staring around him. Vicky had grown up here—the most amazingly huge, thoroughly intimidating, multiacre estate he'd ever seen, one that he knew must be worth somewhere in the neighborhood of a couple hundred million dollars. Sure, he'd known Vicky had money. She had a trust fund, for goodness' sake. But this...

They'd stashed him out in the picturesque garden that stretched around him for at least an acre. Stately trees and blooming shrubs—the flowers potently scented—sprouted around a gravel path. That path wound away from the main house like Dorothy's yellow brick road. Wealth. Power. Prestige. It was all evident here.

And to think, on his way here he'd entertained the notion—however briefly—of having Vicky sign a prenup now that his fortunes were changing and he might actually end up richer than her one day soon. But then he'd admitted, Vicky would likely have his head if he were to ask such a thing so he'd decided not to ask. Now he admitted she would be within reason to ask *him* to sign something, that was if she even agreed to see him.

"Brandon?"

He turned and saw Vicky standing on the pebbled walkway, her long hair loose around her.

"There you are, VanCleef," he pretended to grumble because he had to do something. If he didn't, he'd pull her into his arms. "I've been waiting for you for the better part of an hour."

She stopped just in front of him. She wore a floral dress, and it suited her. She looked soft and feminine and more beautiful than he remembered.

"Oh, yeah?" she asked in an exaggerated drawl. "Well, maybe I'll make you wait another hour."

That's what he loved about her, he realized. Vicky would never let him push her around. She would never be the type to stand by while he worked at something alone. She'd be there, by his side, day in and day out—and more than likely giving him what-for.

"I thought you'd refuse to see me," he said.

Suddenly she went still. "Why would you think that?"

He walked toward her, took her hand. "Because I was a fool."

"But you're here now," she said softly.

"And I'm still scared you'll say no."

"Well," she said softly, "maybe you should ask me your question first, whatever that question might be."

He smiled. "Maybe I should," he said.

She placed a hand against her stomach as if she might have butterflies there or something.

He knew how she felt. "Victoria Prudence VanCleef," he said, taking her hand. "And I can't believe your middle name is Prudence—"

"Hey," she half laughed. "It's for a favorite aunt."

"Well, we're not naming one of our kids Prudence. *That* I draw the line at."

"Kids," she said, tipping her head up at him. "I thought you didn't want kids."

"I thought so, too," he said. "And I'm still not so certain I'm up to the task. My own upbringing, it was so messed up—"

"But we're different."

"I know," he said. "Or more importantly, you'll be what's different. We'll have each other, and with you by my side, I feel as if there's nothing I can't do."

"Oh, Brandon."

He grabbed one of her hands, got down on one

knee. Inside the black velvet box he held open was her mother's two-carat ring—compliments of her father.

"The ring I got you was three carats," he said, noticing she'd gone absolutely still. "And it was gaudy. I like this one much better."

"It was my mom's," she said in a low, tear-filled voice.

"I know," he said. "And I'm hoping it fits, because, Victoria Prudence VanCleef, I would really like you to marry me." He heard her inhale deeply, and when she didn't immediately answer asked, "Will you?"

"That depends," she said, tugging him up.

Leave it to Vicky to turn a marriage proposal into a negotiation. "On what?"

"If you'll kiss me again, just so I know this is real, that this isn't a dream…"

He cut her off. To be honest, it was his favorite way to silence Vicky. *Her* favorite way, too, judging by the way she kissed him back, and then he forgot all about three-carat rings and children named Prudence because she'd opened her mouth and he knew that he had his answer. She slid her hands around his neck, drew him closer. There was joy in her kiss, and tenderness, and passion. Oh, man, a whole helluva lot of passion....

"Now, now, you two. That'll be enough of that," someone said.

They broke apart, Vicky staring up at Brandon with love in her eyes before she turned to the woman who'd spoken.

Elaina stood near them, and miracle upon miracle, she was smiling. "We don't have time for passionate kisses," she said, tapping her watch. "*We* have a wedding to plan."

Brandon glanced at Vicky. "Well?" he prompted. "Do we?"

And she gave him a smile unlike he'd ever seen before, one full of love and happiness. "We do," she said softly.

EPILOGUE

"THEY'RE HERE," Vicky said, racing down the steps of their recently refurbished ranch home and into the spacious family room where Brandon sat waiting. "I saw the bus turn into the end of the drive. They'll be pulling in any second now."

"Vicky," Brandon said, standing. "Calm down. You could have broken your neck coming down the steps like that."

"Nah," Vicky said. "Not today. Not with our very first kids arriving."

Their kids, Brandon thought. Is that what these kids would end up being? Their surrogate children? He had to admit, it was a possibility. The children on the bus were from a variety of backgrounds. They'd put the word out months ago, asking the directors of public-assistance programs to give them the names of children who might benefit from their newly developed program, and now those children were here.

"Scared?" he asked.

"No," she said. Then her face softened. "I'm not scared of anything with you by my side."

He pulled her to him and Vicky sank into his arms willingly. They'd poured so much of themselves into their boys' ranch. Well, Mathew and Kristen Knight had helped, too. So had a number of his fellow drivers. As a result, the Rocking "B" Boys' Ranch had turned into a state-of-the-art facility consisting of six modular homes, twelve-stall barn, corrals, a learning center, a gymnasium, cafeteria and a whole host of other things too numerous to list. He and Vicky had been humbled and overwhelmed by everyone's generosity.

"I love you," he said softly, because suddenly he couldn't speak.

"I love you, too," she said, leaning back. But her face fell. "Brandon, what's wrong?"

"I don't know," he said. "I think I'm scared."

"About what?"

"I'm thinking to myself, what if this was a stupid idea? What if everything we've put together falls apart?"

"Brandon Burke, don't be ridiculous. The kids will love the Rocking B. It's fantastic. We've hired the best counselors. We found kids who need our help. And right now those children are about to see for themselves that somebody *loves* them. They may not recognize that love at first— just as you didn't—but eventually they'll come to trust you, just as *I* did."

Brandon stared into the eyes of the woman he'd married. She was his anchor in rough seas. The one thing that was right on those days when everything seemed to go wrong. The only person in the world who knew all his deepest, darkest secrets…and still loved him.

"What would I do without you?" he asked.

She placed a hand against his face. "Race cars. Drive car owners crazy. Make headlines, but not in a good way."

He chuckled. She was so right. In the past year he'd nearly made the "Chase for the NASCAR Sprint Cup," signed a new contract with KEM for triple the money he'd made before, and, more importantly, used the money from the contract she'd negotiated to open a boys' ranch that would, with a little luck, help troubled teens turn their lives around.

"Now. Are you ready to go outside?" she asked.

"No," he said softly. "I want to hold you a moment longer."

"You better hold me for a lot longer than a moment," she teased, eyes bright. "You better hold on to me for a lifetime."

"Oh, I will," he said gently, bending to kiss her. He meant it to be a quick peck, but as always happened when he touched Vicky, it quickly grew into something more.

"Now, now," someone said from behind them. "None of that."

They sprang apart. Elaina VanCleef stood there, a chiding expression on her face, her formerly glamorous appearance a little more rumpled nowadays thanks to her tireless help with their project. "Don't you realize you've got a bus full of kids out there?"

"We know, Mother," Vicky said, but there was a smile on her face.

Elaina came forward and kissed Vicky on the cheek. She did the same to Brandon. "I'm proud of you two," she said softly.

"We couldn't have done it without you," Brandon said.

"No, you couldn't have," Elaina said with a mischievous grin. "Now, let's go outside. I want to be on the front porch when the kids step off the bus. I can hardly wait to see the look on their faces."

That was the biggest surprise of their marriage, Vicky thought. She and her stepmother had grown closer than ever before. It turned out Elaina was born to organize projects like their boys' ranch. In fact, now that she was done there, she'd taken on a similar project up in New York. Granted, the operation would be on a smaller scale, but Elaina didn't mind. She was diving into the project with both feet, just as she'd done with this one. Vicky didn't know what she would have done without her help.

"Come on," Vicky said. "We better get going before she turns into a wicked stepmother."

"I thought she already was one," Brandon teased.

Elaina pretended to be offended, but they could both see the sparkle in her eyes. "Your father's already down there."

"Well, all right then," Vicky said, her heart starting to beat fast all over again. "Let's go."

Elaina led the way, but before Vicky could leave, Brandon pulled her back into his arms. "Just one last kiss before all hell breaks loose."

"What?" she said. "You afraid of a few boys?"

"Terrified," he admitted.

"Don't be," she said. "You'll do fine."

He would, just as he'd do fine when their own kids arrived, something that was due to happen far sooner than Brandon knew. Just a short while ago, Vicky had taken a pregnancy test. It'd been positive. She was bursting with the news but she wanted to wait to tell him. She'd do it later, when they went to bed and all was quiet in the house.

But it was hard to keep quiet, especially when his lips met hers and joy burst through her soul unlike any she'd ever experienced before. *Tonight,* she thought to herself, savoring the taste of his lips. *I'll tell him tonight.* That would be the perfect end to a perfect day.

"Let's go."

As he took her hand, Vicky knew that today marked a new beginning, not just for them, but for the boys out there, too. Children whom she hoped would flourish with a little love, just as she and Brandon had. Just as their own children would.

As it turned out, that's exactly what happened.

* * * * *

Dear Reader,

Thank you so much for your letters and e-mails. I want you to know how much your words of encouragement mean to me. So many of you have said that my books have helped you through a troubled time. Well, your words have helped *me* through the dark days and for that I'm eternally grateful.

I try to answer each letter, but sometimes I get behind. Rest assured, I will respond to you if you write. For those of you new to my books, I have a Web site at: *www.pamelabritton.com.* There you'll find up-to-date information on *all* my books. For those of you without computer access, you can snail mail me at: P.O. Box 804, Cottonwood, CA 96022.

Once again, *thank you for everything!*

Pamela Britton

REQUEST YOUR
FREE BOOKS!

2 FREE NOVELS
FROM THE ROMANCE/SUSPENSE
COLLECTION PLUS 2 FREE GIFTS!

YES! Please send me 2 FREE novels from the Romance/Suspense Collection and my 2 FREE gifts (gifts are worth about $10). After receiving them, if I don't wish to receive any more books, I can return the shipping statement marked "cancel." If I don't cancel, I will receive 4 brand-new novels every month and be billed just $5.49 per book in the U.S. or $5.99 per book in Canada, plus 25¢ shipping and handling per book plus applicable taxes, if any*. That's a savings of at least 20% off the cover price! I understand that accepting the 2 free books and gifts places me under no obligation to buy anything. I can always return a shipment and cancel at any time. Even if I never buy another book from the Reader Service, the two free books and gifts are mine to keep forever.

185 MDN EF5Y   385 MDN EF6C

Name _____ (PLEASE PRINT) _____

Address _____ Apt. #

City _____ State/Prov. _____ Zip/Postal Code

Signature (if under 18, a parent or guardian must sign)

Mail to **The Reader Service:**
IN U.S.A.: P.O. Box 1867, Buffalo, NY 14240-1867
IN CANADA: P.O. Box 609, Fort Erie, Ontario L2A 5X3

Not valid to current subscribers to the Romance Collection,
the Suspense Collection or the Romance/Suspense Collection.

Want to try two free books from another line?
Call 1-800-873-8635 or visit www.morefreebooks.com.

* Terms and prices subject to change without notice. N.Y. residents add applicable sales tax. Canadian residents will be charged applicable provincial taxes and GST. Offer not valid in Quebec. This offer is limited to one order per household. All orders subject to approval. Credit or debit balances in a customer's account(s) may be offset by any other outstanding balance owed by or to the customer. Please allow 4 to 6 weeks for delivery. Offer available while quantities last.

Your Privacy: Harlequin is committed to protecting your privacy. Our Privacy Policy is available online at www.eHarlequin.com or upon request from the Reader Service. From time to time we make our lists of customers available to reputable third parties who may have a product or service of interest to you. If you would prefer we not share your name and address, please check here. ☐

pamela britton

HQN™

We *are* romance™

www.HQNBooks.com

PHPB0908BL